MW00438233

TOR BOOKS BY PHYLLIS GOTLIEB

Flesh and Gold
Violent Stars

* * * * * * * * * *

MIND*Worlds*

Phyllis Gotlieb

A TOM DOHERTY ASSOCIATES BOOK
NEW YORK

This is a work of fiction. All the characters and events portrayed in this novel are either fictitious or are used fictitiously.

MINDWORLDS

This book is printed on acid-free paper.

Edited by David G. Hartwell

A Tor Book
Published by Tom Doherty Associates, LLC
175 Fifth Avenue
New York, NY 10010

www.tor.com

Library of Congress Cataloging-in-Publication Data

Gotlieb, Phyllis.
Mindworlds / Phyllis Gotlieb.—1st ed.
p. cm.
ISBN 0-312-87876-1
1. Human-alien encounters—Fiction. 2. Life on other planets—Fiction. I. Title: Mindworlds. II. Title.
PR9199.3.G64 M56 2002
813'.54—dc21

2001058355

First Edition: May 2002

Printed in the United States of America

0 9 8 7 6 5 4 3 2 1

and this one's for Jake

I would like to thank Science Fiction Canada
for having patience with my occasional groans
and many requests for research help.

* * * * * * * * * *

MIND*Worlds*

PROLOGUE ✶

Fthel IV, Montador City: *The Company*

The restaurant's bubble-shaped tower rose on its thin stem a quarter-kilometer above the roofs of the city but from inside at the table near the wall Tyloe was looking around at a panorama of endless marshes humped with pulpy succulent growths; among their twining branches were colonies of dreaming Lyhhrt who never woke. Somehow he knew this without seeing them.

But only at a glance. Tyloe was wide awake and sitting there to guard Brezant, not admire the scenery.

Brezant's teeth were on edge. "Lorrice! Stop that damned stupid whimpering!"

She was biting her knuckle. "I can't help it, I'm scared of them. They're lumps of slime inside machines, they know everything about you—"

Brezant's finger and thumb circled her wrist like an iron cuff and she shrank back, but could not pull away.

Tyloe, stationed at her other shoulder, might have raised a cautioning hand then, but there were other watchers, owned by Brezant, sitting at this and other tables. All wearing much the same muted cylon zip, chosen by Lorrice. Brezant had bought the restaurant for this night, and he owned Tyloe as well.

Brezant said through his teeth, "We know that, Lorrice, but they aren't paying attention to you, they know nothing about you, they don't give a shit about you, you're none of their business, they—"

"Madame would choose a cordial?" The very sober waiter with the down-the-nose look might have been a robot, or a Lyhhrt, or a very experienced elderly man. He was clearing the table with thick-bodied grace.

Brezant let go of her wrist. Lorrice rubbed it and said, "Bourbon. No water."

The restaurant was one of a chain that specialized in exotic environments, and its decor was based on whatever the designer could convey of a Lyhhrt's "vision" of its home world. It suddenly struck Tyloe that the eyeless Lyhhrt species would never have known what their world looked like if aliens had not come to show them.

On the concave wall across from him the sun of Lyhhr rose in a double set of halos studded with parhelions and the sky turned mother-of-pearl . . .

Then a Lyhhrt rose from the lift in the center of the floor among the blue marble tables, and another followed: they were hominid forms, one in conservative dark bronze, the other more expansive in brass inlaid with arabesques of silver. Their heads tilted in courtesy-nods.

Brezant's impervious helmet was tattooed under his scalp. He wore an external one for show, its network plated with gold and studded with diamonds and emeralds at the cross points; neither of the two would deter the Lyhhrt from esping him, but he had nothing to hide from them, even Tyloe knew that. Lorrice wore no helmet at all. Brezant would not let her. The necklace with its tiny gold five-point star marked her as ESP-one, but only a Lyhhrt could reach the mind of another; Lorrice was there to esp not the Lyhhrt but Tyloe, and the lawyer Cranshawe, the secretary Istvan, and all the other suits and muscles that enfolded Brezant wherever he went.

The two Lyhhrt slid themselves into the green luxleather chairs. "Andres Brezant," Bronze said, "You come well recommended, citizen." His machined voice was warm and expressive as any Lyhhrt's, and his *lingua* unaccented.

"I make sure of that, Ambassador." Brezant did not ask his name, because Lyhhrt do not have them.

"You live on this world?"

"Sometimes. I come from Earth, in the Sol System."

Both Lyhhrt already knew all of this, but neither party had much small talk.

"Tell me what you can offer us then, citizen." It was no question.

"We will give you freedom from the shame of being enslaved and revenge for the neglect of Galactic Federation."

Brass-and-silver said, "We had that freedom one Cosmic Cycle ago before the Ix attacked our world and laid their eggs in our bodies. It did us very little good."

"And five years ago, when the Khagodi needed your help, you freely sacrificed yourselves and your ship to save their world from being destroyed by the Ix. No one thanked you for that. Not Khagodis, nor the Federation."

"And you believe it is thanks we need?"

"We can bring you reparations."

"Truly! And we are to sign a new Oath and be slaves to you now, instead of the Ix?"

"A business agreement. Lyhhr has withdrawn from trade pacts with three worlds in the last five years. If you kept on doing that your world would regress—I am willing to say boldly—to its primitive state, before the Federation pulled you from the swamps to make those workshells, before the Ix, before anyone knew you at all."

"We are very much aware of that, citizen. Some of us believe that state is—you would say—heavenly!"

Brezant did not bother to ask the Lyhhrt if he believed this. "Without skills and without the materials to practice them. Without any kind of protection or defense. But the Khagodi are still afraid of your anger, and especially so now that Lyhhr has stopped importing platinum and iridium from their Isthmuses District, when so much of their world's economy was based on that trade."

"You have educated yourself well," Bronze said. "I believed only Lyhhr and Khagodis knew that. I voted against those actions when I served on my world's Council. But I and those who agreed with me were voted down—some considered us suspect because we had left our colonies to work on other worlds and were felt to have become overindividualized, heretical. Even contaminated. So much for rewarding our services. But I still serve as well as I can."

Brezant nodded toward Brass-and-silver. "May I ask if that's your companion's feeling?"

Brass focused his diamond eyes on Brezant. "If it was not I would not be here."

"And on your world there are still others who feel as you do . . ." It was a half-question.

"There are enough, citizen."

Bronze said, "The Khagodi must find new markets for their ores, and that serves them right, but because of our foolhardy Council's votes and our broken trade pacts we can't build our ships or the instruments that run them."

"I'll make my offer then. You can sue Khagodis for reparations. If they refuse I can bring a force of up to ten thousand troops with small arms and hypersledges to make sure you get them—"

"Get what, citizen?"

"Control of their Isthmus Territories, twenty-five to thirty-five of their richest mines. We will ship the ores anywhere you choose, as long as we get one-half of the profits. Khagodi are heavy and slow. Their culture is low-tech and their aircraft are flown mainly by the Kylkladi. They have produced a few clumsy gladiators, but seldom warriors, and never mercenaries." *Or we need not bother with chatter about reparations and simply raid them.*

A moment of silence. The thought resonated so strongly that even Tyloe could sense it . . . but no one else in the room so much as flickered an eye. Tyloe for an instant wondered if he had been suddenly gifted with telepathy and in the same instant realized that Lorrice had opened Brezant's mind to him. By way of the Lyhhrt. It closed with a snap.

They're so sure of themselves they don't care who reads them. And she wants something from me . . . what?

I'll find out later. He doubted he would escape finding out.

Brezant's flash of greed did not seem to disturb the Lyhhrt. Bronze said, "Any sudden attack would be very unwise, citizen. We have not dealt much with Galactic Federation lately, but they would take us before we had dug much ore from the pits. Then we might all end up digging in the Urgha Mines, where there are coals and not platinum. And Lyhhrt never do such things without warnings. Wounded we may be but we are not yet devolved."

Brezant was easy. "If you agree with my proposal—"

"Not quite so quickly! You want more from us than an excuse to make a raid on Khagodis's mines . . ."

"Your skills. Do what you like with your half of the profits but design and build our electronics, our satellites, our ships—"

"For your world—and its colonies?"

"For us, and our enterprises. This Company."

"And your weapons? Those we would never build."

"We'll put that aside. With Lyhhrt skills and precious metals from the Isthmuses we would be very satisfied."

"It's an intriguing proposal. You understand that we cannot answer at this moment."

"How long do you need?"

"We may need three or four of your thirtydays to gather a consensus."

Brezant's nails danced on the table. "I thought you came here ready to deal!"

"You may have your forces here, Citizen Brezant, but most of ours are on Lyhhr. We cannot bend all of the laws of reality to quicken communication."

"I can't keep all my people on standby for very much longer." Brezant did not move to wipe the sweat from his face.

"Perhaps you have presumed too much," Brass-and-silver said.

Tyloe was always conscious of a vibration, a trembling, coming off the surface of Lorrice's mind. It twinged like a tuning fork up the back of his neck into the base of his skull now.

Brezant's knuckles hit the table-top four quick light raps. "Maybe I invited you here for an evening of entertainment! Maybe the fun is over and it's time to go home!" Darkness was beginning to climb the walls of the Lyhhrt world; its sky had many stars but no moon.

Both Lyhhrt were silent for a moment. "Citizen, we said nothing on purpose to offend you. Both parties have too much invested in this meeting to give up on it. Once we communicate with our base we can reach an unalterable decision in five of your minutes, but twenty thousand spacelights more than all the thousands we have broadcasting now couldn't relay our messages faster. We need a minimum of two thirtydays to bring you the answer."

Brezant nodded. "That's done then."

"But remember this, Andres Brezant. Whatever our decision is, it begins with a mission to Fthel Five and a complaint to Galactic Federation." Bronze and Brass-with-silver rose and flowed away down the lift.

Brezant waited a beat after the floor closed over them, then grabbed Lorrice's empty bourbon glass, flung and smashed it against the wall. Tyloe could have caught it but didn't dare.

Lorrice sat still. Her tuning fork rose an octave.

Brezant made a gesture, and his guards and flunkies moved away from him to the wall. Tyloe got up, but Brezant waved him to his chair. He found a handkerchief and patted his face dry. "All right." He turned to Lorrice, his voice caught a roughness and he swallowed. "You're the ESP, what did you pick off from them?"

I don't think it's the Lyhhrt she's afraid of.

:You think too much, Tyloe!: the mindvoice said.

"They weren't lying about wanting the deal. They believed what you said." Lorrice dug in her gold-skinned handbag, offered him a Zephyrelle, an expensive mixture of weed and dope encased in purple and gold, put it in her mouth and lit it for him.

He accepted it, drew in deeply. "Yeh. What else?"

"Ah, this restaurant reminded them of a Lyhhrt decontamination chamber—"

"I don't give a shit if they think it's a pigsty. Go on."

"Nothing rea—"

"There's lots!" His head turned. "Isn't there, Tyloe? You looked as if you were hearing something."

What does he want from me? Tyloe, the newest member of the guard, wasn't eager to be an advisor. "Only what everyone else got. That they believed you, but they needed to consult."

"Yeh." The heavy stubbled head turned again, and then Tyloe's armpits sprang a sweat of relief. "All right, Lorrice, out with it!" Brezant bent toward her. The smoke fell from his nostrils in thin streams.

She was pale, and gauntness aged her face. Her hair glimmered faintly in the dying light. "They—they said themselves they weren't speaking for all of Lyhhr . . . but," stumbling, "they never once referred to themselves as 'I/we' or 'we/us' and—the three or four Lyhhrt I've known have always done that at least once every ten or fifteen minutes to show they're connected to others even if they're alone."

"So?"

"This is a group that's split off from their world, and, ah—"

Cranshawe, the lawyer, rescued her. "We can't tell how big that group is, and how much of Lyhhr they represent."

"They're enough for me." Brezant pushed himself away from the table and stood. "Let's get out of here." His shadowed men and women rose around him.

The lift ran down the stem of the bubble, a long way down, and Tyloe was crammed in beside Lorrice with her scent and Brezant with his smoke. Brezant's hand ran down Lorrice's hip and began plucking at her dress, rubbing a fold of black chiffon between thumb and finger, not quite pinching or touching, his pink hand a small animal gnawing the twist of fabric.

Lorrice's mind retreated to some area she had created for herself; Tyloe wanted to look the other way, but there was nowhere else.

The beggar with upturned hands who waited by the restaurant door in the stem's base was an O'e, a remnant of the old Zamos clone factories. At its peak the Zamos Corporation had created thousands of clone slaves for underwater mining, personal service and prostitution. The O'e had been left over as detritus when the Corporation fell. This one had the hominid shape and grayish skin of most of them, along with an eye eaten out by skegworm and the warped body of one who dug in garbage heaps for scraps of rotted food.

Brezant, coming out of the door into the hot night, found one of the beggar's crooked feet in his way, kicked it aside, dropped his burning Zephyrelle in the beggar's cupped hands and passed by heading for his landcar.

When he was out of sight the beggar pinched out the hot coal with his fingers, plucked a transparent envelope from his dirty rags and tipped the Zephyrelle into it. He crawled away, painfully slouching down the lanes and alleys that threaded the ancient palaces of a fallen civilization, until he reached the back-door garden of Galactic Federation's World Headquarters. The door was opened by a Lyhhrt in a gunmetal workshell, who let him in and followed after.

He stumbled across the too-big rotunda, even bigger at night, to where Willson was working late in his closet of an office. The lamp was just bright enough to show the gloss of sweat on his face. Gunmetal moved to close the door, but Willson said, "Main power's out, cooler's gone, this is too bloody hot."

"I hadn't noticed," the beggar said.

"No, I guess you wouldn't."

"Here." Digging into the stinking rags, he found the envelope and placed it on the desk between Willson's hands.

"Eh, this looks like something. Get some good genes off it. Wait'll Greisbach sees this!"

"I/we hope so." The beggar pulled off and flung aside his rags and skin, and became another Lyhhrt in a brushed silver casing.

"You think this yobbo is one of the leftovers of Zamos's little empire?"

Gunmetal said, "Do not make 'humor' about Zamos."

"Awright, awright! No offense meant."

"Whether this is a remnant or not, it's dangerous," Silver said, "and we will find out what."

"It's sure lucky he had that cigarette."

"That was not luck. I made sure he wanted one."

"A risk, though. Watch you don't outsmart yourself—eh," calling through the open door, "Greisbach, is that you?"

"No, but I will do instead," the voice said. Both Lyhhrt saw through Willson's eyes the figure with the dark gleam of wrought iron striding the rotunda, heard the *tzuk!* of the bullet, felt Willson's life dissolve into nothingness, *tzuk!* again and again—as Gunmetal exploded, Silver, who had been the beggar, fell crashing against the wall, the intruder's hurried footsteps echoed off the marble floor of the rotunda. . . .

My Other! Gunmetal's workshell lay in ruins, oozing with the thin pinkish ichor that was Lyhhrt blood.

The surprise of the attack had shattered Silver's control of the workshell, he had twisted helplessly in his attempt to dodge, and the explosive bullet, aimed at the midsection where his body nested, had missed and gouged the tip of his shoulder, showering the room with a thousand minuscule silver flakes.

Lyhhrt cannot run in hominid workshells that would batter them like shaken babies, and by the time Silver could begin to pull himself out of that black shock he saw Willson slumped dead with his forehead on the desk. No cigarette butt in an envelope. No telepathic traces, and the Lyhhrt did not know of any ESP more powerful at shielding than himself or another Lyhhrt. So one of the Lyhhrt delegation had twigged him and followed. Outsmarted.

One flash of thought: *Willson, wife, children, hopes*—and his livelong partner the Other, of the pair the Lyhhrt travel in to keep their sanity, an empty reverberation.

And another voice called, "Hullo? Hullo?" That was Greisbach, hurrying; she'd been diverted, probably, not killed at least, the enemy hadn't bothered with her, yet. The Lyhhrt wanted to be moving away quickly, and far, but not to make himself suspect by his absence. He had lost everything and he had nothing to tell her, except that Brezant and his brass and bronze Lyhhrt had made a tentative agreement. He did not even know where Brezant's ten thousand troops were stationed—some expert had locked that byte deep into Brezant's mind for him.

The Lyhhrt set his silver workshell on self-repair and pulled on his rotten beggar's rags, listening to Greisbach's heel-clicks on the marble. Knowing that when he left this uneasy moment death was waiting to follow.

Before Greisbach could begin to comprehend what he told her he had gathered the strange belongings that Lyhhrt carry with them and was pushing them down the cobbled streets in a beggar's barrow. His mind was blank.

ONE ✳

Khagodis, Burning Mountain: *Hasso Deconstructs an Archive*

"... and as my first example I offer you in all humility my own dissertation ..."

Hasso son of Evarny leaned harder on the lectern to ease his wasted leg, and faced the hundred-odd other Khagodi men and women squatting on their circled places in the Hall of Learning. The Hall was a beautiful structure in the shape of a Kylkladi bower, and in fact had been erected by Kylkladi to house Galactic Federation's Interworld Court. But its heat in Khagodis's equatorial summer had been detested by so many other Interworld jurists that it was finally being given up.

The students, young and healthy as they were, did not worry about heat in this winter season, when cooler winds hushed through the bower's leaves; they tilted their heads eagerly toward Hasso's lectern, the scales glistened over their massive bodies in colors that were bright and fresh, and their heavy tails were tightly wrapped around them.

Hasso hated public speaking, and in his law studies had carefully avoided any direction that led to open court. But he was determined to make his own young generation as passionate as he was about creating archives. Now he was proud to be standing in this historical setting and, bracing himself for a new and scholarly endeavor, he stood tall, gulped air three times—"but before I build the structure, I will show you the building materials,"—and launched himself into the great work of his life, speaking at times by swallowing air, at time by esp, sometimes with gestures, occasionally rubbing down his scales to keep them from rising in the heat of his passion and devotion:

On the world Sol Three that they call Earth the people are born one by one, and kept together in a jumble of sexes and ages crowded into only one single dwelling where they can barely breathe, and whatever faults or flaws they have are intensified. Where there is goodness they beget wonders, and where there is evil they grow demons. I thank all of the Saints that I have dear friends among Earthers, but when I think of the Zamos family my head begins to steam! We grow bad eggs enough but we keep them carefully apart from the healthy.

Two hundred years ago Zamos and his clutch of families became a Corporation specializing in fraud, money laundering, extortion and prostitution, and eventually bought a company called NeoGenics that created specialized human clones for serving on worlds with extreme conditions. They began a special branch of that company to manufacture clones for sexual exploitation and built hundreds of brothels—legal brothels—on seven worlds—and even on this world!

—a pause to settle the little stir of shame—

—and all who worked in them were slaves! And there were those of us—of us!—who became slave masters.

For Zamos discovered gold in the waters of our Isthmuses and dropped down its cloned undersea workers to collect it. It was Chief Justice Skerow, then wife of my father Evarny, who first discovered this horror. At that time, the Saints preserve us, I suppose we were smug enough to think no such evil could touch us... but we were slavers in the Isthmuses and brothel-masters even here in this city of Burning Mountain!

While all these evil things were happening two more worlds had come to haunt us, and these were Lyhhr and Iyax. The Lyhhrt we have known long and been uneasy with because their telepathic power is so much greater even than ours, and they are so frightened of being separated from their equals. The Ix nobody knew, nor wanted to when they did—

—everyone knew someone who had known someone who had seen an Ix and its specter rose up before them in chitinous black six-limbed horror, its sting-smell of hallucinatory pheromones and the spaceless black-flaming sparklings of their aura, and all shivered—

—because they were egglayers who had so fouled their home world that they could not produce the nourishment to incubate their young... and by exploration of other worlds they found this in the bodies of Lyhhrt.

Neither world belonged to Galactic Federation. The Ix had been unknown. The Lyhhrt were neutrals with some Federation ties, and they begged GalFed for help but no one would risk the money and the manpower.

Zamos came to their rescue.

In their laboratories they created an artificial egg-hatching medium, and from the Lyhhrt demanded their service to Zamos for one Cosmic Cycle, one hundred and twenty-nine of their years. The Lyhhrt had no choice, except to destroy themselves. Zamos gained the use of Lyhhrt robotics, surgical techniques and telepathy, and the Lyhhrt took away nothing but shame. Though Zamos's fall came as that Cycle was ending, the Lyhhrt had spent what seemed to them an eon of slavery helping Zamos create slaves and monsters to serve on ten score worlds . . . sacrificing their souls to save their lives . . . and when that reign was ended and they were freed they helped to save our world and got little thanks. . . .

Another Mysterious Stranger

Hasso thought there was no place on the world Khagodis, or in the whole universe for that matter, so pleasant as the rooftop of his house in the city of Burning Mountain. The white winter sun, faintly gilded with mist, hung between afternoon and evening; its light fell softly on the rainwashed pastel walls of the stuccoed houses and shops clustered on the slopes down to the river.

At the other corner of the sky two alabaster moons were launching themselves, and the brightest stars and worlds were flaming in the deep sky. The air was wonderfully warm, not the choking heat of summer, and several of his neighbors were out on their roofs enjoying it with him. Hasso could just hear the peaceful *tink!* of the goldbeater's hammer from the jewelsmith's across the way.

He was waiting for his stepmother Skerow, who always came down from her home in the Northern Spines to celebrate the GreenWreath Festival with him on her way to the Raintree Island Poetry Conference. Both had been invited to attend the Consecration of the New Interworld Court, a recently finished complex, now based deep in among the cold mesas of the Southern Diluvian Continent, that would replace the old bower, and house World Government as well. But Skerow, recently and gratefully retired from the lectern and from power, had declined.

"I do wish you would come and enjoy the occasion with me, goodmother."

"I am coming to your warm land to be with you, Hasso, and though I love my own cold desert I needn't go to another one." She was stubborn as always, and Hasso tilted his head and gave up.

The chimes rang at the entryway downstairs as he was brewing a pot of sprigwort tea for himself. He had bought a jug of white-thorn essence for Skerow, who liked something stronger; the grill was fired up, a good shank of crockbull waiting on its platter. . . .

Skerow would never ring: this was a stranger. With a spit of annoyance Hasso set the teabowl down. His servant was gone for the day after lugging all the crockery up to the roof and helping him set up the grill, he'd left his impervious helmet below in his kitchen, and, weary from his stint propped on the lectern in the Hall of Learning, he did not want to crawl all the way down the stone stairs and up again for someone he didn't know.

He felt no telepathic emanation, and no ordinary citizen in the street goes about wearing a damned heavy scratchy helmet only to be fashionable. Stranger . . .

"Eh." Not good news. An alien perhaps. After the trials that brought the Zamos Corporation down at last, the ranks of jurists and packs of journalists had diminished offworld toward the newest sensation, leaving a few tourists, clusters of diplomats and the merchants supplying them to maintain the alien contingent.

Hasso sucked in a bellyful of air, said, "I will be with you in one tick of a stad!" and picked up his staff. He began limping his way toward the top step of the long downward passage.

"I will come up if you permit," the low resonant voice said boldly.

Having no better answer, Hasso said, "Come." The street was in shadow and no light came from the entrance below. He settled back on the broad base of his tail and waited as the dark shape rose.

Its edges were not quite clear. Khagodi, whose sight and hearing are slightly duller than those of non-ESPs, depend on each other to verify them. Now the neighboring roofs seemed to be empty, and the goldbeater's hammer had fallen silent.

The visitor was an outworlder, likely an Earther, Hasso thought, from his hominid form. No shorter than Hasso, he was wearing black clothing, with a dark wide-brimmed hat, and seemed to pull in light without illuminating himself.

Hasso did not have time to open his mouth before the stranger said: "You are Citizen Hasso known as Master of Archives for Sector 706.394 inclusive of systems Fthel and Darhei." He spoke very standard unaccented *lingua*.

Hasso would not have claimed so great a territory for himself; it included his sun's worlds and also those of Galactic Federation Headquarters. He forced himself not to step back from this aggressive speech and said, "Citizen Hasso, yes."

"I have been advised by the world Lyrrh to inform you that you will be called as a witness in an action being brought against your government for negligence in refusing to support and defend Lyhhrt action against the attack of the world Iyax in local year 7514."

Hasso drew a slow depth of air. "Who are you, citizen, and what is your authority?" Whoever he was he was not a guest, now, but an opponent. "There is no Lyhhrt ship in orbit, and Lyhhr no longer has a permanent embassy on this world. Show me identification."

"My genitors are Lyhhrt." The stranger's hand flashed the gold disk: the Cosmic symbols of Lyhhr swarmed on it. Hasso's scales rose, and for a moment he thought he was going to be hypnotized. But in an instant the emblem vanished somewhere in that body or its clothing, and Hasso knew that his visitor was truly a Lyhhrt. In anyone else's hand the disk would have turned ash-white and crumbled.

"I will presume you are satisfied that I am Lyhhrt?"

But Lyhhrt, those brain-sized lumps of protoplasm, walk the streets of alien worlds encased in brilliant workshells of beaten gold and bronze, not imitations of Earthers' flesh and cloth. "Yes, but not that you have authority."

"I live on this world with the permission of your government, and my people have made use of my citizenship to send you a message. They have certainly begun this action. They will arrive on Khagodis within three thirtydays to bring it to Interworld Court. The message is from them, not me. I have had unofficial information that if Lyhhr is not satisfied there will be an actual attack. Although I am an exile from my world and I can find fault with it, I cannot believe it would ever bring any kind of army or armada to any world."

"Are you warning me, citizen? I have no personal authority. You ought to tell this to World Government, and I must tell you, it is well documented, that all of this world's council offered to sacrifice themselves to save the Lyhhrt. So why come to me?"

"You may have that dangerous frailty, a withered leg and only one heart," the Lyhhrt said calmly. "But I am the only Lyhhrt on Khagodis and I have no power or influence."

"But how do you exp—"

While Hasso was drawing in another of those deep and angry bellyfuls of air the chimes jangled a warning, and Skerow's telepathic voice said, *:He doesn't mean to insult you, Hasso.:*

"That is quite right," the Lyhhrt said abruptly, "I meant no harm. Lyhhrt rarely do." To emphasize the words he shrank his height, and his long coat pleated on the flooring.

While Hasso struggled to find sense in what the Lyhhrt was saying—Lyhhr attacking Khagodis!—Skerow was mounting the stairs with unusual speed. The Lyhhrt turned to meet her, rose in height and extended a hand to help her up the last step. "Sta'atha Amfa Skerow, the respected Justice and distinguished poet," he said.

"My fame precedes me ever." Skerow's tone was both gracious and wry. The breath was whistling harshly in and out of her gill-slits. She did not need to tell him that she was a retired Justice.

Nor did Hasso bother introducing her to the nameless Lyhhrt. "Citizen," to the Lyhhrt, "I hope you will be able to tell me more clearly what Lyhhr intends, and what I have to do with it." He said this much more civilly than he had intended.

"No, Archivist, I have spoken enough. You know all that is necessary for now." He turned in a swirl of cloth without any hurry and . . . flowed down the stairs, gone. The sky brightened, and Hasso saw that his rooftop neighbors were enjoying their meals.

"Eki, goodmother, what a strange one."

"Indeed so, Hasso—a full complement of Lyhhrtish tricks! But let us have our dinner before your tea turns sour and the sun cooks that delicious cut of meat."

"I must know of that Lyhhrt in some recorded source if he is a genuine citizen."

"You will remember eventually. But don't brood now, Hasso dear. I am delighted to be with you and ever so hungry."

And for a little while Hasso and Skerow did no more

than share a dinner with pleasure and affection. Although there would always be a shadow standing between them, however faint: Evarny, who had been Skerow's husband for twenty years, until he divorced her for infertility when their young daughter died. The woman he then married to give him his Lineage had been able to bear only Hasso, and Evarny had died before knowing his wife and son would ever meet. Or that they would form a powerful bond.

Skerow dipped her tongue into the bowl for the last drop of the fiery essence. *:You know that Lyrhht, Hasso. I am sure you know him.:* Then, on taking thought, *:Unless, perhaps, a robot . . . :*

"No no! The Lyhhrt would never send a robot in the shape of an Earther on Khagodis! They are far too esthetic—and that awkward clothing was ridiculous—"

"That's true. He seemed to realize he was ridiculous . . . you know, Hasso, I believe that fellow was probably very frightened, and that clothing was meant to make him inconspicuous."

"Yes, goodmother, only it didn't work very well! If he truly is the only Lyhhrt on Khagodis, most likely he—eh, I have got him now! You and I both know of the Galactic Federation agent who was present when he was born—helped him to be born! Eki, I suppose I should not expect to keep everything in the top of my brain. The agent was that Earther fellow Ned Gattes that you must remember."

"I certainly do. I know no more Earthers than I have fingers!"

Hasso's mood darkened even further; the long and agonizing history still flickered in his mind as darkly as the Inland Sea of Pitch on whose shores he had spent his youth. At that troubled time five years ago when the orbiting Ix had demanded the subjugation of Khagodis, the two Lyhhrt who were on the world then had given their lives and their ship to destroy the vast and lowering Ixi vessel, the greatest one of its kind. But before they did so they had conjugated to produce one descendant who would tell their story.

"Yes, we know who this Lyhhrt is now." *:But why come to me, and in an Earther-shaped workshell, why anyway is he a citizen of this world?:*

"Perhaps he became too well known on his own," Skerow said. "An individual, and one who drew too much attention to himself."

"A heretic in the minds of others, then. He ought to have been honored on his world, and able to find all Others . . . no use thinking of that, I suppose. But why come to me?"

"No insult. Most likely he wanted to warn someone he respected, and whom he felt was as vulnerable as himself."

"You believe he was really trying to be *friendly*? I wish he would not have spoken in riddles! I cannot believe the Lyhhrt could want to stir up any kind of war. I must find out whether the Ministry knows of this."

"I'm sure he meant for you to tell them."

"He left me a heavy burden. I hope he finds himself lightened of it."

:Poor fellow, I hope so too.:

Crouching with joined minds in the last of the reddened sunlight as the shadows rose and the rising night wind sparked the fading coals in the firepot . . .

Fthel IV, Cinnabar Keys: *Crawlers*

Around the time Hasso was giving his lecture on archive construction, Ned Gattes was just about to step off the train in a place he wasn't sure he wanted to be. Three days earlier a voice on his comm had told him to come to an arena in Lisboa today at fifteen hours, there was money in it.

Lisboa was a town on a local rail line about a hundred

and fifty kilometers from his home in Miramar, and he'd fought in the arena occasionally to earn a few cred. But he hadn't been there, or even fought seriously for years, just in exhibitions and giving lessons for not much money, and this call promised a good handful.

Since Zamos had collapsed there hadn't been much of it for a used-up pug with a wife and three kids. Galactic Federation had left him alone, and he wasn't calling them either. In the past he and Zella had made most of their living fighting in Zamos arenas on five worlds; Zamos's corruption-riddled empire had given work to millions upon millions, and with its disintegration the vast realms of gambling houses, arenas and brothels had shrunk and devolved into small businesses and private clubs.

Live pugs now fought down back alleys in smoky rooms where Ned and Zella did not want to go, and the gladiatorial school where they had been teaching young pugs their moves had gone out of business: now fights were mainly fought by robots—even the cockfights were robotic. And most of the live fights had become criminally controlled and much bloodier.

He wouldn't let Zella go to those places, and ducked them himself. He had some hopes for this one.

The train let him off at the usual station; its clay tile roof was crumbling and the stucco walls were cracking. Ned tried not to see the shabbiness of the main street and its loungers, the rutted roads and dust-spewing landcars. On most blocks the walkways had stopped moving and the treads were buckled.

It was mid-afternoon and the westering sun was fairly kind to the small shops and eateries he was passing. At the first street branching north he turned right and after the corner fruit market, there was a door, the same thick slab of wood-comp he remembered.

A big red-lit sign above it said: The CrawlSpace!

That was new, and so was the slot for i.d. He paused. *Private club. . . .* The back of his neck prickled and he rubbed at it.

But he'd spent more than an hour on the train and he'd be stuck here for two more hours. He slotted in his District Worker's Permit.

The door clicked and buzzed, slammed back in its socket, ricocheted once and slid back again slowly.

Beyond it was a square room with a high ceiling and skylight. All kinds of crests and shields hung on the walls, naming champions and associations that Ned had never heard of. The ring in the center was bedded with clean sand.

As he stepped inside Trax came forward with his old fighter's strut, grinning with new white teeth. He was otherwise exactly as Ned remembered him, with the same bald head and hairy arms and legs. "Come on in, Neddo, welcome to the CrawlSpace—we got some good times today!"

He came closer, where Ned could smell his sweat. "It's chebok, your specialty, innit?" And in a low voice through his teeth, "Today you lose."

Ned took one breath. "I don't fight to lose."

"You do if you wanna be paid."

Ned smelled *bloodfight*—that often hinted threat he'd managed to dodge in Zamos arenas.

Behind Trax he could see in the white bloodless light that along one wall fifteen or twenty men, one Varvani, and one or two women were crouched on stools and folding chairs. The youngest were middle-aged with reddened faces and wrinkled foreheads; they wore snapcaps and leather pea jackets, half had thick gold chains and rings. There were curls of jhat smoke rising from their fingers and mouths. They did not speak but every once in a while one would lean over to give a pat on the head or shoulder to a much younger man in leather breeks who was sitting on the floor in front of them with legs crossed. The champion.

"Here he is!" Trax's face was all teeth. "Jammer, the winner of the silver Terra Cup, just waiting for you, Ned-boy!"

The youngling stood up, stretched, and did a little dance in place. He had dark curly hair and smooth skin, looked strong and graceful enough, and well-kept, rather like somebody's pet. Ned did not waste time wondering who the owner was. His mind was spinning.

He refused the offered refresher bottle, then shucked his jacket and top and dropped them in a corner, baring his years of scars. Nothing to show for them either. He accepted the chebok, a mailed fist with sharp steel spikes, very new and shiny. And the heavy leather buckler with metal studs that had never been scratched. Chebok fighting went with the trade, but Ned did not like it; he didn't mind a taste of blood and a touch of fear, but chebok meant too much of both.

Jammer danced forward snarling and feinted with his chebok to cover the lunge with his shield meant to drive Ned's own spikes into his flesh. He had frightened eyes, Ned thought; he blocked that and caught a couple of scratches on his jaw: first blood that fell in a spatter on his shoulder. There was a crackling hiss of breath from the audience.

Jammer followed hard with his chebok and Ned, dodging that, was caught off guard for a fraction of a second too late, and left himself open to a slam on shoulder and cheekbone from Jammer's shield. He lost balance and landed sprawled on his back. Winded and dizzy, he heard the hissing deepen to a low roar: *Give it to him, Jammer!*

Jammer leaped forward to kick at him, an illegal move, but Ned caught him hard on the leg with his own chebok. Dripping blood, Jammer hopped on one leg, screaming, "I'll kill you! I'll kill you!"

Silence. Somebody said, "*Yes.*" Ned pulled himself to his feet, stood back, and waited. His head was still ringing and he had sparkles in his eyes. He shook them away.

Jammer stumbled forward frantically, eyes in a stare. Ned took pity on him, knocked the chebok out of Jammer's hand with his own and pushed him down with his buckler.

Empty hand, a legal end to the fight.

The audience rose and roared like a thousand. *C'mon! Let's get'm!* Ned stood watching them for a moment, while they shook their fists. He waited for them to step forward, but they did not, yet. Two or three of them gathered around Jammer, *Get up, boy, you ain't hurt bad!* There were no guns here, but throwing knives were common enough. Now, though, maybe the jhat had dulled their aims as it was slurring their speech.

He'd seen all these men and women, or others too much like them no matter what their species, standing in the doorways of their offices in casinos, brothels, arenas, waiting for the money to be counted. And now that the empire they had served was fallen, they had laid their money down on such small hopes he would have felt sorry for them if he could afford it.

He picked up the other 'bok so that he had two of them, and clashed them together, in case anyone had ideas. No one came near him. "Go kiss your boy where it hurts and send him back to the nursery," he said.

Trax was kneeling beside Jammer, bandaging his leg. He screamed at Ned, "You crazy bastard, you ain't getting paid for none of this!" His face was purple, and he was shaking.

"I guess not," Ned said. "I guess you won't be, either." He dropped the weapons, picked up his clothes and was out of there.

He went down the street quickly, wiping blood off his jaw with a cloth that had gone through many launderings, and eventually put his top and jacket back on. No one came after him, and he spent the rest of the time sitting on a hard bench in the station, reading the graffiti and watching local news on the sputtering screens.

He had a bad time of it with Zella when he got back, with that black eye and the slashes.

I can't believe you didn't know what you were in for!

She was crying, touching him, dabbing him with wet swabs and antiseptics.

I didn't, Zel! The pay sounded so good!

I'm going to be afraid to leave you alone. . . .

As he would be left tomorrow. Zella and the children were leaving for Montador to wait at the deathbed of her mother, with whom she had never gotten along, but who had relocated here from her pioneers' world for an easier old age. Zella usually did this two or three times a year. Her mother specialized in deathbed scenes.

I'm a grown-up boy, I'll get along all right.

I don't care about the money! It's not going to happen again!

He agreed with that. They found a minder for the kids and went to Dusky Dell's for beers.

Spartakos Cuts a Deal

The fight going on in Dusky Dell's sea-front bar in the Grottoes district of Miramar was a different kind; the awkward punching scuffles weren't rare around Happy Hour when Dell gave out three for the price of two, and Ned was safely niched in a dark corner with Zella. He was touching his rough fingers very gently to that spot on her neck just over the second cervical vertebra, that was still soft as a baby's. She hunched her back like a cat. "You're tickling."

"It feels so good."

But the back of his neck was still prickling, along with the hurts and his anger. There were other reasons for twinges of the spine that did not account for this one, and one of them was Spartakos, the robot created by the Lyhhrt as an exhibit, servant, calculator, storehouse of secrets, pet. At their first meeting Spartakos had declared Ned his friend, and when Galactic Federation and the Lyhhrt took them into service and sent them into danger the two had saved each other more than once. Five years ago the Lyhhrt, in releasing Ned, had left the robot with him.

Spartakos was no longer a servant or an ornament, but a world-citizen. He had vowed to serve the O'e, the slave-race his makers had created: he was up on Dell's stage now, dancing with an O'e woman and a Varvani who had also become his friends. For this display he had transformed himself into a serpent twining among the limbs of the other two while a couple of Bengtvadi played a nose-flute and a bucciphone. An audience clustered around the stage clapping in time, while drinkers slammed their mugs on tables.

Dell paid Spartakos a lot of money: he had doubled and redoubled her business. He used the money for energy and upkeep, for tending the O'e with food and medicines wherever he could find them. That took most of it. And what was left over he gave to Ned and Zella.

That bothered Ned deeply. *No way to fight, what can we do? We could find cheaper digs and at least keep the kids in school. . . .* Better than sponging free meals from Dell and letting Spartakos pay the rent.

Money meant little to Spartakos and could not do much more for him than supply energy: when the Lyhhrt had left him with Ned they had deserted him, and he had no way to cure the deep tarnish of his gold-plated head and hands or the flaking of his chromed body, and lately his coordination had begun to suffer. Even if there were automaton specialists who were skilled enough to restore him to blazing brilliance, none of them would have dared touch a Lyhhrt work. Spartakos would have self-destructed.

There was a sudden eruption from the fighters who, borne by the circulation of the audience toward the bar, had reached a bottle-breaking stage in their battle. The Varvani raised his hand to stop the music, jumped down from the stage; the customers parted for him as the sea had done for Moses: he was a head taller than everyone else and had arms as thick as taqqa trees. He plucked up the fighters by the scruff, carried them through the exit and tossed them over the railing into the sea. At this level of the Grottoes it was not deep and had no hungry beasts. The Varvani returned and the dance went on.

The room calmed, and Ned turned his mind back to whatever else was giving him that twinge at the back of his neck. Out of the corner of his eye he had noticed the workman—at least a fiercely weathered Earther in denims with a neckerchief and shabby cap—who seemed to be looking at him with a peculiar intensity. Now as he thought about that he felt himself forced to turn his head and look again. For a moment he thought this might be someone from Lisboa after him.

No. This was a telepath. Looking at him, pushing at his mind. His anger rose and was damped down by that push. Before he could shake free of the effect the workman rose and squatted by the doorway.

The show was finishing with a flourish and a bow, with Spartakos reforming into his still handsome self; in the quiet that followed Dell came onstage to announce last round and saw the workman, a stranger. "Hullo, mister! Looking for work? I'm not hiring on right now but I'll give you a meal." He was not one of the kind she'd hire anyway, too awkward and sullen-looking.

Blue-shirt looked up at her with strange eyes, and Ned could see her eyebrows rising at whatever message he was giving her. Dell was an old fighter friend of Ned's, muscular enough to be her own bouncer, and Ned thought she was paler than usual. She crooked a finger at Ned. "That one wants you. Don't ask me."

"I don't like the looks of him," Zella whispered.

"Nor do I," Ned said. But he got up uneasily and headed for the doorway. Spartakos came down the steps to join him without being asked. Ned realized: *But he has been asked. Radio signal. That boyo is a Lyhhrt.*

Blue-shirt said, "I am not one of those from Lisboa. Come out of here where we can talk."

"What about?" Ned said. "You never come near me unless you want something. Eh, I guess you want Spartakos back. Well you'll have to ask him nicely now you've made him a world-cit."

"That's not what he wants, Ned," Spartakos said.

"Something else? No, wait, I know. You have a little work for me. Get blown up, beat up, shot at—"

"Please listen, Mister Gattes!"

Ned followed him out to the grotto stairway and down a few steps with a very reluctant tread. The night was warm and the sky full of stars out there, and the sea swept with the crossed paths of two or three moons. "Whatever it is, no," Ned muttered.

The workman said, "Listen, *please!* There is not much you owe Lyhhr, but you can give us that."

Ned reflected that, since he and Zella had been living off the avails of Spartakos for the last half-year, he owed him that. He settled himself on the stone step; it was warm, but he felt cold.

The Lyhhrt began: "I/we are—we were, I and my Other—attached to the Lyhhrt Embassy at Galactic Federation Headquarters on this world. Our Embassy did not know that we were also GalFed agents investigating—"

"Wait a minute! This sounds like very high-level business—you sure you really want to tell me—"

"A block has been on you since I took sight of you, and if you refuse my request you will forget this conversation. We were placed here because our world government suspected that the Ambassadors were assuming authority they were not given. In fact they are claiming to represent all of Lyhhr and threatening to bring an action against Khagodis for some imagined insult! We had been gathering evidence, they found us—" The workings of his shell began a barely audible hum and he paused to control it.

"Last night in Montador City one of them killed the contact I depended on, murdered my Other, and shot at me—and that murderer was one of them/us, one of our own people—who is searching for me now and he will find me before the police find him!"

Ned stared at this ragged creature who was like nothing he knew of as Lyhhrt. "How do I know all this is true? And if it is, what do you want me to do about it?"

The worker pulled the collar of his blue shirt down from his shoulder. His self-repair had filled in and reshaped the steel-mesh matrix where the shot had hit him, but he had no time to replate himself; he was working in economode, and there was a jagged star of blackness on his surface. Then he pulled the shirt back over his shoulder and hit Ned with:

> *Brezant bloody overtures in Montador/ESP woman-fear/Bronze and Brass-and-silver and ten thousand dropdown Khagodis*
> *smashglass/smokeflick———beggarcurb* WATCH YOU DON'T OUTSMART YOURSELF *says Willson———*
> *(greisbach is that you?/*NO BUT I WILL DO*/Lyhhrt/Tzuk! Willson!/omygod nononothing/TZUK! AND AGAIN!/*
> */*SMASH!
> *I-WE/US-MY OTHER!!!MY/BEING—my LIFE—I* still living?
> —alone with white-hot thoughts crashing rebounding reverberating against the seared walls of the mind—
> no tears for eyeless Lyhhrt. . . .

"I understand, I think," Ned said. "A chukker named Brezant, wants to send an army to attack . . . Khagodis?"

Workman calmed himself and told the story. "It has to do with what happened on Khagodis when you were there five of your years ago."

"And was it this Brezant that sent the Lyhhrt to kill you?"

"I cannot tell that. One of the two he had with him might have done it, but I didn't dare esp him. . . ."

"And you want me for—"

"There is nothing you can do about any of those—I am trying to explain my desperation. We have never lost sight of you and this artifact"—a nod at Spartakos—"even when we had no need of your services, and I am grateful to have found you here—"

Ned believed Lyhhrt did not tell lies; he assumed that this one was telling what he thought was the truth. "Because now you need me—"

"Lyhhr needs—"

"—to go down all those alleys through the garbage heaps where people have dirty faces and forgot to shave, where you couldn't go even if you dress up like one of them, and want to send me instead because you think I'm one of them!" Unconsciously he rubbed his jaw, which had been badly repaired and grafted long ago, and tended to flame or whiten when he was upset. Now it was red with slashes under the padding.

"No!" *:I might have shut your mouth but I would not.:*

"Thanks."

"My maker means well, Ned-Gattes-my-friend," Spartakos said unreproachfully. Ned wondered how he managed this.

"Ned!" He had not seen Zella slipping through the door and waiting in the shadow. Now she grabbed him around the shoulders and whispered, "Stop it, Ned." And to the workman-Lyhhrt, "He's not doing your dirty work!"

"Listen, Earthers! Listen, Edmund Gattes!" The workman crouched and thrust his arms out as if his body was truly a fleshly one, and the skin split over the crown of his head for a moment to show a glint of metal. "I am trapped on this world without a ship or even a shuttle, I have money that will not buy me protection, because of the work we have been doing I have no public accreditation, and the one person I trust to speak for me is running for her life—*(Greisbach, is that you?)*—and I cannot go back to the Embassy when the Ambassadors are plotting a war!"

The workshell gritted under the false skin from his effort to control himself. "Who can tell me from any other Lyhhrt now? I am alone, I have no Other, I have no accreditation! Only my genome can identify me, and I dare not show myself as long as I am hunted! The worlds of strangers are all too glad to be rid of us, but I cannot get off this one! Yes, I/we ask those like you to do dangerous work, and it may be in rubbish heaps, but we need you most because we trust you. We chose to look like common people now because other species are so frightened and suspicious of us, and come to you again because a fighter who is not a thug is the most valuable person to do this work for us—help me escape from this world and carry a message to the world Khagodis that anyone who threatens to attack them is a vicious criminal and not a representative of our people!"

Ned was taken aback at the longest speech he had ever heard from a Lyhhrt.

"Please! Say that you will consider helping me/us do this! If such an action came to pass Galactic Federation would become involved, there would be threats and embargoes, then military operations, and our already crumbling world would be completely shattered!"

Ned muttered, "I have a wife and children." He was breathing hard, and Zella was still clutching him around the neck, with her fists a knot under his chin. *And I'm over-age for a pug.* The lesson had been well drummed into him a few hours ago.

"The Khagodi know you from your work there five years ago," the Lyhhrt said. "They owe you favors. And when I/we can find help we will take care of your wife and children while you are away—and later you and your family for at least as far as the third generation. After that, if things go on as they are doing, we may be incommunicado."

"I don't see how it could get that bad."

"It may seem like a local quarrel to you! But our Councils, which we would never have needed one Cosmic Cycle ago, because we were One, have been torn into factions over the states of individuality, kinds of individuality we can allow among us, what we can afford to accept, and what we must refuse.

"All because of our trade, travels, explorations. Every day we grow a megamultiple of dogmas—why need I tell you this? If we are drawn into any kind of exoplanetary action there will be complete chaos!"

"And I'm to say all that to the Khagodi?" Khagodi were six times his weight and nearly twice his height, and looked like that dinosaur—

"Allosaurus. Say anything you like as long as it keeps Khagodis from believing we will attack them! My Other has been destroyed and I have nowhere else to turn, but I will make myself their hostage."

"But will that work!"

"Your friends Skerow and Hasso will know you, and Spartakos will be our own best represent—"

"One moment, my Maker," Spartakos said in a voice even deeper and warmer than the Lyhhrt's.

"—representative of—what? what?"

"Do you say that you want me to go with you, Maker?"

"Of course! You would be—"

"You are not asking me whether I want to go! I have had a useful existence here finding friends and taking care of the O'e, whom you made and then deserted when you gathered yourselves in. You made me a world-citizen, if you remember, with volition, and I want to stay where I am."

The Lyhhrt seemed thunderstruck. Spartakos was the one being among the worlds that he could not esp, and now was not allowed to touch without permission. The Lyhhrt stared at him for a speechless moment and Spartakos stood straight before him as if his splendor had not dulled.

"I need you, Spartakos," the Lyhhrt said weakly, almost wheedling, "to be our representative of Lyhhr's mastery of crafts Khagodi have depended on for—" He stumbled a bit and then recovered his passion: "Please! If we can carry out this mission we will give you new bearings of sapphire and titanium, replate your head and hands with newly-refined gold, and coat your steel body with rhodium! We will tip your fingers with iridium, give you fingernails of nacre from the finest shells of the hugest pearls in the seas of Xirifor, we will burnish you!!!"

Ned's only thought was *if.*

Spartakos stood silent for a moment, then said, "Will you also take care of the ones I have been serving?"

After the same scrupulously timed moment, the Lyhhrt said, "I/we will."

He turned to Ned. "Of course, we will give you risk pay also." And as an afterthought, "And we will rebuild that ugly jaw with newly grown skin and real bone."

"If I get back," Ned said. "I'll take you up on it."

"Ned!"

"It's all right, Zel. I have to risk it. I'm damned if I'm going back to Lisboa. This way everybody gets taken care of and that's how it's gotta be." The sloshing of a wave at the sea-wall made him jump, and he stared as a thick hairy arm came over the edge and got a grip, pulled up a soaked head with a draggled beard. "What—"

The Lyhhrt stood up and bent forward; Ned caught a flash of truly alien suspicion and terror that nearly cracked his skull. He gasped, "Watch it, man—that's Geordie, he drinks here!"

Zella cried, "Ned? What is it?" No one else had noticed the flash, and Ned shook his head; he'd learned something else he didn't want to know: that a Lyhhrt could be caught off guard.

The Lyhhrt hunched his workman's shoulders once and then the hand reached out of its sleeve further than an arm ought to go, he gripped the fleshly one, another hairy arm grabbed the railing, and it was one of the tavern brawlers who finally dragged his thick body up and over to stand dripping on the steps.

"Much obliged."

"Any time."

Ned said, "Hey Geordie, where's your friend?"

"Over by the pier waitin till his head stops spinnin!" He pulled himself up the Grottoes steps into shadow, with no idea how narrowly he had missed—what? Being struck down? Dropped back into the sea?

The Lyhhrt, for all his admitted weaknesses, his lack of the usual splendor, once again gave Ned a sense of being bound in deep and uncontrollable forces.

There was a silence, full of thoughts that might have been spoken but were let pass. After a few moments the Lyhhrt broke it.

"Ned Gattes, now you know everything I know. I beg you, as soon as you are able, take a walk at noon in that market up the road from here." He slipped away down the Grottoes stairs toward the darkness.

Ned and Zella did not watch him go but, arm-wrapped,

climbed the steps upward toward home and bed. Spartakos looked once at his friends, then turned and followed his maker with footsteps faintly ringing.

Good Night

"If your old man was such a sonofabitch what are you doing here with Brezant?"

It was a house, a hotel, a castle, it could be anything, they'd been travelling in darkness, and now they were here, alone and hidden in the depth of a forest. A place with stucco-effect walls, and its doorways were arched. Tyloe had hardly seen the light of day since he joined up with Brezant. Tyloe and Lorrice had adjoining rooms, too cozy; she'd opened her door into his, and was standing in its arch, her face sharpened by curiosity.

He was just sitting on the edge of his bed digging in his bag for tooth-cleaner. He stood up. "My father wasn't a sonofabitch, he just wouldn't give me room to breathe." Mercifully, she was wearing an impervious helmet, muting the tuning fork; its velvet sheathing looked like crisscrosses of red veins. Her dressing-gown was quilted black satin, an almost too obvious emblem of the darkness of night and the forest around them; somewhere in the depths of forests over the world, ten thousand men. He felt vulnerable, almost virginal, in his paper-white seersucker jams. "Does your ah . . . employer know what you think of him?"

"He knows everybody's scared shitless. He likes that."

"I don't like being scared. What does he want from me? So far all I've done is hang around."

"Well . . . I think you're sort of a reward for me . . . for letting every slimy exo crawl around in my skull. . . ."

"What does he think of this?"

"I'm the one with the esp here, and he doesn't say a word."

He stared at her and his hair stood on end. He was profoundly grateful for her helmet. Picturing those thick fingers twisting the fabric. Keeping his face straight, not put off. *That's his idea, is it?* But he dared not ask that question, or the other one, *What about crawling in my skull?*

"But he thinks you'll make the business look more respectable, give it some class, you've got height and build, went to a bunch of expensive schools, you can talk right. Not like those greasy lawyers and thick-butt thugs who sit around playing skambi all day."

"I was kicked out of all of those schools."

"But they chipped off some of your edges just the same, didn't they? Otherwise you wouldn't be here."

"What about you? You're here too, and I know you're a registered ESP."

"Ah, yes, one star." She grimaced. "The Registry sent me out here. I thought I was going to be the high-salary hostess of a wonderful luxury entertainment complex, know just what everybody wanted or needed and make sure somebody else got it for them. But Zamos blew up and I fell into a cheap whorehouse where the johns were scared I knew their secrets . . . so I was getting beat up in S&M fantasies until Andres found me, and I'm grateful for that, and I'm loyal, even though he is nervewracking. And he's—he's even kind of exciting . . . but you—you ran away from all the ones that wouldn't let you breathe. Do you breathe easy here? What are you loyal to?" Stepping forward, closer to him.

He found himself mumbling. "Maybe I never found out. I wanted to be something completely different. Thought I might be a pug and even went to a training school, but with my height I'm more of a target than a weapon and they all went out of business anyway. Like with you. Right now I think all I wanted was another chance to start over. Save up a little money and go home."

She said nothing to that, and it occurred to him that staying with Andres Brezant and starting over were mutually exclusive possibilities. Tyloe knew he was naïve, but he wasn't stupid. Brezant, after all, had allowed him to see and hear everything. "But this minute I'm loyal to Andres Brezant, and you can tell him whatever you want." Almost, in his mind, "him" with a capital H.

"I'm damned if I'll tell him anything." She grabbed his wrists and took backward steps toward her doorway, pulling him with her; she had strong cool hands, very white on his brown ones. "I'm the one that picked you off the street, and I'm here to make sure you have plenty to do." Drawing him over her threshold, flinging open her black quilted satin to clench him against her nakedness, crinkled jams and all.

What she wanted. No mirrors in these ceilings . . . not a Zamos whorehouse, but . . . *anybody watching?*

TWO *

Khagodis, *Gray-green Great Equatorial River*

Khagodi rarely travel by air because they weigh at least three times as much as any other species in Galactic Federation; Galactic Federation ships take them to whatever worlds that need them as judges, scholars, or telepathic therapists; their air cargo carriers are piloted by feathered Kylkladi.

Hasso was resigned to the lengthy voyage on the paddle-wheel barge down his world's greatest river on his way to the world's greatest institution, the Interworld Court. Hasso had already informed World Governors' Office of the Lyhhrt's message, and appointments for further discussion were set; so that with the three-thirtyday window he had been given by the Lyhhrt there was minimal urgency to his mission. But he could not help feeling resentment at the burden he was bearing. Being obliged to declare that Khagodis was under the threat of Lyhhrt attack had parched his mouth and choked the voice in his throat.

The wheel splashed and flickered, but its wake hardly puckered the smooth and heavy breadth of the river, whose other coast, though deeply forested, was faint with mist. There was no quiet aboard. Khagodi in official red and blue shoulder-sashes were mingled among Dabiri with braided tails, bright-feathered Kylkladi, and Bengtvadi with tattooed heads: tourists or embassy staffs on winter holidays, chasing after scattered children; in the mind silence underneath the whickering and squawking the Khagodi carried on their esp conversations, careful to focus them away from their alien neighbors.

At every stop on the long way traders boarded, mainly Kylkladi, to hawk jumbles of oxycaps, dried zimbfruit, fresh sea-stars, dopesticks, vials of allergy spray and necklaces of imitation Pstyrian fire-beads. Heavily muscled blue-skinned Varvani followed to push their creaking wagons for them.

Hasso, who rarely wore a helmet, rested in his circled place and was grateful to be distracted with noises and colors, multi-tongued arguments, children's counting games, calls from passing boats. The afternoon rain was loosening in the clouds, and the bargehands unscrolled the long green awnings with ropes and squeaking pulleys.

The sky flickered, but the lightning that struck Hasso did not come from the clouds. It was a psychic cry of grief and anger uttered by a woman—no, a girl scarcely older than himself, for Hasso in spite of his position and dignity was not long past adolescence.

She had ripped the strap off her impervious helmet, dragged it off her head and flung it away somewhere on the deck, where it rolled and clattered among the peaceful travelers who jumped as one and radiated a wave of surprise.

Hasso caught one glance from her tear-bursting eyes and knew a thousand things at once:

What is happening to me!

Dear Saints, I love that woman!

He was not only instantly in love—but in the grip of an embarrassing surge of lust that made him twist where he crouched. He yearned, with his whole being, with everything he had suppressed for all his life, with all the passion of the one heart he had been given instead of the Khagodi's double-hearted birthright, with all the effort he had put into learning and seeking in dusty records for grimy secrets—

All those around him should have been staring, snickering, jeering. No one stirred a limb or lifted a scale. The young woman's companion, a big southerner in brilliant scales and flash helmet, was grasping her arm, was about to twist it, she was shrinking away, his eyes squirted blood that splattered his blue official sash—too obviously a Khagodi with high blood pressure and a bad temper—

And all at once Hasso *knew*, as if the world had cracked open and spilled every secret of its millions, that the lout in the blue sash and the helmet crusted with false jewels was an Emissary of the Governor of Western Sealand, whose borders half-circled those of the Isthmus Territories, that the mother of the young woman was a widow whose husband had once been wealthy but left her in poverty, and having failed to win the Governor for a husband, had succeeded in selling him her daughter, and that this daughter, in her despair had cried out—

Just as Hasso's mind was about to boil over, in the instant when he was wondering how he knew all of this, he felt a peculiar stillness and almost knew what was coming next. *Knew* what was coming next.

An exceedingly sharp mindvoice aimed at him alone said:

PUT ON YOUR HELMET QUICKLY, ARCHIVIST! YOU DO NOT WANT THAT ONE TO RECOGNIZE THE MASTER OF ARCHIVES WHO CAN SEE ALL THINGS AND FIT THEM INTO ONE.

Hasso did not need to look: he knew the Lyhhrt was settled beside him on a three-legged stool, still wrapped in his ugly clothing. "By Saint Gresskow's Seven Bastards!" He actually heard himself whispering this unaccustomed oath. In a moment of breathless silence after he had hastily pulled on his helmet, he added, "Lyhhrt, whatever are you doing here?" He realized that he knew everything because impervious helmets mean nothing to Lyhhrt.

All was calm now. A child ran to fetch the tumbling helmet and the young woman meekly put it on. With a touch of the Lyhhrt's mind her guardian had let go his grip on her arm and forgotten his anger. He fished a wipe from his kitbag and absent-mindedly dabbed at the blood drops on his face and official sash.

But Hasso's spirit sank. With his glimpse into her mind he had given her one into his own, and in that instant she had seen kindness and the hope of help. And he did not repel her—surely not when she considered what she was travelling toward! Because Hasso had no blemish but his weak leg, though the pains he took to move his body neatly deepened the lines in his face.

But on a thinly populated world where reproduction was all-important, Hasso did not expect that any woman would risk her fertility with a man who had a wasted leg and only one heart, no matter how many times others called him a prodigy and a genius.

"Why are you here, Lyhhrt?" he asked again.

The Lyhhrt wrapped himself more tightly into his thick clothes and pulled down his brimmed hat even further. "A duty I have been forced into . . . no matter how I tried to shirk. . . ." And went on: *:I was conceived on this strange world and carried in the metal body of a robot to another one. That fellow you call Ned Gattes who guarded me sent me home safely, but by then it was I who had become too strange for us/my others, and they would not let me be One. I made my un/one self a gold and silver body and marched about like a bejeweled fool, but no matter how hard*

I worked for Galactic Federation I was no one and had no true being.:

:I had forgotten that you worked for them.:

:It is worth forgetting, except that they pay me a pension!:

:For a being five years of age by GalFed Standard, you are surely not a failure!:

:If you say so, Archivist. Finally I came back here where my genitors conceived me, where they at least had a few moments of sweetness before their sacrifice, and I keep watch, to honor them . . . my only us/ones.:

:You watch very well, Lyhhrt. Now tell me what danger it is that you've kept me from. The governor of Western Sealand has not much to do with me.:

And will have even less when she *is his wife.*

The Lyhhrt did not answer the private thought. *:You recall that Zamos bought a tract of land in the Isthmuses, a decayed estate belonging to the impoverished branch of a wealthy family. They bred clones and also found gold there. That governor—:*

:Of course! He's from a branch of that same wealthy family, they were named Nohl and he is Gorodek—and he bought up that land after Zamos was disbanded . . . yes, the gold ran out, and it was put up for sale . . . a worthless piece of land, but . . . its eastern border is only eighty-five thousand siguu from the Great Platinum-Iridium Field! He had bought it in his first wife's name, I had heard the rumors—and even sent for the documentation to keep in my Zamos archive—because an elected official is not allowed to own land in another country, and he was being investigated! I was only distracted and put it out of my mind because you dragged me into this business, Lyhhrt!:

"But it is all the same business," the Lyhhrt said.

"I can see that it is a dangerous one," Hasso muttered, *:when that land can be used for a staging area if the Fields* *were to be attacked . . . I must keep my skin well away from Gorodek.:*

And the woman he will marry. But he could not stop himself from yearning for a touch of that mind once again. *:But how Gorodek is connected to Lyhrrt only you can tell me.:*

"I know nothing to tell you now, Archivist, but I would like to stay near you for a while because I am frightened, as you have already noticed."

Lightning cracked the clouds and the rain beat down on the awnings like stones, and splashed into the river, as it beats at the end of the third quarter of every day on Khagodis's equator.

Hasso did his best to smile. "Lyhhrt should not be frightened, especially when others are so fearful of them. And I am ever so grateful to have an ally beside me."

But how can I leave her in such despair and misery? And how can I, how dare I help?

:Forgive me for saying so, Archivist, but you don't dare even try to help. It is not only dangerous—but if she has no strength of her own to grasp it, your help is useless.:

Then both fell silent. They understood each other too well now to need anything but silence in mind and voice.

Fthel IV: *Ten Thousand Men Plus Ned*

Ned could remember his mother singing the verse, if not to him then to his sisters and brothers in the crammed little house on the other side of the world in New Grace City:

The grand old Duke of York
He had ten thousand men,

He marched them up to the top of the hill
And he marched them down again

She'd got it from twenty generations of kids in the street who were too poor to watch KillerQwark on the trivvy or play ZammBanza with the plug-eye. The Lyhhrt had given him this number, along with everything else he knew of Brezant's meeting with the renegades.

The verse and the ten thousand kept buzzing in his mind while he packed a change of clothes and a bed-roll, his usual travel gear when he set out for dangerous places. The apartment was ringingly empty. Zel and the kids had slung backpacks and left before he was fully awake, he had felt their muzzy kisses and Zella's silence. No more talk about risk, danger, dread.

But Ned was thinking of that number alongside his experiences fighting in Zamos's gameplexes for twenty years, places like Shen IV, where there might be five thousand guests and two thousand or more staff.

I can bring a force of up to ten thousand troops with small arms and hypersledges. . . .

On Shen IV even discounting atmospherics for fifteen species there were endless freights of food, drink, performance equipment, computers and robotics rolling in on kilometers of underground corridors, so . . . No strategist, Ned tried to imagine where ten thousand troops plus hypersledges might be forming the militia Brezant had in mind, on this world where colonists had made themselves at home in the ruins of ancient cities among forests, jungles and endless archipelagoes. Especially a world where equal thousands of GalFed's civil servants took their vacations. And how Brezant would move them to Khagodis if his plans worked.

Of course not ten thousand yet; a nucleus that would grow by drawing on shifting populations of laborers, factory workers, old pugs who scuffed for work, malcontents like

Brezant's woman who had migrated with big hopes that got shrunk . . . and the big problems: where Brezant was going to find the ships that would carry his thousands and his sledges, and stay out of the range of suspicion, find the transport shuttles that would reach those ships, where he got the seed money—

Not my business.

He picked up the bed-roll to sling it on his back, and began to think of something else. No one knew yet that he was going away with Spartakos, and the less and later they knew, the better. The Lyhhrt had watchers, and so would he.

He unpacked the bedroll and stowed it in its cupboard, shucked his top and jeans and pulled on the thin shadowsuit (an old but good Lyhhrt artifact, fine as spider-silk) that would turn him into mist if he jumped out of his clothes and pulled its hood over his face when he was running late for GalFed. Topped that with the clean clothes he had unpacked, didn't know what his laundry prospects were. Folded his impervious helmet small and tucked it in his pea jacket because few had ever seen him wearing it. Then buckled his wrist into another agents' souvenir, an interworld trans-comm that looked like a cheap local message pad. Done.

In the mirror he found a fairly presentable man who was out of work, a well-used pug something under forty, good muscle and no belly yet. Scarred mug turning a bit weatherburned, and dark blond hair bleached from the light of five suns; not a deep thinker, hardly ever learned anything on purpose except fighting. But smart enough to suit his surroundings.

That's you, Ned.

The weather was cloudy and close to rain, and he was glad of this, because it dulled the ache of leaving home—not knowing where he was going. He hunched his shoulders against the wind, and when a tree branch whacked his face and made him turn he realized he was being followed.

He frowned over his carelessness but didn't dare change his pace. Couldn't make out who, kind of pudgy, vaguely familiar. He had that old feeling of being very isolated. He didn't dare use the comm to call for help because the Lyhhrt was in too much danger already. Nothing to do but keep moving.

The road was opening up into Plaza Square, and his mind dodged about for bolt-holes among the old buildings that made casings for new shops. He stared unseeing at the Tarot cards, sex aids, beers from forty-seven breweries on five worlds, cashbooks, dried sea-stars from Khagodis, and ganja (ge'inn and karynon in the back room). Follower ducked and lingered among broken columns that had become decorative statuary scrawled with graffiti. Ned did his own ducking toward the one place he could hope for help, and began to run.

The tracker lost patience and came out in the open, panting, his puffy face red with effort. Ned knew him. The other fighter in the bar; not Geordie.

Lyhhrt's anger and terror flashing:

Watch it, man—that's Geordie, he drinks here!

Hey Geordie, where's your friend?

Ned found the alley he was looking for, and the entrance, slowing to take a couple of long breaths and calm himself: he could afford that much.

Waxers Works was a small gym set in the ruins of a once-beautiful stone grotto, an old and now shabby place with dirty floors and peeling walls where Ned and Zella used to work out once or twice a tenday, and usually found some old friends and fighting partners. They'd given it up when the money ran down. Nobody around today but Hammer Head and Knuckle Duster dueling with sliver-sticks, both wearing baggy purple pants and black and white checked jerkins, their near-identical freckled faces grinning with big teeth, flaming red hair flying. They were good.

"Hullo, girls! What's doing here?" Ned wiped sweat from his forehead.

"Heyo Ned, ain't seen you in whiles, got new work?"

The pair were sisters whose real names were Daphne and Prunella, but they answered to Knuck and Ham readily enough.

"Lookin' for it, you heard of any?"

They stopped and thumped their sticks on the floor so that the little bells on the tips of them jingled. "Nah, we're too old for the porno, just slivers or chebok. But we got too whizzo for 'em nowdays, everbody gets pissed cause we're not bleedin. So whatsit, Ned, we help you look?"

"Thanks-oh girls, but whatsit is a boyo tailing me, he's comin' up the street there, an' I dunno what he is but I don't like 'im." He glanced out the window, saw the edge of a shadow.

"We wipe 'im for ya, Neddo?"

"Nah, just scuff him a bit, change his mind for him."

"We do." The sisters were half-a-head taller than Ned, and each weighed half again as much. "You want to take a dekko out the back way?"

Ned was tempted. Then took a thought and added, "I'm gonna open up here easy one sec 'cause if he's just some gormless wacko I'll be in real trouble, so you just keep by me, hey?" He did a little two-step to warm up and launched himself out the door, question on his tongue.

There was no time to ask it. First he saw nobody and then a glastex dagger with a fat-fingered hand gripping it ticked him under the chin. It had wavy double edges, looked longer than it was, and sharp, very sharp. It shone white under the white sky.

Ned gripped the wrist of the hand holding it with his left hand and shoved back into the fat face till the elbow joint growled, Attacker yelped, Ned kicked his shin for him, and when the knife flew from his fist Ned slammed his nose with the heel of his right hand.

Geordie's friend stared gaping. A thread of blood slipped down the cut that ran from forehead to jaw while his nose turned crimson. Ned ducked back in before he could pull himself together, and slid the door closed. He was suddenly, sharply, unreasonably aware that one of the local gendarmes in his khaki slops and cheap elastic gunbelt was shuffling down the lane toward his refuge.

"Eh Ned, y'done it y'rself! That's a steal!"

"Y'were here when I needed." He was heading for the back way, *just to see if Geordie—*

:HE WAS BUT WE ARE HERE NOW,: the Lyhhrt said from somewhere in that sharp mindvoice. Ned stood still and began to shudder, found himself giggling a bit. "Nothing's wrong, ladies, there's nobody out here, it's all right.... Thanks a lot, darlings, just go on fighting and you didn't see a thing."

"Bangers an mash tonight, Ned, you come on over?"

" 'Nother time!" He gave them a wave goodbye, they thumped their staffs till the bells jingled, and he took a good last look at them standing like an Anglo-Saxon version of Ashanti warriors.

When Ned closed the door behind himself no one was in the back alley. There was a thought-trail and he followed it, but his mind was still jingling with Knuck and Ham. He took a long calming breath. Yes. They were the kind of warriors Brezant might think he needed, but Ned wasn't going to steer them.

The Lyhhrt had holed up, literally. At the very base of the Grottoes, past where Geordie's friend had squatted and the sea just touched the lip of the weathered platform, was a weed-choked cavern too small and wet for use by others.

Ned bent to crawl into the dark and reeking hole, side-stepping rippling pools and dodging the patches of slime on the walls. The floor rose gradually and after a half-score steps opened up into a small dry room lit with a coldlight standard and neatly fitted with a narrow set of shelves; Ned felt the bubble-pop of a force-field as he stepped into it: the air was clean here. Spartakos was standing against the wall motionless, with his afferents turned down.

The Lyhhrt was shelving jugs, jars and instruments. He had removed his artificial skin and was now a smaller figure in brushed silver. He turned his electronic eyes toward Ned, saying, "All that I own now is here. . . ." but Ned was looking at Spartakos. He had never seen Spartakos new, and the robot was far from that now, but the Lyhhrt had found something in his magic shelves powerful enough to remove any tarnish, recover most of the lost gloss, polish the pearl fingernails. He gleamed.

The Lyhhrt said, "Would you resume your afferents, Spartakos."

The diamond eyes opened. "Hello, Ned!" Spartakos moved his arms up and out and added with innocent relish, "Am I not beautiful?"

"You are," Ned said.

But the Lyhhrt spoke without warmth: "Now, Helper, what have you to say?"

Ned was frowning. "Did you know who those chukkers were last night?"

"I realized eventually, yes."

"You pulled that Geordie out of the sea, and that was his fat friend trying to shuck me."

"Should I have let him drown? I've taken good care of both of them. Now—"

"And they knew me too!"

:They knew you from Scudder's Inn, Garden Vale, State of Bonzador five years ago when you saved the child of our Others. Like you, I would not have touched them until I was

sure of that. Now tell me how we will go ahead.:

Ned took a sharp breath and a step forward, eyes up. "You want a hop between stars, Lyhhrt? I'm sorry you're lost and have no Other with you, but for all your money you have no ship unless you can find one to hire, and I haven't heard of any, and you have a helper who is just a pug. The only way we'll get to Khagodis from this hole is with all the other pugs and scruff that hires on with Brezant and let him pay our way."

A Hot Box

Life went on for a day in the forest mansion, and no one looked sidelong at Tyloe. He wondered if everybody else had gone through the initiation. He walked carefully, uneasily wondering how far he could make himself go in the service.

Toward evening a runner came, and Brezant began to scream: Everyone came running.

The room Brezant used for his office had a desk with everything built into its surface, but he was not paying attention to the newstrips, stock quotes, sports-wins that flashed at him from seven worlds. "Whose goddamn dumb idea was that! Thought they'd shuck him in a barroom fight? Assholes! Last thing a show pug wants is a fight he can't control! They wasted their time on him? He's a nit, a nothing, he hasn't been in GalFed service the last five years! Come on, Lorrice, whaddya say!"

The room was stuccoed, its ceilings vast, its massive cabinets in dark wood with deeply carved doors and knotted brass handles; Tyloe, from his scrapings of liberal education, recognized Varvani work, an art heavy and full of dread.

But Lorrice, she was cool today, he thought, tuning fork muted. Perhaps sex had made her calmer. She said, "I never met him," Brezant snapped his fingers and she added without any hurry, "but Tyloe here, you took fighting lessons from him in that school, didn't you? He'd recognize you."

"That was a while ago, he'd have forgotten me," Tyloe muttered. "I was the wrong shape to get the hang of his style."

"You mean you couldn't beat him," Brezant said.

"I ran into his fist on Shen IV," Oxman said.

"He's been beaten plenty," Tyloe said impatiently. "He's got a mess of scars on his face and a bad jaw graft. Whether or not I could beat him, there were no more jobs for pugs."

Arms akimbo, Brezant surveyed his muster, snapping, "Nobody else got a word here?"

Heads turned back and forth until Lorrice, staring at the messenger cowering in the corner, said, "Frankie, just take that helmet off and let me look at you?" She forestalled Brezant's surge: "I can do it myself, Andres. Just let me." She took the helmet from Frankie's head. "What did Geordie say?"

"Well, he wasn't in very good shape when I saw him in the hospital." He seemed less afraid of Brezant than of Lorrice, cold as a dagger in her gray silk suit.

"He was beat up?"

"No, but his eyes was turned up an he couldn't talk very well. Something gone wrong in his head."

"An ESP attack!"

"They said he'd get better."

"And he said . . . something. Think."

"I don't much want to—awright, I think what he said was, a real weird Earther come in the bar, sizes up Ned Gattes—Geord never saw 'em before, and he was drinkin there a thirtyday, and the first thing he thought it might be a Lyhhrt 'cause they walk funny in those machine shells, even though this one was wearin clothes, and next thing he was dumped in the water and forgot everything else."

"Sonofabitch!" Brezant whirling and snarling, "That Lyhhrt will know everything about us! Those are two I want wiped. You all say yes?"

Nobody said anything except Cranshawe, the lawyer, in his even voice, "You might have other Lyhhrt coming after him."

"Then maybe we just get us some tame Lyhhrt! Go get him you jokers, Oxman and Hummer, you go out there and really whack him!" Sweeping the air with his hands, "Out out everybody, eat high, drink up and sleep tight! Just you, Lorrice, you stay with me!"

He danced there punching the air with high fists, his vital and powerfully sexual essence running over and spilling, "You get it out of 'em baby, no secrets! Love ya love ya love ya," shoving his face between her breasts and snorting. "Do for me baby, do for me! Stick with me and I'll pave your ass in diamonds!"

Tyloe sat in his bedroom holding his dizzy head. *He's crazy.*

Armor

"First, you need a helmet," the Lyhhrt said.

"I have one." Ned showed it.

The Lyhhrt did not dignify it with a look. He reached into his shelves and picked out what looked at first like a bronze armband, fanned it out into a jointed helmet of thin plates lined with fine-linked mesh. "You push this lever to close it, and pull that tab to open it, and the button over here will lock it. This sensor antenna beneath your ear will allow you to communicate with Spartakos wherever he is, and when it is retracted, neither I nor any other Lyhhrt can reach you." He folded it up. "Now try it."

Ned frowned. "I've never used one."

"If you want to join a militia you will need this."

Ned took it gingerly, cringed a little at the vibration in his hands as it sprang open, set it on his head, locked it, pushed in the antenna's tip—*a mind all alone in the universe for one moment!—*

"It fits," the Lyhhrt said.

Ned extended the antenna hastily as he gaped at his reflection in the cupboard door. "Eh, Captain Futurismo!" It looked only a little too beautiful. Lyhhrt could not do less. *As long as somebody doesn't kill me for it—*

For an instant he had an image of himself grasping the savage chebok, and shook his head.

"Unless you have a genetic twin it will not work for anyone else. But," the Lyhhrt added with more than a tinge of regret, "if you are truly afraid of theft and murder I will tarnish."

"No." Ned nodded at the dark gleam of his image. "I'll risk wearing it as is." He pushed the right buttons and pulled the right knobs to remove the helmet, closed it and clamped it on his arm under the jacket. It fit.

"Now," the Lyhhrt said, "we are starting out with no ship and no allies and men wanting to kill us. How are we to move under those conditions?"

Ned, who had spent a lifetime thinking on his feet, said, "You've been saying Brezant promised those Lyhhrt he can bring a force of up to ten thousand—am I right?—if he gets a go-ahead from Lyhhr. We can't tell whether he was just blowing hard—"

"All I know is what I learned from their ESP woman. If I/we had tried to esp him deeper we would have been killed without learning anything at all!"

"—but from what you've said those two Lyhhrt believed

him when he claimed to have troops on standby, so we have to assume he's been enlisting, or his staff is doing it for him."

"All we need is to find them—do you know where to look?"

Ned shrugged wearily. "How could I know for sure? And that's not all we'd need! His 'troops' could be all over the world, but if he hasn't got that go-ahead, he'd have to be crazier than he is to go very far."

:All of them are crazy,: the Lyhhrt said, not bothering to single out anyone.

"We have to start somewhere. If he was here with his whole staff he'd likely base himself near Montador City to be near the Embassy when he's expecting news—"

"The ESP woman gave no indication that Brezant would move away."

"—and I'd count on his recruiting first in Earther colonies like here in the Cinnabar Keys or on the Continent. That's cheapest. His ESP is an Earther and so are all his staff. His nearest lift-off from Cinnabar Keys here is Port City in the Basalt Desert just twenty-five hundred klicks away, it's all handy. I'd want to start by looking for the kind of people he'd hire in those districts and find out what they know."

"And where start then! Where start!"

Lonely Lyhhrt gradually became psychotic, something else everybody knew. Ned swallowed. "This is a small town with no kind of work that needs the military. In my home colony overseas I served a year in the reserve and then conscription got voted out—the military isn't important on this world, there were no 'aliens' when we settled here and the wild animals are slaughtered or in cages and parks—"

"*Where—*"

"We do have some time! And I'm doing my best! There's legion halls where old soldiers get together, and there's still people who want to handle guns and march around in ranks and files. But not around here. Port City is probably the best place to look for them."

"And they will all know who you are, will they not?"

"Brezant won't be marching around the barracks telling us to keep our back straight, will he? He sounds like a businessman, behind a desk while the officers work in the field. And *you* know, Lyhhrt, as long as we have Spartakos with us it's gotta be hard to hide no matter what shape he takes. The whole world knows Spartakos, he's the only world-cit in the Twelveworlds of Fthel who's a machine. But"—he nodded at Spartakos and then at the Lyhhrt—"you two can defend yourselves well enough." *If not me.* "The old dogs I'm looking for just want a chance to fight and be paid for it, they don't have anything against us, and if we can mix in we'll only be like performers to them." *Some kind of clowns.* "Maybe I'll even know some of them if they were pugs like me who fought on five worlds." His throat had dried up and he wished he had a beer.

"I don't know what is clowns and I have no beer. Here is water."

Ned took it on faith and drank it. "We have no choice and that looks to be the only way we can reach Khagodis. You choose the way you want to get to Port City."

"We'll take a private monorail car, reach the station by the path that runs along the sea-wall. It's rough and not many use it."

"And when do you want to leave?"

"Not tonight. We would reach there after midnight and we have no base for ourselves. We will stay here tonight, I have provided a hammock further back with an oxylator so you will sleep with enough fresh air, and here is a prepared meal for you. We will leave before dawn." He took a glassy package from one of his shelves and offered it.

Ned accepted it doubtfully. It looked with its paper fork and tiny square of napkin almost like any takeout from any shop that sold them. He was far from asking where the Lyhhrt might have bought it or by what alchemy he might have made it, only squatted with his back against the wall and pulled the heatstrip. "Bangers an mash? Eh, I guess that's what comes of hanging around ESPs."

He ate watching the last of the red sun's rays bouncing off the tide pools' ripples, rings of light growing and fading on the mossy roof of the cavern. Spartakos, with nothing else to do, stood motionless beside the cabinet. The Lyhhrt had disappeared into some corner of it.

The food tasted as it should, and the mild stink of the briny air did not spoil it. During a day of sweat-popping fright Ned had forgotten hunger and weariness. But the tension of keeping the Lyhhrt right-side-up had stiffened his neck, the fright had not left him and was very near panic—*Goodbye Zel and kiddos, this crazy business got me killed!*—yet his eyelids began to close as soon as he ate the last scrap; and he fell into a half-waking dream in which he watched the Lyhhrt opening a folded shelf into a table, touching a place in his neck to open little doors in his silver abdomen, a miniature cabinet.

Ned pulled himself up and staggered to the back of the cave where he found the same kind of sturdy canvas hammock he had slept in on several other worlds, dinged the oxylator, climbed in and . . .

Lyhhrt reached in for the transparent globe that held his naked self in its liquid, one and a half kilos of brain that looked like a giant cowrie shell with pseudopods holding almost invisible remotes; its thin and glistening skin was mottled in mauve and rose.

Lyhhrt was dreaming in his marshy world with its sundogs but no moon and its multiple millions of *our/selves*, while he directed his workshell to set the globe on its table, unplug it and add fresh nutrients from squeeze-droppers and vials of powder.

Ned dreamed with him. . . .

—what to do then? We wanted to be left alone to live as One and we were attacked by Ix, we begged for help from Galactic Federation and were ignored, Zamos gave us back our lives but made us become slaves and create more slaves for them—

—you say it would have been better to die and be forgotten—

—be One with the Cosmic Spirit—

—you think so! The Cosmic Spirit is life, we are part of life, and life battles to exist . . . the Ix attacked us to save their own lives when they could have asked—begged and pleaded as we did—for help . . . and who knows whether they did and were refused as we were by some other Federation of worlds . . . now Zamos is gone and if not completely destroyed its head has been smashed and nothing is left but flailing limbs—

Ned, dreaming, asked himself if there was a congregation of Lyhhrt in this cave or if he had been transported to their world, and realized, dreaming, that there was one Lyhhrt with generations of teeming minds in one brain telling each other the story of one people. . . .

—we were supposedly saved from Zamos, but the work we did for him we do still and the difference is, we are paid for it . . . but are we saved? We dream impossible machines and clothe ourselves in them and create ships and weapons for flesh-covered souls to destroy each other—what kind of freedom is that? We go out alone and isolated in metal casings and spy for others and make ourselves insane—and if we refuse, stop selling, stop destroying, want to live in peace, in One, on our own world, they say—

:Wake up!: the Lyhhrt said. *:They are coming.:*

Ned's eyelids were stuck together and he had no time to

rub them apart before a tongue of flame darted into the mouth of the cavern. His first thought, *oxylator!*—no, the Lyhhrt had turned it off, the flamer's whip of fire curled back on itself against the Lyhhrt's force-field with a hiss as it drowned in the pool at the cave's mouth. One tick after that a gun's barking shot sent its missile tearing through the field, it caromed off the corner of the Lyhhrt's cabinet, cut the strings of Ned's hammock—

Ned was halfway to the floor by then anyway and the bullet exploded in the ceiling and sent splinters into his neck and shoulder, no, his collar and sleeve.

Then there was quiet.

Ned understood, was made to understand in the chaos, that the attack-suits of their assailants had been programmed to fire as soon as their sensors identified the targets. Spartakos had jammed their electronics as soon as their signals reached him.

But: "That force-field was an error on my part," the Lyhhrt said calmly. "It delayed the signal."

Ned had not enough handkerchiefs to wipe his sweat off, and said through wildly chattering teeth, "Oh yeh." No force-field? Saw himself licked to ashes by that sharp flame tongue. He pulled himself up, still violently shaking. He had been skimmed by missiles before, but never two at once.

Where are they?

"Come and see," the Lyhhrt said.

There was rage in the voice and thought. Ned did not want to follow, but the cave was a dead end. He stepped carefully past the charred walls over the ash-strewn floor, avoiding the puddle. The sky was still dark with brilliant stars, dimly lit with a pink streak in the east.

Two figures were standing immobile before the cave's opening. They were crying out faintly through the thick bubble helmets, a thick man in dark glasses, a tall woman with yellow hair; since their electronics had been disabled they could not move in the flame- and bullet-proof suits. The suits, heavy akrytex dark as charcoal, could have stood by themselves anywhere, like the rocks at Stonehenge. "They're from Brezant?" Ned asked.

"Yes. They did not send their barflies after us this time." He walked around the two figures, came back to stand beside Ned and pointed at the weapon, suit glove still gripping and aiming it at them. Ned knew it, the long-barreled Quadzull: the one weapon Zamos originally had forced its Lyhhrt slaves to design for the Ix, and this one had been modified for Earthers.

"If you've been shielding me how did they track us?"

"Sweat, spit, skin flakes. We have not moved very far from your bar."

Not a very good choice, Lyhhrt. One more "error." "We better move away from here pretty fast." For the first time Ned noticed that the Lyhhrt-workman had reshaped himself back into the O'e beggar he had been at the curbside beneath the Lyyhrt-world restaurant. *To be less noticed.* Oh yes. Ned sensed Spartakos at his shoulder, fixed in a stare at Lyhhrt-as-O'e.

As the Lyhhrt-O'e was intent on the two attackers. "What shall we do with these?" A question half to himself and half to the man and woman in the suits, the one with the gun and the other with the flamer. "I wonder if those suits would still protect at close range. . . ."

Ned sensed more than mere toying with the thought. The pair were frantically twisting and crying out, their bubble-helmets misted with their breath.

Spartakos had begun to say, "No, Maker—" but Ned overrode him. "Lyhhrt, neither of these is the one that killed your Other, and this is my home. I come around here two or three times every tenday and I live five minutes away with my wife and kids. If I disappear and two bodies turn up there's gonna be more people after us than even Spartakos can count."

After a long moment the humble O'e face turned away. "Yes," the Lyhhrt said. His voice cracked. "Time to leave."

"Do they have enough air?"

"They have enough air. Whoever comes by in a boat will find them." He turned to Spartakos, who could not take his eyes off Lyhhrt-as-O'e. But neither said a word as the Lyhhrt went back into the cave to lock up and hypnoform his shelves, flick off his lamp. He led the way out: not to the east up the Grottoes steps where Dusky Dell's Happy Hour had folded itself up until noon, but westward around the jut of the cliff toward the much larger steps an ancient civilization had hewed out of the live rock of the cliff's face.

Ned forged his way up the giants' stairway under the blaze of stars that seemed now like the constellations of another world, a day-and-a-half away from being at least half-contented to hug Zella and drink beer in Dell's.

"What—?"

Spartakos and the Lyhhrt were standing motionless three steps above him. Ned's heart jumped and he scrambled to see what was keeping them, at first a dark shadow and then by its dry and musty smell the body of an O'e who had crept there to die under the hot sun, eaten away by diseases that brute evolution seemed to have spawned for the purpose.

Spartakos was very still. The Lyhhrt was beyond impatience—almost sparking with electric tension—but he only said quietly, "This one even you could not have helped."

Spartakos bent to pick up the gnarled and now sexless body and let it slip into the sea. He went on in silence on the path along the sea-wall and the Lyhhrt said sharply, "Come along, Edmund Gattes."

Lyhhrt hate names and use them most often as something

near insult. Ned raised his head from the sea and said levelly, "You chose me, Lyhhrt."

"You had better begin thinking of me as O'e," the Lyhhrt said.

THREE *

Khagodis, **Steaming Around the Diluvian Continent**

:What are we to do?: the Lyhhrt asked Hasso sadly. *:If we refuse to sell them our powers, build their ships and weapons, make ourselves sick with loneliness—try to live peacefully on our own world, they say: but you create wonderful instruments of surgery, heal bodies and minds with them, teach us to think thoughts we never dreamed of, and if you refuse that, what are you?:*

Hasso said carefully, *:Lyhhrt, perhaps there is more than one way to serve the Cosmic Spirit.:*

:It may be so, Archivist, though it would be difficult for me to tell that to my Others short of heresy . . . and what are we to do in the meantime?:

If Ned found it difficult to think of his Lyhhrt employer as O'e, Hasso could hardly keep from thinking of his own Lyhhrt companion as the Baby; he seemed so much like a lost child. Though a powerful one.

At Ocean City most of the barge's passengers had disembarked and boarded a much bigger coal-powered vessel for the journey southward around the coast of the Diluvian Continent. A long three days this was, and would have been longer and harder if Hasso had not been able to afford a sleeping basin. Nothing to see but the ocean's curving horizon to starboard, and to port the deep mass of the continent; beginning thickly green, it gradually eroded to pale granite that shifted from pink to gray as the long shadows slanted.

Hasso was hard put to keep his mind on the dangers around him, to restrain himself from trying to catch glimpses of the young woman—*:Her name is Ekket,:* the Lyhhrt had said—who had seized his consciousness at one blink. *But I cannot throw away everything I have worked for all my life in one moment of foolish desire. . . .*

She was standing by the railing looking out at the red line of the sunset; between her and Hasso three or four children were playing knucklebones and jumping up and down with triumph or dismay. Hasso was grateful for their distraction.

The Lyhhrt said suddenly, *:Look!—no, don't look!—but now the young woman's guardian is encouraging her to remove her helmet and cool herself . . . I believe that's a trap, he may have caught a trace of you in her thoughts . . . perhaps I wasn't shielding as well as I believe. Keep your helmet on, friend.:*

Hasso obeyed, with regret. But he got one instant's flash of her thought, perhaps by the young Lyhhrt's compassion for a lover, or merely a momentary breach of his shielding:

my mother
has sold me like a
whore

a thought shaped in the *seh* form that Skerow had written in all her life, brevity bursting with passion in nine syllables, created by a poet's tendency to fit a thought into such a waiting form, sometimes the inability to think it without forming it.

Hasso kept his eyes resolutely away from Ekket, but he could not help noticing that at this same moment the girl's guardian startled, and sharply ordered her to replace the helmet on her head.

Quickly Hasso and the Lyhhrt cleared their minds and focused on blankness to avoid an entirely different and dangerous thought: *:There is another Lyhhrt traveling with us, who knows everything we are thinking, and he is working for Gorodek. I am sure he let us into the young woman's mind to trap us, and we must take care, Archivist.:*

They finished their last day of voyage without speaking, and the last night in fighting back their dreams.

In the morning the landscape to portside was one great heap of rocks after another, with scrubby clumps of blue-green growths among them; eventually the ship passed through a breakwater into the harbor, where it tied up at a rough temporary dock built with newly hewn stone pilings and heavy planks of gubthawood still glossy with fresh waterproofing. The docking was the first at this location, since the New Interworld Court was truly new; the travelers would go through Imports and Registrations, a cluster of stone buildings as new as the pilings, and entrain for the Court on new steel tracks.

Hasso disembarked with a deep sense of foreboding that the gray skies reflected, and kept preventing himself from looking around at every step. He had his helmet latched tightly and the passes and ticket ready in his sling-pocket, and knew where to board the flatbed train. "Will you be coming along with me?" he asked the Lyhhrt. "I'm traveling on the third platform behind the engine."

The Lyhhrt was ignoring the stares of some of other passengers who, having been dissuaded from paying attention to him earlier, now suddenly noticed his awkward clothing and lurching walk. "I have a cheap ticket," he said. "I came on such short notice."

"Let me come with you on your car, then."

"No no, that's crowded and uncomfortable for you, and I travel easily in my shell. But I will meet you as soon as we reach the Court."

"Let us both take care, then!"

The Lyhhrt somehow edged away and became invisible once more.

Hasso felt very much alone among the bustling passengers, and stood still. The visitors he had expected to spend his time with were arriving by solar airship, an expense worth a year and a half of Hasso's salary, but he was mildly surprised that, with all the effusive invitations he had received, no one at all had come to meet him.

As he was thinking this he became sharply aware that the young woman Ekket was standing, alone and unattended, only a few siguu away from him. She seemed bewildered and was looking searchingly in the flow of incurious travelers.

Hasso did not move toward her. *I was foolish enough to allow myself such strong feelings, but I cannot blame her for that.* He could not keep himself from taking a good swallow of air and calling out, "Are you in difficulty, dems'l?"

"Eki! I have lost my escort, who went to such great trouble to keep me close to him." She spoke lightly, but with some bitterness.

Hasso did not dare to look for the fellow. "I'm sure he will come to claim you soon."

But before he could move away from her, an official who was obviously the portmaster's deputy by his red sash with brass studs, came striding forward, followed by Ekket's guardian waving his arms and crying out, "I tell you he has been smuggling it for the purpose of overcoming and befouling the Governor's bride! And that Lyhhrt, that you allow the freedom of this world, was conspiring with him, I heard their whispering—and now that creature has escaped!"

The portmaster's deputy placed himself in front of the guardian and spoke gravely, "What have you to say of this, Hasso son of Evarny?"

Hasso was completely at a loss. "Say of what?"

"This fellow Sketh is the aide of Governor Gorodek, and he claims that you have conspired with the Lyhhrt citizen to import an illegal substance, a dangerous aphrodisiac, for immoral purposes!"

The accusation left Hasso both breathless and voiceless; he swallowed air desperately and managed to cry out, "That's ridiculous!"

"Nevertheless I must ask you to allow the search of your luggage."

"I—" Everything was becoming unreal to Hasso, and his head began to throb. "I—if I must, I will allow it—but you will find nothing improper, nothing!"

The baggage handler fetched Hasso's small case, almost the last one left now, and the deputy conducted Hasso into the office, where his assistant unlatched the case and carefully removed the contents: his formal sash, with its Seal of Honor, carefully packaged; his rather bulky comm unit; his rain-clogs, a flask of dirib oil, a jar of sea salt. . . .

The karynon was in the sea salt; after all else had been unfastened, shaken, and poked at, the assistant's probing fingers plucked out the two small packages.

Hasso was trembling. "That is not mine!"

"It was found in your belongings," the deputy said quietly, "and until this can be investigated you had better stay with us. We have a lodging for you in a holding area, and of course Sketh will remain here too. He must repeat this claim when the Peace Officer comes, and also tell us how he came to have this information."

Sketh did not look pleased, and the deputy addressed him: "The young woman in question has been met and taken in charge by a new escort, has she not? It may not have been wise for you to let her go without giving her an opportunity to give us more information. At any rate, you have no pressing business, I believe, and are also free to remain here."

Free to remain! Hasso would have pulled off his helmet and opened his mind to the whole world, but esp evidence was nowhere accepted, especially not in GalFed territory. And the train had left.

Sketh cried with an explosion of breath, "You will hear from the governor!" But the deputy was an even larger and more imposing man than Sketh, and there was no more argument.

The deputy watched Sketh being led away and said to Hasso, "I know your honest reputation, Archivist, and I deeply regret this action, but there is the evidence—and we are situated in a new Interworld Area of this world where we must codify the Law as we go." He swallowed. "Ek! No consolation, is it?"

Hasso Alone

The holding area was a dusty square cell with a dry sleeping basin in one corner and a square window of thick glastex. Hasso could see nothing through it but a blur of gray sky and scrubby vegetation. All of his possessions had been left with him except for the incriminating jar of salt, but within a few moments of closing and locking the door, the deputy's assistant returned with a bowl of fresh sea salt—"Local, and very good!" he hissed—and Hasso could barely croak a thankyou. He was so dispirited that he stood in the center of this room leaning on his staff and did not want to move.

He did not know what to think. It had flashed through his mind that his own Lyhhrt friend might have been working with this fellow Sketh—Hasso had no way of knowing otherwise—and that his claims of keeping Hasso safe had been false, and his fears and tremblings nothing but deceit.

Hasso had thought that Sketh might be working with another Lyhhrt . . . *but perhaps there was no other Lyhhrt. It may well have been my Lyhhrt, the Baby, that I trusted, who betrayed me and led me into a trap, who would not let me travel with him because his ticket was cheap . . . if there had been another Lyhhrt among us he would have known everything we were discussing without our knowing, and he could surely have struck us dumb and without memory if he wished, but he let us be, and then suddenly—yes, suddenly he found a way to strike me dumb, here, in this place. . . .*

Eh, I am sure that karynon belongs to Sketh, and he is the one who uses it!

And a neat trick he played.

He recalled a case of Skerow's in which a Galactic Federation agent, an Earther named Lebedev, had been set up and falsely charged with smuggling karynon, had spent a year in a violent prison—unfortunately he was really smuggling Earther foods called *barley* and *chickpeas*, a foolish misdeed usually absolved by a small fine. Hasso did not know who was going to absolve him. And few prisons were as violent as the ones on Khagodis, whose psychotic telepaths could not be subdued by the most powerful of the sedating drugs.

And all because of my suspicions about the Platinum-Iridium Field?

Into the second quarter of the day the assistant returned with a bowl of fresh braised sea-stars flavored with sprigwort. "Cooked them myself," he whispered like a conspirator. His eyes would not meet Hasso's. He turned the taps to fill the basin and tossed a handful of salt into the water. "Rest if you like, citizen," he said, and crawled out in an agony of embarassment.

Hasso was humble, so much so that he was sometimes accused of working at it. Whether he was or did, he did not like being humbled—and although the civility of his keepers blunted the sharp force of his anger, his contempt for their fear of the Governor of Western Sealand left a dull ache in his belly. But he did not believe that Sketh would be served with fresh braised sea-stars. He forced himself to eat, slowly, and then moved to lean against one of the four walls. He did not want to sink into the basin and lose himself in sleep.

He pulled off his helmet and let it drop to the floor. The room was shielded; though he had his comm with him he could not use it. And he had no secrets.

I am sure there must be many others who suspect Gorodek of having designs on those Fields . . . I have no proof of that, and surely no one believed I would run off with the bride! Yet I must have some secrets, or Sketh and his master would not be afraid of me.

Gorodek's purchase of the Nohl estate had nothing to do with me, I have no power and I stay away from those who have it. My only interest in the documents about it is to complete my Zamos archive. I do nothing but read and listen and gather dusty facts. . . .

Skerow had once said: *Take care you are not seen as The Man Who Knew Too Much, Hasso. . . .*

What I know is my only power, and whoever feared me would be afraid of what I know. Should he be afraid?

Back against the wall, grasping his staff, he contemplated the room, the dusty cube of dim light.

My Lyhhrt friend warned me of Gorodek, I cannot blame him for being frightened and running off. The thought came unbidden and comforted him. *My back aches horribly, but my mind is clear. . . .*

If I were home in my own study—and how I wish, instead of leaning on this dirty wall—if I were home that window would look out on my street with its stucco houses and blowing trees. My set of shelves would be on that wall beside the basin . . . my clay tablets and styluses at the bottom where they don't have far to fall, the sealed packs of damp clay beside them; next up my three-screen comm with TriV and players for spools, wire, tape, optic, and those disks with old local ordinances I really should throw out, up to the top my vellum scrolls of WorldGov Records going back two hundred and fifty years . . . the fan humming to keep the dust out of them and the almost annoying perhaps sometimes comforting buzz of the humidifier that keeps them from cracking to pieces . . . and in front of all those my lectern and the thaqwood scroller with silver knobs that dear Skerow gave me after I had presented my dissertation. All of my secrets are on that wall. Everything to do with Zamos.

And what has Gorodek to do with Zamos? Since WorldCourt still sends me documentation of everything to do with Zamos though the trials are over and there are no new prosecutions—at the moment in any case—the Court was sending me documents about Gorodek and his land purchase with reference to Zamos—what would be new there?

Think, if I were to step on my ladder and reach up to those Earther books with spines and leaves, codex number seven. Testimony of witnesses—all of whom went to prison.

Yes: that land in the Isthmuses was bought from the Nohl family in the name of the Interworld Trade Consortium and managed by a gang of felons who were stealing its gold and selling it back to the Consortium. And let me leaf through past their words to—I do remember that I stuffed these extra leaves of copy into this volume because they were of Earther paper and did not read them more than once because symbo lingua *does make my eyes sore.*

Description of lands—and the deed itself, as sold to Agga, the wife of Gorodek who soon inherited it! No, I saved it in that Codex not only because it was paper, but because it was connected to Zamos. Of course that was why it was sent to me. . . .

The purchase was revealed three years ago, but his wife had bought it three years before that. She was also a member of the Nohl family and she bought it cheap because it was swamp land and there was no gold left. Of course there was a fuss about her owning it when her husband was the governing official of another land, but she claimed, or he claimed for her, that she cherished it because it had been in her family—a nostalgic sentiment!—but as I recall, if you looked more closely at the evidence during the trials, you would find that piece of land contained a clone factory, an experimental laboratory of excruciating tortures, a nest of Ix that reached out northwest even to Burning Mountain—sentiment indeed! And much of that was still there after they'd bought it. Yes. The last leavings of Zamos's empire.

There is no provable evidence that Gorodek or his wife knew of that, or had anything to do with it. Though I do wonder how she died. No children at any rate, that's why he wants that young lass I dare not think of. Eki, Hasso! You have no luck!

But I would not be surprised if there were Ix on that land when they bought it, and he knew that. But why did he buy it? He may be thinking of using it as a staging area but that was not why he bought it, six years ago.

Hasso dismounted from his imaginary stepladder. The thought of Ix had made him dizzy for a moment; though he had never met one, he had once fought off an Ix attack by the force of his mind; that was meeting enough for him.

And his father Evarny had been killed by an Ix.

In the Interworld Court, in the same bower where Hasso was lecturing a few days ago, at the end of the testimony during the first round of trials, everyone making the first move to leave . . . Hasso had made Skerow tell him everything, on one of those days on the rooftop under the winter sun, brewing tea and pouring the whitethorn:

Skerow: *Myself standing up at the back thinking how wonderful it was that justice was coming to pass, watching Evarny come up the stair to meet me, how bright and sharp he was, how quickly he stepped—then saw the sparks, smelled the ozone, felt faint and dizzy, could not help looking up where* it *was crouching in the roofing branches, holding that gun in the black claw hands, long-barreled silver gun, lightning-bolt against blackness, meant for me because I had made the first move to destroy that monster of evil Zamos and—*

She could not go on, but he had seen it clearly enough in her mind:

No! no!—his father—*my father!*—throwing himself in the way and the reverberation of the bullet exploding in his body.

And the gun, the long-barreled Quadzull, that the Lyhhrt designed for the Ix, to their credit the only weapon they ever made. No threat could force them to design another once they saw how that bullet exploded in a body.

That gun.

Let me reach up again, so hard, so tired, into those shelves. No justice for that murder, the Ix escaped and was almost certainly killed later, but those guns? Lying under that case of wire spools beside the psi-resonancer there is the printout on flaxskin sheets that I sewed together with red oilthread, World Court and Interworld Court Reports on Illegal Weapons, yes, Quadzull is an Ix name but we manufactured the guns on Khagodis, as that report told, like it or not, in that place, whatever is its name, Eki, I have dropped my staff, I am so dizzy and my heart beating fast and faster and such an ache in my ribs—dear Saints, let me not die before I discover—in a factory they claim is now closed, shut down, levelled to the ground on Five Point Island, a protectorate of Western Sealand, Gorodek's land where they made guns for Ix to assassinate Skerow and murdered my father instead. I—

Hasso fainted.

Fthel IV: *Night*

In the forest house karynon came in two dermcaps: the aphrodisiac and the antidote. She had pressed the one on his wrist where the veins were; the other was in a tiny jeweled box set into a gold bracelet on her wrist. Brezant did not need them; he wanted dangerous extremes. There was half an hour on the timer, after that madness and death. He lay alone on the immense four-poster watching as she dipped her fingertip into perfume and ran it up the inside of one thigh and then the other. Rubbing a fold of her skin between his thumb and finger.

It had been another day of rage: bigger risks and more losses. She and Tyloe had held him down, soothing and cajoling, and the little doctor had supplied a big dose of calm.

Now Tyloe watched through her eyes, in his bedroom or wherever he happened to be, because she wanted him to watch. She was not afraid of him, and didn't care that he saw her fear and desire.

:Enjoying yourself, Tyloe?: This thoughtvoice had a new tone. *:You did. Now it's time to stop. You watch* them, *Tyloe. Istvan, Cranshawe, Demarest—you watch all of them.:*

What she wanted him for.

She loves him.

And a Good Time Was Had by All

Ned was staring out the train window at the landforms that rose and fell, the shoulder-high strawgrass and the semi-succulents like towers that had spines as long as his arm. Thinking about nearly having been murdered. "Those fighting-suits," he said, "Lyhhrt didn't make them, I guess?"

The Lyhhrt said, "If we had you would be dead."

"I bet they cost a lot just the same. They wouldn't put all the troops in them?"

"Maybe front line attackers if they were using flamers. They would still cost."

"And if they didn't work they'd cost a lot more." He did his best to think of other things.

Port City was the first real city built and settled on Fthel IV. Inland southwest toward the center of the continent, it rose out of a wrinkled basalt desert, the overflow of an ancient volcano. It had been built prefab in straight lines, there were few gardens or gracious lives there, and the air was always hot, not warm. Its citizens sneered at effete towns like Miramar for their boutiques and historical atmosphere, and most often referred to them as The Refinery.

Only at night did the city flower with coldlight and neon designs on every building, and then it burst into riots of color, and occasionally riots of whacked-out navvies and construction workers stopping in for a boost on the way home.

Ned stood on the main street's walkway, gripping the handrail, Lyhhrt to one side, Spartakos to the other. Below him the monorail hummed, and far across shuttles lifted into the evening sky on spurts of fire aimed at orbiting ships. The passersby, who had already seen everything coming and going, paid no attention.

"Where now?" Hire-hall and Legion Hall had come up empty, and Ned wanted a beer and a sit-down. He sighed. "I know two or three places around here. . . ."

"Let us go, then," the Lyhhrt said.

The bar was as Ned remembered it, down a long lane, very much like the one he had run with his heart thudding only yesterday, behind slivered boardwood doors between a PiKwiK and a CashNow. Ned pushed through the doors into a blazingly lit room blaring with drums and cymbals, and centered with a canvas-floored ring where three beefy life-forms of indeterminate sex and species had wrestled themselves into a grunting pretzel-knot.

On the walls the same winking, gesturing holograms of buccaneering men and women who had piloted the traders/smugglers of the spacelanes in the last couple of hundred years; in a corner the same chrome-plated form of a giant woman with classic features and breasts tipped with spigots: Goddess of Beer. She carried a lightning bolt in her left hand and her right hand held a copper mug, which she lifted stiffly to her mouth with bended elbow and set down again with a clank, lifted and set down again. In moments when the music paused her joints gritted faintly.

Spartakos paused to stare at her. "That is not an *auton,*" he said.

No friend for Spartakos there. "No."

"That's not seemly, Ned."

"The beer isn't very good either," Ned muttered, wishing he'd chosen some other place. His nose prickled with smokes and perfumes. A lot more of the jhat here. He searched for a table, sidling through the usual crowd of rawboned sweatband-headed men with skin half sunburn half tattoo, wrapped around hefty women wearing real jewels. Mostly they were workers around the port or on permanent time-and-a-half in mines, factories, construction and on derricks, and most of them knew Ned, mainly because of Spartakos.

:Look who's here: the way the Lyhhrt transmitted it, seemed to flash through all the minds at once.

"Here's the one lives off his robot like a fucking pimp," a voice said.

Ned had sometimes run a couple of whores in an earlier life to cover his work for GalFed. He looked hard at the voice's blue-jawed owner. "I want work. Who's hiring?"

"Nobody wants pugs no more. This is a port here with rousters and tuggers, and around it's factories, mines, construction. If you're good at that you'll find it."

A woman came from behind the beer goddess to take orders: she was an O'e, and the look that passed between her and Spartakos, and then at the Lyhhrt-as-O'e, was a laser beam.

Ned touched Spartakos's shoulder.

The woman said nothing except with her eyes. With difficulty, Spartakos turned his eyes away. Ned almost felt the circuits flashing.

Drinkers jeered at the O'e and put out legs to trip her, but she was nimble and stepped over them neatly. Ned turned his glance away carefully and Bluejaw dug his snout into his beer.

The wrestlers unraveled themselves into a Varvani woman, a bulked-up male Dabiri and a genuine Asiatic sumo wrestler. Ned found his voice to say, "I been to all your hirehalls."

A quiet thin voice said from a dark corner, "Been a lot of hiring for offworld."

"Depends where."

A loaded silence. Then, "Aren't we choosy," Bluejaw said with an elaborate titter—

—then something like a shifting of viewpoints, or—

The O'e woman was whispering to the Lyhhrt, "You are so lucky to have Spartakos protect you!"

—a sense of infinitely reflecting mirrors, of minds rebounding from each other, of a heavy body with silent feet, powerful swinging shoulderblades, a whacking tail, thirst and hunger . . .

. . . resolved through the doorway into a big red cat with red eyes flashing green eyeshine, a black V stripe running from her forehead down along her flanks. Her telepathy marked her as female, an Ungrukh woman.

The Ungrukh, a mutant version of Earth's own leopards, were, along with Lyhhrt and Khagodi, one of the three species Galactic Federation depended on when they needed telepaths. But Ungrukh did not like following orders and were not very sociable, even with each other. They worked only to feed themselves on their fierce and rocky world.

Ned, about to sit down with his squeezer of beer—he had never drunk from the beer goddess—stood watching the Ungrukh. The bar had fallen silent; the drinkers knew this cat and their eyes were on Ned now.

The Ungrukh woman came straight to Ned, stood on hind feet and clapped her paws on his shoulders.

She opened her jaws and said in raspingly guttural English: "Harroo Ned Gattsss! You mooff here naow?"

Some of the drinkers spluttered in their beer, others laughed, and the rest twisted their mouths in disappointment.

Ned grinned. "Just visiting, Rrengha—what about you, sweetheart?" Her saber-teeth were so close to his face that his breath made her whiskers quiver. He was panting, but he stood quietly and let her finish her little joke. "I wondered what happened when I didn't see you around the plaza in Miramar."

"That's a long story." Rrengha relaxed into competent *lingua* and dropped to the floor. "All because I am trying to get to Khagodis." She looked up at Spartakos, and then at the Lyhhrt-as-O'e, and did not mention that she knew what he was.

But the whole room seemed to be listening now, or perhaps Ned's uneasiness had become paranoia. He stepped off the razor edge he had been walking on and sat down a little calmer. "Let's hear it."

"First,"—the bartender himself was approaching with a big bowl brimful of chunked raw meat to set down in front of her—"my dinner." After she had gulped this down and slurped the last drop of blood she said, "For now I am earning my living as the guardian of peace in this place." She looked about and found everything peaceful, while Ned took a suck of his beer and left the Lyhhrt to brush away the O'e woman.

Then Rrengha panned the room with a look and the customers kept their eyes to themselves. "It is some years ago that Galactic Federation tells Ungruwarkh there is a request from Khagodis for consultation with us because both of our species are so strange. Neither one grows out of the life on its world. We originally believe the god Firemaster comes from our volcanoes to make us in the colors of our land and his fire, but now even the most ignorant of us knows that a powerful alien being from the depths of space picks animals off your old world and makes us Ungrukh out of them for his amusement. That is hard to swallow, but we manage.

"The Khagodi are also not related to any other of their life forms, and they have ten times ten kinds of religions to explain their beginnings. But when they dig up an ancient ship that comes from some other world their scientists and priests want to know the truth and ask us for advice.

"Not so simple. Nobody is offering any money." She gave a meaty belch as politely as possible for an Ungrukh. "We never have much and there is little to find when all you want to buy is knowledge. And you know we don't care much about writing our history when it is mostly about old battles. Khagodis is having trouble with politics and the Ix and the Lyhhrt, and they don't care what their learned people want.

"Galactic Federation says, what Khagodi want is not our business, but after a lot of arguing they agree to pay one person's way to Khagodis by whatever route is cheapest. My people say, Rrengha, you are here on Ungruwarkh four times ten, and ten again years, your mate is dead of old age and your cubs have grandchildren, you are not much use around here, so it is your turn to tell those fools on Khagodis what they want to know, and let them pay your way home.

"All very well, next delivery of cattle embryos on Ungruwarkh that ship picks me up and by one or two jumps here I am in this ugly city—which is somewhat nearer to ships and cheaper than your beautiful one—still waiting for the lift that takes me to Khagodis."

The Lyrhht said suddenly, *:And you found this place. You would not be working here if there was no information coming.:*

:There is a matter of being given admission, Lyhhrt . . . they must trust me first.:

:And they had better do it soon,: the Lyhhrt said. *:We also would like to do a favor to Khagodis. Not to wait.:*

"Yeh, that is a long story, Rrengha," Ned said, playing up, and also wondering how Rrengha and the Lyhhrt had become so close so quickly.

Rrengha said in a mindvoice that was like letters of fire, *:We two peoples know each other many long years, Ned Gattes.:* And then, loudly, "Aar! Pretty soon I get tired of moping about here. I want lots of space and fresher smells!" A thump of her tail signified that the conversation had ended.

Ned, because he was an old hand at the business, felt one of those synapses, at once insight, resentment, relief: first the realization that Rrengha was a Galactic Federation agent, at least a temporary one, because GalFed never deals out any money without exacting service, if only on a while-you're-at-it basis; resentment at adding another member to the team at the risk of making it unwieldy; relief that the new addition was as powerful a force as Rrengha.

Even though Ungrukh and Lyhhrt had had their disagreements during their long years of history. Spartakos, at least, was peaceful, having pulled away from his concentration on the O'e woman and shadowed himself in a corner.

Ned muttered, "We can't hang around here forever. In the meantime there's no bloody lift." He rose and sauntered to the dark corner where the man with the quiet thin voice had said, *Been a lot of hiring offworld.*

:Be careful with that one!: the Lyhhrt said sharply. *:He is well armed.:*

Ned said, *:So am I.:* If Lyhhrt/Spartakos/Rrengha with their minds/lasers/fangs were not weaponry, what was? He sat down at the small corner table and regarded the man, who looked back at him mildly enough. "My name's Ned Gattes."

"Lek here." He was a scrawny man with rough-cut hair, a scrag moustache and a point of beard under it. He was wearing clothes as worn as himself and a conical felt hat with a curled brim, and had no woman or jewelry to show off. He drew on a dopestick and let the smoke curl away from his mouth. "I know of you, and everybody's heard of Metallo Man but that other one doesn't look useful."

"They come with me, that's all."

"Are they worth anything?"

"Depends what you want them to do."

"That half-rotten O'e?"

"He'll fight for my sake."

"I can find a fight for you—not in any arena, not in this bar either . . . not on this world. You'd have to pick a side."

"That's what you expect in a fight. What kind of sides?"

"What kind do you want?"

Ned sucked the last drop from his squeezer. "The one with the money."

"Good choice." The O'e woman came forward to clear the table and Lek set down his mug, and smiled. She turned her head and shoulders away as if she were warding off a blow, and hurried away quickly. He watched her beaded helmet glittering and the swirl of her flowered gown and said, "Some of them aren't bad looking if you don't look too close. . . ."

"Yeh," Ned said, and waited. He could feel a hot trickle of sweat running down from his left armpit and wished he had taken his jacket off.

"Your robot friend collects them, doesn'e?"

"Lyhhrt made both of them. Birds of a feather."

Lek snorted. "They fight for Lyhhrt?"

"The O'e I know will do anything Spartakos wants. I guarantee it. And he'll fight." *For the ones I know he will, anyway.* "Who's hiring, and where offworld?"

"There's a hot spot on Praximf's moon, Calidor, always some bunch wanting to build a base there—"

"And none of them ever comes back from anywhere near Praximf, do they?"

"If you say so . . . you've been to Khagodis, no? Some work for the Lyhhrt there?"

"Lot of good it did," Ned said bitterly. "They never came back either."

"But you know the place."

"I would if I was paid to know it. Is recruiting your business, Lek?"

Lek gave a closed-teeth grin. "No—but it's my business to find out if the recruits know the place they're going to . . . eh, what about that cat you're up close with?"

"Rrengha knows the world."

"She bite?"

"Never bit me."

"Heh, I dunno if that's saying much. That's it, then." Lek pinched the coal off his dopestick and dropped the butt in his vest pocket. "I can't guarantee I've got work for you, but I can tell you if you want a cheap doss drop my name at the Sol3City on Main at Fourth, and you'll hear from me. They may not want the Big Red that place, but I guess she has her own quarters." He got up, thin and loose-limbed, tipped his hat and left.

:That was very dangerous. Especially if I had been forced to strike him down.:

Rrengha would have taken care of that a lot faster. "You want me to be the mug that deals with the other mugs and that's what I'm doing." Ned had half-expected those lazy eyes to look up, the thin lips sneering: *Don't I remember you from somewhere, somebody saying you did odd jobs for GalFed?* He found himself longing for the backup of somebody he knew and cared about. Zella had been that in arena days past, she had always been a fiercer, sharper fighter than he; while he liked a taste of violence, she was often afraid of her own anger. He felt lucky it was not usually directed at him. He said to Rrengha, "Lady, you want to come with us or make your own arrangements?"

Rrengha grinned, "Not to sleep with you, Ned Gattes—and I owe a night's work here, but when you want to leave this city I am with you."

They left her curled up neatly beside the doorway, heavy head resting on her crossed forefeet.

Outside Ned found a cool night where few trees whispered when the wind blew; down the lane toward the street coldlights were fading and neons blinking out. "Good to be out of that smoke," he muttered. It hadn't mixed well with the beer. "At least we got out of there without a fight, and that's more than I can say for some places."

The Lyhhrt said in a very low voice: "We have a follower."

Ned turned to look, saw a dim figure, saw it stumble and then heard a crack, very much like a head hitting the pavement. It lay very still; Ned crept up to it and the Lyhhrt did not prevent him. "Dead?" It was one of the bar's customers, a thick dark-bearded man trussed with the usual weapons. Ned only vaguely recalled him, and was momentarily disappointed. He'd been wishing it was Bluejaw because that chukker had a whack coming.

:A concussion.:

He looked up at the Lyhhrt, who had nothing else to say. "Did you do this?"

A shrill voice cried out, "I did that, I! I!" The O'e woman came out from the doorway she'd been hiding in, shivering, hugging herself in the sharp wind while her robe blew about her in mad patterns. "He was running for me, me," her angry eyes picked out the blue and red glints of coldlight and neon. "And he thinks he has the right, always him and those others, he splits us like axe on wood and lets us burn for his heat!" She grabbed at a fold of her robe to wipe her eyes, a slit opened in it and Ned saw the knife harness strapped to her thigh. She pulled the cloth together, crying out through her tears, "I put out my foot to him," repeating the gesture, "and if he has split something so much the good for him, that piece of shit!"

She stopped to catch her breath and Ned felt he needed some too. "We won't say anything to anybody, but you better get back there before they miss you—and let us get away from here too." The unconscious man began to snort and twitch. "Let's go—"

"No! I want to come with you, with Spartakos and this other one you have along and give shelter to—"

"No, dems'l," the Lyhhrt said, civilly enough but with a shade of panic, "we must get away from here before—"

"Please, no!" she cried desperately, "Spartakos! Let me come with you wherever you are going! Please, please take me with you and share your freedom with me!"

Ned and the Lyhhrt were already on their way, but Spartakos was standing still. His head turned, from the O'e woman to Ned and back again. He moved deliberately to pick up the groaning man and set him on his feet, where he fell immediately to all fours and stayed there for a moment, moaning and snarling, and gradually began to crawl away—probably, Ned thought, with a boost from the Lyhhrt. Spartakos came to the O'e woman, laid a hand on her shoulder and said, "Dems'l, the ones we are going with will not treat you any better."

Ned thought of the way Lek had been watching her.

"Please! If I can stay alive in that place I can do it anywhere!"

Ned said desperately, "Miss, it's worse than you could think!" His own words gave him a shiver.

She bowed her head into her hands and wept.

Spartakos looked at the Lyhhrt, and at Ned. "This one will not lie rotting on the steps down to the sea." And to his charge, "Come along then, we will find a safe place for you."

Nothing for Ned but to follow, and the Lyhhrt, like the O'e he was pretending to be.

Ned, frightened, exhausted, stewing in his own sweat, wondered about the crawling man, of whom the Lyhhrt had said nothing, but was not so curious that he wanted to find out.

FOUR *

Khagodis, New Interworld Court in the Southern Diluvian Continent: *Hospitality*

Hasso thrashed in fearful nightmares, drowning in heaping seas, twisting in swaddling bands on flaming pyres, battling the squirming monsters that leaped out of his mind, and—

"No need to throw yourself about, Hasso my friend. You are quite safe now!"

Who . . .

Hasso forced his sticking eyelids open.

"Yes, it is Tharma, your old friend from Burning Mountain!" The lively crinkled face and the voice with its sharp West Ocean accent certainly belonged to Tharma. "You never expected to see me by your bedside." That was true enough, though Hasso had known that Tharma had left her Police position in Burning Mountain to become Head of Security in the Court. Beyond her there was a white wall and arched ceiling, even a round window with morning sunlight coming through its quarter panes.

When he tried to move he found himself bound on a linen-covered mattress by wide bands of elastic cloth that limited his movement without stopping it; his head was encased by an impervious helmet in the form of a padded bonnet to keep him from harming himself as he flung it to and fro. His mouth was so fearsomely dry he could not speak, and a medic in a red sash came forward with a bowl of water while Tharma loosened his bonds.

After taking a few sips he gasped and croaked, "What are you doing here, Tharma?"

Tharma took his trembling hand. "Your friend Lyhhrt saw what was happening and sent me a message right away. If I had not been forced to leave the Court for only two days this would never have happened and—"

"But what—"

"You were found unconscious in a faint because of a disturbance of your heart rhythm and of course you are being given drugs to counteract it—"

Hasso swallowed air mightily. "My heart! Dear Saints, I am not enough of a wreck but that I must be tormented further!"

"I spoke one or two words to the Director General about that—"

Hasso slipped the knot under his jaw and flung the helmet away. "Shut into a cell and tied up here too! Really!"

"Because you were fighting so hard, Hasso. You were put to sleep to calm you down. With the drugs you are taking you will be quite well in a few days—and this is the finest hospital in the world."

"And then I will be shut back up in a cell, I suppose!"

"Absolutely no—"

The door opened then and Hasso shut his mouth at the sight of the Director General himself, the employer of his employers.

That official, whose name was Vannar, was a large and

dignified man wearing a white flax-seed sash with gold buttons of office. Hasso had seen him on TriV many times but they had never met. He put out his tongue courteously at Tharma, turned to Hasso and said, "Archivist, I speak for myself as well as my Customs Officers when I say that we owe you the deepest apology."

In this moment Hasso was putting his mind in order and it seeped in that he was not to be put back into a cell. "Your Honor, those officers had evidence that it might have been dangerous to ignore." *But even safer to run an identity check on the accusers instead of being so frightened of Gorodek.* The DG, massively helmeted in brass and silver, was safe from the criticism.

He squatted beside the bed, looked down at Hasso and said gravely, "It will not be of much importance now." Hasso became frightened again, but Vannar swallowed air and said, "That fellow, Sketh was his name, I believe? who accused you is—how can I put it otherwise?—dead. In fact, he was killed. Murdered."

"Dead? He was in a ce—holding area like mine. How—"

"We have no idea how—and even less, why! One of those small window panes was melted away—"

Hasso's mind became concentrated very quickly. He had an idea, and was glad of the Director's helmet.

"—and the officers found him dead from an arterial wound in the neck. He had no weapon with him, and none was found. What is, what is more," Vannar stammered a bit, "the autopsigram and psychopitron readings showed definite signs of karynon deformation syndrome in his brain and blood cells as well as traces of other illegal drugs . . . eh, whereas there was no sign of such in your own tests."

The Director held up his hand for patience and took time to draw air, "And as well, there was a scale fragment of his found in your travel-case, clear enough evidence that your baggage had been tampered with."

"And I am exonerated," Hasso said quietly.

"Of course! Completely!" Vannar began to rise out of his squat.

"If my exoneration and your apologies are well publicized I will not consider taking legal action."

"Understood," Vannar said stiffly. Then he crouched down again and said more warmly, "My dear Archivist, I can hardly tell you how grateful we are that you are alive and in good care. You would not believe the horror our officials felt when they found both of you collapsed in that manner."

"I am sure I can well imagine it." Hasso said civilly. "Thank you very much for your kindness in being so frank, Director." With a twitch of eyelids Vannar made a sober exit.

Tharma waited until the door had slid closed. "Not a bad fellow, but a bit slow on his feet," she said. "You may change your mind about legal action. That experience must have had an effect on your heart."

"It brought out something I may well have been born with." Hasso began to stir himself and felt his heart's flutterings. "And I don't need such an ugly weapon."

"I have informed your stepmother, she was eager to come here, but I hope you will excuse me. I told her not to make the long hard journey."

"Quite right, thank you. And what of my Lyhhrt? Is he safe?"

"He has a small room to himself in a servants' lodging house. There are better outworld lodgings, but . . ."

He is too fearful.

"All of your friends here have asked after you, but I'm afraid your troubles have been rather eclipsed by the excitement of the murder."

"The less gossip the better," Hasso said. "Has no one else tried to contact me? I have an appointment with the Director of Interworld Relations—"

"You must rest for a few days, Hasso."

"I suppose so . . ." But the matter lay heavy on him.

Before Tharma left, Hasso weighed the padded helmet in his hands and confided, "Such thoughts as I was then—or now—thinking I would not want to be the property of others. . . ."

Tharma gave him her deep smile again. "No one here would dare go near your mind for fear of drowning in facts, Hasso, so you have nothing to worry about there! If I see you again I hope it is in greeting."

Once alone Hasso took a quiet moment to consider that miscreant Sketh. A flash of thought, perhaps accidentally sent him by one of the medics, gave him a vision of the crumpled figure in its gaudy sash collapsed on a dusty floor with its stream of clotting blood flowing from him. Whatever else he had become, Sketh was once a healthy and vigorous man; now he had been scoured and peeled into a piece of evidence. But a darker thought followed him.

A Lyhhrt is the only kind of being here that could have forced its way through that tiny window and done it . . . I had believed before all this happened that there was another Lyhhrt aboard . . . and I am so relieved that it was my friend Lyhhrt who kept faith with me and brought Tharma to help me, but . . . he was also the messenger who brought the bad news about Lyhhr and its claims on Khagodis.

. . . Sooner or later they will think of our friend and say, Eki! a Lyhhrt has done this and here is the only Lyhhrt we know, so it must be—

I must make sure that does not happen.

Later a police constable questioned Hasso briefly, but he had nothing to tell: he knew who Sketh was, but the two had never exchanged so much as a direct look before the accusation; his imprisonment was a blessing in that he had been under close surveillance while Sketh was being murdered.

After two more lonely days of being prodded, injected and manipulated by ticking, grinding and stuttering robots, he was shown into a private guest-house room where he found a beautiful marble sleeping basin with bronze and silver faucets, and flasks of fine unguents on the rim. His baggage was waiting for him, sea-salt and all.

As was his friend the Lyhhrt, in his thick mournful clothes.

"I am so happy to see you, Lyhhrt!"

"And I so sorry that I could not free you earlier."

"I'm not much the worse." Hoping that bitterness had not tinctured his voice.

"There is a banquet tonight, and everyone expects the only Lyhhrt in the world to attend. But I will not go unless you do. Will you be there?"

"Of course. Otherwise everyone will think I am either dead or in prison!"

"I will see you there."

Alone, Hasso stood looking out of the pillared bay window at the sandstone plain far away to the east where New World Mesa upthrust itself into the last flame of the sunset, bearing the great alien ship on its table-top like an offering to the Cosmos. It had been carried far and long since its discovery in the Northern Spines near the Pearlstone Hills, Skerow's homeland.

The ship was the source of the greatest mystery in the world. Because there were no aboriginal peoples on Khagodis; its citizens had no line of descent from or genetic relationship with any other life forms.

If the Khagodi had some other home world or people, they did not know them; they knew only that thousands of years of exploration and digging had never linked them to any other species in the world. There were branches of Khagodi religions that considered these conclusions heretical: the Diggers and Inheritors contended that no one had yet dug in the right place; the Watchers and Hatchlings who believed that their ancestors had been delivered by burning gods in enormous eggs. Perhaps this ship was one. The scores of life-forms preserved in it had come from many worlds, some still unknown, and no one knew where it had originated.

Hasso regarded it from a gleaming room in a magnificent palace and wondered whether this generous lodging and beautiful prospect would have been assigned to him if he had not suffered that heartcracking experience. Then pushed aside his fears of frailty and dressed himself in a deep green sash with gold threads, the one in which he had delivered the dissertation that made him Master of Archives; finished by picking up his staff to set out for the WorldGuests Welcoming Banquet. He did not wear a helmet; the non-act was his form of dare.

The banquet was the culmination of a long schedule of official welcoming events with a lot of fuss for an hour or two and not much food. This fête was a genuine evening meal, held in a grand hall roofed with many-colored genuine glass panes in extravagant shapes, and floored in mauve and blue marble with inset circles of coral for guests to settle in while they ate or talked. Hasso found one for himself, as usual halfway between the center and the circumference of the crowd.

Though the men had brightened their scales with unguents and the women wore colorful robes, their attitudes were stiff and reserved: murder cast a shadow on them. Only the few outworlders, Dabiri with tails brilliantly dyed and braided, and Kylkladi with gilded feathers, seemed lighthearted.

Hasso could not see the Lyhhrt, and did not look for Ekket; she was beyond even his timid dreams now. There was no sign of the consul who was to be his contact, an old friend from the Northern Spines, now working here; but he was relieved to find friends coming quickly to surround him, several minds chiming in at once:

:We couldn't find you anywhere, Hasso, there was a fuss and a stir, and you were taken away! Vannar told the whole story . . . but did not want to let us visit and tire you out.:

No, he kept me well wrapped in bedclothes and padding, Hasso did not say. He leaned on his staff and let his friends bring him sea-stars, fingerclams and crisped winterbracket from the round dining table.

:But how could that Sketh have possibly been murdered?—everyone's talking of it. And why . . . ?:

Hasso was not sure why, but the man was a bad-tempered brutal drugger who could not be trusted to take charge of others—particularly a young woman like Ekket who knew little of the world beyond her home. Gorodek had been a fool to trust him. *Perhaps it was planned to murder me and his Lyhhrt chose the wrong one. No. That Lyhhrt would not choose the wrong one.* Hasso took firm control of these thoughts, and kept them buried under many heaps of other thoughts, beneath all of the facts that Tharma assured him would frighten everybody away.

Across the room he could see her, a big hearty woman who looked too serious now to be approachable. He was still searching for his Interworld contact when Isska, a retired Court Recorder so bent with age she was not very much taller than he, brought him a bowl of soothing petal-brew and sipped from it herself first. *:Never know what can fall into these concoctions:* and Hasso was struck by the sense of conspiracy and expectancy that Sketh's murder was fostering, thinking that fear and suspicion always found fertile ground.

Expectancy was fulfilled soon enough by a stir in one corner that sent a wave of reactions among the guests: those wearing helmets raised their hands to check the latches. This movement almost amused Hasso for a moment; his friends were mild-mannered academics and minor officials who might have liked to have more interesting secrets than they did.

Hasso heard a whisper of *ek, there's Gorodek!* and the stir swelled into a close procession of burly men in liveries of copper-colored silkweed sashes with thaqwood staffs and rattling clogs. Hasso had never seen the Governor of Western Sealand in person, and had not paid him much attention on TriV. In a space between one fellow's snout and another's tail he saw a little shrunken man with a pot belly taking two steps for every one the guards took.

And Gorodek's sash was also dark and narrow, its buttons of copper like his simple mesh helmet.

Behind him, in blue-green moiré winesilk and too many heavy gold necklaces, Ekket followed, stepping in her sandals as if she were treading beds of coals. She did not look to left or right.

The sight of her was a tightness of the heart; Hasso turned away and would have left the feasting then, but the procession stopped before him, and Gorodek came forward, harshly drawing air: "Hasso, are you!"

"Yes, Governor." Hasso showed his tongue.

Gorodek wagged his massive head back and forth: "I don't see your Lyhhrt friend around here—perhaps he's shy and doesn't care for our company!"

Nor I yours, Hasso very nearly said aloud, but was saved by a mindwave that swept him with relief: "He's sure to be here, Governor. Here he is coming now!"

The crowd fell away on its own to let through the slim and brilliant figure.

"Yes. It seems I was mistaken," Gorodek said. He was staring as if his eyes could penetrate that casing. "But we are all delighted to see him, are we not?"

"I certainly am," Hasso said meekly. "I am sorry for the loss of your aide Sketh."

"Are you truly? Be grateful that you still have yours,

Archivist!" Gorodek turned away and his troop fell in around him.

Hasso shivered, not from fear but because in Gorodek he could see himself shrunk into embittered age, and he thanked his Saints that he had never wanted power over people. He turned to the Lyhhrt. "You make this time and place bearable to me."

:You see, Archivist, that I have decided against being fearful.: The Lyhhrt could make sure that no one paid overmuch heed to him, but now he was splendid in gold with star patterns, centered with diamonds. He had called himself a bejeweled fool, but had not thrown his jewels away.

Hasso sensed that the display was meant to bolster his own spirit. "That doesn't mean you should not be cautious, dear friend, but I am very glad to be with you here." And this feeling supported Hasso through an hour of pretending to enjoy himself, nibbling and sipping, allowing himself to be presented on the dais as an honored guest, watching the performance of a Kylkladi dance troupe so furious and energetic that it sent their feathers flying, and listening to a brace of Bengtvadi playing mournfully out of tune on nose-flutes. Whenever he shut his eyes he could see Ekket chained in gold, and when his patience ran out he pleaded a genuine tiredness; his body seemed very heavy to him.

The Lyhhrt walked him back down the long cold halls to his room. At the doorway Hasso pushed his mind away from Ekket and said, *:I have not seen or heard anything of our Interworld contact, and that makes me uneasy . . . we will find out tomorrow . . . :*

For one moment the Lyhhrt stood so still that his diamonds did not glitter. Then, *:I believe we are about to find that out tonight, Archivist. May I come in with you?:*

Hasso's scales rose. "Certainly." His hand trembled on the latch, but he pushed the door open and went in.

:We don't need light.:

In the darkness with the Lyhhrt beside him Hasso stood again at the center of the room, leaning on his staff. The moons were rising; they cast the black shadows of the rock spurs and the mesa that was barely of a size enough to be the platform of the great ship.

:Over there . . . :

His attention sharpened as he caught a movement at the corner of his eye and found a shadow that had not been there before.

A new mindvoice said, *:I have been waiting for you but I have not much more time.:*

:Who—: But Hasso recognized the mind of a majestic woman named Reddow, a former protégé of Skerow's who also lived in the Northern Spines: his contact from Interworld. She was crouched outside the building in the angle of pillar and window, alone and in tears.

:What are you doing here, Consul Reddow? Go around and come in!:

:I cannot. There is a switch on the pillar to your left. Touch it and come out.:

Hasso did this and the glass pane slid away; he stepped out onto the esplanade into sharp moonlight. The Lyhhrt did not follow.

"Don't look at me," Reddow said sharply. "There are spy-eyes in that room. Pretend I'm not here. If you are seen talking to me it will go badly for you."

:I have shut down those eyes,: the Lyhhrt said.

Hasso could not keep his own eyes turned away. "What happened?"

"I have simply been sent away," Reddow was trembling. "Told my services were no longer needed." She went on bitterly, "They gave me tickets—"

"Who are 'they'?"

"The court clerk and two attendants, people I hired myself! Tickets for the barge leaving empty at midnight—a cargo vessel—to meet the ship that will take me home in the morning, and a sum of money that they said was the rest of the salary due me—and I will be so disgraced I will have no way of finding work except in my own local office!"

Willy-nilly, Hasso found himself in her mind, tasting her hot tears, and sensing an odd blankness. "Did no one give you a reason?"

"No—but I believe it must have to do with what we were going to discuss. . . ."

Hasso said slowly, "You were—you are the superior officer of those clerks, Consul. Why did you allow them to treat you that way?"

Her head rose slowly. "That way?"

With care Hasso said, "It's you who have power over them. You needn't have obeyed them."

Slowly her body lifted from its crouch. She said wonderingly, "It never occurred to me not to do so."

"Yes," Hasso said. "I believe your mind has been under some stranger's influence."

"Who is it?"

"I'm not sure," Hasso said, although he was. Except for his own friend there was only one other being who might have the power. "I think you will find everything as it should be if you go back to your room now . . . and we needn't discuss our important business for a day or two . . . we do have that much time."

"But what am I to do with the tickets—and the money?" Reddow said faintly, trying to fight through the mist lingering in her consciousness.

"My impulse would be to say: Tear up the tickets and keep the money—but I believe it might be safer to return them to your clerks. Tell them: Take care of these. They might not have realized the seriousness of what they were doing, and that way you will not ever be accused of theft. Are you feeling a little better?"

"Very much so, Hasso, and thank you."

"I think it will be safe to leave now."

He did believe that it was safe.

The shadow moved away from the esplanade.

:You handled that very well, Archivist, and it is *safe for now,:* the Lyhhrt said, as Hasso snicked the bolt on the glass doors. *:Now I will go take care of those clerks. If they should ever realize what has happened, they will not mind my help in reversing such embarrassing actions. And eventually I will find that Other. . . . :*

The Lyhhrt's loneliness burned like Reddow's tears.

Fthel IV, In the Forest House: *One of Those Days*

Tyloe spends his time looking and listening for he doesn't know what, he eats and drinks and works out on all the machines in a big high vaulted room with arched windows filled with a hushed green light, among all those snaking steel tubes and springs, it's like a gothic torture chamber; sometimes a couple of the thick bluejawed men or hardknuckled women will spar with gloves or the chebok, nobody asks him, few speak to him other than Brezant and Lorrice, the only ones that trust him. And she wants to keep him onside. So after the errands and the workouts and watching trivvy locked on Brezant's favorite porn station, it's eat and drink some more.

Now he's sleeping it off after another day of all them snarling over wasted supplies, money not come yet and a bunch of shitheads getting lost looking for enemies in the wrong direction. Another night of her thoughts drifting into his dreams, though more often lately, mercifully, she's been wearing that red lattice helmet and closing her mind down against him, she keeps her sexual feelings for her employer. . . .

But now the dreams are flowing into that dim room where—

—in jeweled shoes and red silk stockings with gold cord garters she's crouching beside Brezant on the bed while his hands run over her everywhere, dermcap on his wrist giving off a bead of lamplight while the karynon darts into every branch and rivulet of his bloodstream, his eyes flash with every pulse. The timer ticks faintly.

I love you, she whispers.

Yeh sure, baby—gimme, baby, gimme right now!

She mounts him mouth on his, heartsbeat!—heartsbeat!—it's the height of the history of the Universe!—he pulls his mouth away to roar his violent joy!—

(Tyloe in sleep feels this)

—and now they're boiling into the room, doorslam, Istvan, Oxman, Demarest, thick men in shadow-suits pulling her off him, falling on him with beating fists grunting—*thought you were the whole Big Man you stupid arsehole hireling*—ripping the bracelet with its poison-cure off her wrist, shoving her in the corner, screaming she staggers up to grab at the bracelet, they punch her down, she's sobbing, breathless, Brezant howls *Give me! Give me!*—

The timer rings.

Tyloe jumps up every nerve-end firing, no, not a dream, flings off covers and runs, slamdoor through her room, to Brezant's through that other adjoining, heavy ancient door, Tyloe's on them—

—grabbing the nearest pair of feet and hauling till the rest of the body drags off the bed and the head hits the floor thudding, does not quite duck number two's fist shaving his skull, but backs himself on the bedpost and raises a knee to shove a foot in the thick belly twice before Two is flung back and flattens Three, pulls up Lorrice by the arm in rough haste, Brezant thrashing and screaming—"I can't stand it! I can't! Give me—give me the fucking—"

Tyloe's got a grip on his arm, panting, "Help me, help me get'm outa here!"

She's yelling too, "It's poison, it's killing him! Where's the—"

Istvan is on hands and knees retching but Oxman and Demarest are scrambling up reaching for stunners, and Tyloe, who has depended on speed, can't match the strength of any of them; through her mind Tyloe senses the dark figure of Hummer outside the door, waving her zap—"Lyhhrt here! Lyhhrt landing!"

"Money!" Oxman drops everything and runs out.

Demarest yells, "What about them!"

"He's done for an' we'll shut'm up later, come on!" Demarest follows, Istvan pulls himself up and limps after them, rubbing his belly. The door frame glimmers for a moment as Hummer welds the lock shut with her zap.

Tyloe thinks: *Lyhhrt? What Lyhhrt?*

Brezant who's been gasping and choking suddenly loses consciousness.

"I got it, sweetheart," Lorrice pulls herself up. "I found it, there's some left, I found it! Here!" Her hands are trembling so hard she can hardly push the half-broken dermcap against the inside of his wrist. "Now help me, Tyloe—"

"Help you what? We can't get out anywhere!" One eye half shut, he's craning desperately for exits, door welded, no others, windows strong as stone walls.

"Here." Lorrice presses a curlicue in the patterned wall beside the bed, a door slides open, a wood-paneled elevator beyond it. "Lots of different people have lived in this place." She flings a silk robe around herself and grabs at Brezant's wrists. "Come on, wake up, Andres! Get going, Tyloe, for God's sake!"

Tyloe looked elsewhere into blankness. "I—he's dead."

"No! No! He can't be!" She threw herself over Brezant's body, clasping his face in her hands. "Andres!"

"He's dead, Lorrice. It was too late and not enough antidote left."

"But he's screaming—he's screaming in my mind, help me, help me!" She hunched over the body as if it was her child, glaring at him.

Tyloe shook his head, and said, "Only in your own mind, it's not him, he has a subdermal helmet," and reached over her to close the staring eyes. He closed his own for a moment to ease the headache the glancing blow had given him.

She had warned him, surely she had seen this coming—how could she have let her guard down?—but her absorption in that figurehead of a man had been as strong as any helmet... *and I'm not much of a guard, they thought I was a pretty boy too weak to bother with—*

He saw himself in her furious eyes, his swollen eyebrow, his terra-cotta skin, that showed him the son of diplomats from half the peoples of Earth, smeared with dead black blood over his cheekbones, ugly to her now. The messenger.

She collapsed into sobs. "He can't be dead! Money was coming in and we were gonna have everything!"

As if she had really believed that. He grabbed her by both arms. "Lorrice, listen! What does it mean, their saying, the Lyhhrt is here? What Lyhhrt? I haven't seen or heard of any Lyhhrt beside the ones we met in Montador! Why all of a sudden have we got one now?"

"Lyhhrt?" She stared at him and whispered, "I don't know." Her eyes were blank.

"All right then, let's get the hell out of here! How can that lift get us out?"

"Down the cellar, there's an exit—that's why Andres—Andres and I rented this house."

"Let's get going."

"No, wait, I want to take him!" She was hauling at Brezant's body by one arm.

"Where, Lorrice? He has no clothes and neither have we. Do you think we could bury him?"

"I can't—" Her eyes overflowed with tears suddenly.

"If you want to live, leave him, just as he is, otherwise if they don't find him they may think he got away somehow and come looking—and maybe, just maybe if they find him they won't think we're worth chasing—"

"What can we do there with no clothes or food!"

"We'll have to find out, because we can't stay here!"

The cellar was a vaulted cavern fairly clean and well ventilated; things skittered or flapped occasionally but nothing touched them except falling dust. Air, cooling and electrical systems were just perceptibly humming, and the darkness was broken only by their maintenance and warning lights. They found a bare place against a wall, waiting until their eyes accommodated.

"What's happening? Can you tell what they're doing?"

"Oxman's talking to the Lyhhrt, the others—they've broken into his room—" She let him see through Oxman's eyes: a Lyhhrt in a black steel workshell that looked like wrought iron.

Oxman saying: *Shit, there's nobody here! Just the body!*

They were not likely to find the particular curlicue that opened the door.

Where the hell they gone?

Better have a look around—

Lorrice whispered, "They're coming down here! The Lyhhrt will know where we are!"

"Do the others know?"

"I can't tell that—but he'll know *we're* here."

I did not expect there would be two bodies—that's dangerous. You will get rid of those.

"That's him, he's talking to Oxman! Oh . . ." She leaned her head against his shoulder for a moment, and he felt her tears through the cloth. "Cranshawe's dead . . . he was trying to keep them from . . ."

Tyloe saw the sprawled body through her mind and eyes. The Lyhhrt was nodding toward Brezant:

Absolute incompetent. Hiring him on was a great mistake and it was time for him to go.

Wasn't easy trying to get on with him either.

Here are cashbooks, and you will receive whatever else I've promised when the ship leaves. Now clean this up, dispose of those bodies, and when you're through here get down to Bonzador and work on that army. As for this house—

The owners will come, the lease was about to run out anyway.

You will not speak of this to anyone. Goodbye now, you'll see me again.

"I think he's leaving," Lorrice whispered. By now Tyloe and Lorrice were sidling along the walls looking for niches and open doors; Tyloe could feel panic rising in the back of his throat.

:Tyloe! There's an entrance here.:

Locked.

Demarest and Hummer were coming, their footsteps skittered down the ramp. Lorrice, fighting her own rising panic, felt around the doorway, found the i.d. panel and pushed savagely, Tyloe joined her and without warning the heavy door opened in silence. The door closed behind them; light flowed from the ceiling.

Tyloe stared. "Christ, this is the first place they'll look!"

Three walls were lined with crates, the fourth with racks upon racks of sample weapons: Karnoshky flamers, Gothenburg stunners, Uzi MarkVII/Gimmels, Zepp darts and almost every other kind of gun that could fit into human hands and limbs.

"I never knew of it," she whispered.

"Do these jokers know?"

"Everything I thought I knew is wrong."

"Come on! D'you think this arsenal was for the 'army'—in this house?"

She sharpened. "No! they'd have been in a storage depot. The i.d. for this place must have been caught up in our own security code when we wired it."

"I'm afraid whoever does own it will sniff us out when they find they forgot to lock up. Why wouldn't the Lyhhrt give us to his slaveys?"

"That'd be four bodies to dump, and we aren't going to tell anyone else ever. I'm sure he saw to that." Trying not to think, *he may be saving us for something.* Shudderingly trying not to think of *Lyhhrt* at all.

The thoughts from Demarest and the last stragglers drifted outward from Lorrice's mind:

Nah, they ain't down here. Anyway when we shut this place up tight they'll be locked in and they got no food.

This was a damn good kip. . . .

Plenty more of those when this job ends.

"I wouldn't bet on that," Tyloe said. "I don't think they know everything either."

The figures drew farther away, the thoughts faded. . . .

"They're not going to find us here," Lorrice said, braver now.

"Yeh." Tyloe was trying to keep himself from thinking:

Rats in a trap. "Listen, I want to get this straight about the Lyhhrt."

She seemed to fade. "I never knew anything about that."

"Brezant was a figurehead, and those jokers seemed to have known the Lyhhrt a long while. Did he hire them all on?"

"They were here when I came . . . I told you how Andres found me, and I think he hired Cranshawe, that's all. . . ."

"But you were the ESP! You were supposed to be esping them!"

Lorrice had become even paler. "I guess I wasn't, then, was I? Just made to think I was."

Tyloe said wearily, "All right, then. Tell me how we're supposed to get out of this trap."

"Here," she reached for the door-latch. "Come on."

"No, no! If we're safe in here we can stay long enough to make sure they don't forget something and come back."

"There's no goddam place to pee."

They waited sitting on the floor, backs to the wall. Every so often she turned her head away from him and wept for Andres Brezant, for his death and for his final humiliation; finally she fell asleep in his arms. Her stockings were tattered and her shoes crack-heeled; she was so wan and dark-ringed under the eyes that he did not want to abandon her in spite of everything.

Tyloe did not realize he had fallen asleep until he woke and found Lorrice staring at him.

"You kept saying you couldn't fight," she said dully.

"Not as a pug! My father kept driving me, I learned all kind of martial arts, and won prizes, but that's mostly posing around—and where would I need to fight, on my father's estate? That was all the trouble with my father, he had me taught everything and trained in everything, everybody telling me how wonderful I was but it wasn't good for anything and I didn't give a shit about anything except to get away from his pushing."

"I bet you do now, if it's only for your own ass."

"I risked it free enough trying to save your bullyboy."

Neither of them had much to say then. But Tyloe knew: *It's the only way I could have gotten out of this place.*

"You're right about that," she said bitterly. Then, suddenly, "That Lyhhrt has nothing to do with the lot Andres was dealing with, he had a different . . . smell to him, the way he said, 'You'll see *me* again' . . . he's a loner."

Tyloe braced his sore head against the wall. "They're all the same bastard to me."

She was silent for a long while. "I could have saved him."

Tyloe said wearily, "Oh yes. And somebody else would've done him in." He pulled himself up on stiff legs. "It must be near morning." There were no clocks in the fortress of arms. "I wonder what happened to the servants."

"There were only two or three staying tonight. They all flew off in their buzzer when the fight started."

"I hope they got somewhere . . . I hope we get somewhere. We got something to ride in?"

"I have my own aircar."

"Good. Now which way is out? I'm damned if I'm going through that room again."

She said nothing but led him down narrow stone passageways through a massive coded door that opened at her handprint to a maze of wine racks and up a spiral stair into an ordinary pantry.

Upstairs the only sound was of ventilators; there was no one in the long wide-paneled rooms, and Tyloe realized how little furniture had actually been in them. A few wrinkles in the carpets where a dragged body might have pulled at them; one snakeskin shoe lying on its side was all that remained of Cranshawe. Tyloe swallowed hard to keep from retching.

"Let's pick up some clothes and get out of here."

But she had rushed off ahead of him past the exploded door and its glimpse of the vast rumpled bed into her own room, where she rummaged feverishly in wardrobes with sliding doors that slammed and ricocheted.

"What in hell are you doing now? You can't take all your baggage!"

"You can do what you want and fuck off, Tyloe! I'm not working for you!"

Tyloe shut up. Last thing he wanted now was a fight. He went to his room and dressed, nothing too fancy, packed a few things into the same knapsack he'd been dragging around the fight-rooms before he fell in with Brezant. Fell in. He didn't expect to find much use for the kind of rich clothing Lorrice had bought for him with Brezant's money. He did not stop for anything else except a glance into the mirror to see if he was the same man he had been yesterday. He looked the same: the image was not shivering.

When he came out he found her running through the house, picking up bits, jewelry, dopesticks, picking pockets for cashbooks, credisks. He said nothing, but stood waiting for her, a few minutes worth of patience—until he heard her scream.

He ran into the room with the flashing desk where Brezant had held court and found her standing with hands flattened to her mouth, staring at the Lyhhrt sitting draped in that grand leather chair, long and elegant in wrought-iron black with ruby eyes.

"Hello there," the Lyhhrt said. His lips had been formed into Cupid's bows.

"What do you want?" she whispered.

"Nothing right now, but I'll find some use for you. You do have a few more brains than those thugs. . . . Did you enjoy my little toyshop? I'm the owner of this house, and I let you in there, you know. You can run along now, but don't go too far from Montador"—he tossed a cashbook and Tyloe caught it without thinking—"because I like that place, you can have a good time there for a while."

Tyloe and Lorrice could not find words, or perhaps were stifled by the Lyhhrt. Finally Lorrice burst out, "You bastard! You murderer!"

He paid no attention but rose sinuously. "You can run along now, but not too far. I'll always know where to find you. . . ." He elongated himself out of the room in the way of Lyhhrt.

When Lorrice could open her mouth to speak, she said, "I don't know—I just don't understand what's going on."

"I think you were right when you said he was different." Tyloe shoved the cashbook in his pocket. "I/we has become I/myself/alone. Let's get out of here, as far as we can run anyway." He could not keep himself from taking one last look through the multipaned windows and their deep green forest light that once seemed so heavy with wealth.

Khagodis, New Interworld Court: *A Guided Tour*

Hasso woke to the realization, to the resignation that there were people in his world who hated him and wanted him dead.

"You needn't worry about the spy-eye, I disabled that for good," the Lyhhrt said.

"I was sure you would," Hasso said, with a degree of cynicism that he had also become resigned to by now. He grasped his staff and pulled himself from the basin, let it drain and showered down in fresh water so the sea-salt would not crust on his scales.

The Lyhhrt, who had spent the night in his workshell, propped in a corner, said, "I hope you will not mind if I use your basin to change my water and feed myself?"

"Of course you must use it, and I will wait here until you are done—"

"Truly—"

"I promised myself to look out for you, Lyhhrt, and I will do that as well as I can."

He kept his eyes and mind away from the Lyhhrt's self-care, though this Lyhhrt was the least private of his species, and for a few moments watched the sunlight moving slowly above the great Mesa with its pride and burden, and throwing reflected sparks on the walls from the Lyhhrt's moving diamonds. "There is to be a guided tour through that ship at half-past third-quarter," he said. He could not have told the Lyhhrt anything he did not know already, but the alternative was not to speak at all. *Gorodek and Ekket cannot help but be there.* "I do not care to take part in that, but—"

:I will stay here and keep watch over myself, Archivist. You cannot guard me with your fierce mind forever.:

The Lyhhrt also knew that Hasso could not bear to be so close to, so far from Ekket, without end. He said very carefully *:It is a pity that the young woman cannot take courage and break away from that brute.:*

Hasso, staring into that distance, said, "She is only obeying the law of her country, that keeps tight control of their children until they are married . . . many countries do—and, you see, it is our endless worry over fertility."

"Archivist, I think you know too much about the Law."

The fencing and gates to the designated land around the Mesa did not quite bar the long ragged tail of foreign correspondents attached to the delegations, but let in one designated journalist, drawn by lot, at each showing. A moving walkway led from the gate around the mesa to the elevators that were not visible from the pearly towers of the Court. Around the ship was a railing tall enough to keep Khagodi from falling into the canyons and electrified at the top to keep vandals from climbing up.

The commentary was of course recited by a Professional Speaker, not merely a guide, and without the usual air of forced enthusiasm. The whole prospect was so vast that awe was unavoidable, and any exaggeration would have lessened that power:

Twelve years ago . . .

But Hasso knew all that, any quick dip into his well of facts would have fished it out. It had been recorded ten thousand times: the stark cavern lined with the dusty windows of cells holding specimens of extinct animals preserved by a mysterious process that kept them looking alive, and they had been reanimated in computer and plastene models so very many times that every child had worn out three sets of them in the last five years.

And we do not know even how it traveled here, because there is no great engine in it, and no travelers, but only these casings with their interrupted lives. . . .

The line was one long shuffle-shuffle on dulled steel floors, with a deal of tail-jittering. Hasso had hoped Ekket and her surly Governor would not have come along on this tour so far into the Conference, but they had, seven or eight siguu ahead of him—and perhaps they had come to all of the tours so that Gorodek could parade his pandered bride-to-be . . . Hasso wandered out of the opening, nodding at the guard.

"Seen too much of it already, citizen?" the guard asked in a tone less rude than the words. "So have I."

"You are paid for it," Hasso answered with a smile he knew was wan. He walked away along the flagstoned area, unwilling to have even one companion, following the circle of safety-railings *that keep people in*, thinking of the close-shut cell he had nearly died in. The rising cliffs and deeps of the pinkish-gray canyons were more amazing than those petrified remains, he was thinking . . . he wished his eyesight was keener so that he might if only in imagination browse among them—

—and felt a very curious sensation, not sudden, not painful, a feeling of becoming gradually, almost satisfyingly . . . transparent . . . his spirit as the essence of a clear window through which some Looker was watching. The vestigial scales of a prehistoric crest rose on his head and tingled down his back. *I am being looked into. . . .* Not by any invasive telepath. *No, being used as a magnifying glass.*

As soon as he formulated this thought the feeling stopped. And somewhere, and in some time a voice was saying:

no truly it is the people who

Hasso shuddered and stumbled, saved himself from falling by grabbing at the railing, the breath hissed in his gills, he could not have said a word to save his life.

There was a moment of absolute blankness and then a riot broke out.

An old woman Hasso did not know came running out of the doorway, jaws working soundlessly, holding in one hand a helmet that glinted and flashed with jewels, and with the other pulling at Ekket's arm, neither of the two trying to speak at all, with their thoughts blazing, it seemed to Hasso, out to the horizons.

:You must put it on! You must!:—the woman kept pushing the helmet at her—

:I will not! I will not!: Ekket grabbed at the helmet and with surprising strength sent it high over the rail, glinting and clanking down into the vast abyss below. Pulled the gold from her neck and sent it following the helmet.

"Eki! What are you doing!"

Ekket found voice: "I will not marry that terrible man! I will die first!"

"The disgrace! The Governor! Your poor mother!"

"She made a dreadful ruin of her life—I swear that by all the Saints she will not ruin mine!—and as for your Governor, that ugly, horrible—"

By now there were a score of others rushing out, Gorodek's guards and courtiers, the accredited journalists, ambassadors from three worlds, and eventually Gorodek, helmeted but obviously sizzling with fury—"Someone will pay for this!"—then catching sight of Hasso and squawking, "It was him! It was his fault!"

Hasso gaped at him.

Two security guards in red sashes pushed their way through this throng, not gently, and plucked Ekket from the grasp of her chaperone. One of them took a light helmet from a pouch—"Please let me put this on, dems'l, it is only for a few moments—all others of you please stand back and let us have the elevator to ourselves—and you, Governor and your entourage, you may come down in good time—"

Hasso, who was bracing himself against the railings and could not make himself move, tried to sort out all of these thoughts and actions in his mind. What came of them was: first, Gorodek had suddenly announced that he would marry Ekket on the spot, the priest he had with him to bless all his endeavors would perform the ceremony; and then Ekket had begun an outcry of—what?—rape? She had rushed outside, he had seen all of that, and half of the people inside the ship had become hysterical.

And whatever had been happening to him while he stared out over . . . ?

The old chaperone, who was wearing Gorodek's livery, caught sight of Hasso and cried out hysterically, "What are you gaping at, you fool!"

"A spectacle," Hasso retorted, and walked away quickly before he made one of himself.

Ekket

Yes it was true it was all true he did he said he would teach me to obey him if I would not love him and he would not need to pay my mother anything for me that he had me in his grip now like some stupid torturer in an Old Saint's Tale that we learned in school where the Saint let anything be done to her and bore it without complaining and got great honor after she died horribly he grasped me and had two of his filthy guards hold me because I could tear him in three pieces if I only got my hands free and I could not move and faugh! I puked all over his damned marble floor and I thought he would kill me and worse worse he showed me this great vulgar helmet even a whore would not wear and said when we were married he would lock me into it forever and I was afraid he would kill me then and he made me go to the ship with him without even letting me augh! without even letting me clean myself and all this is true I swear by all those stupid Saints you have me here my mind is yours

Chief Security Officer Tharma switched off the resonancer and said, gently for her, "Yes, dems'l, but esp is not evidence. DNA is."

Hasso and Tharma: Covering Everything

Tharma was looking at him kindly; kind looks were her specialty, as humility was Hasso's. "Do you understand, Hasso?" Some intensity along with the kindness.

Hasso found tears in his eyes, and a little of Ekket's nausea. "I don't understand why I needed to learn all that."

"I was considering justice and the law," Tharma said. "I want your legal opinions before all the lawyers go to work."

Hasso would have been amused at her admission of need, if he was in a better mood. Tharma was a woman of infinite patience, but no shame or timidity.

"I know you will keep quiet about this, Hasso, and I will do the same for what you are about to tell me. I believe Ekket was telling the truth, and that tests will establish it soon. I need to know more about foreign law: Will Gorodek give us trouble? Will the young woman? Can we charge him with anything? Or help her? I dealt with international matters for the WorldCourt when it was in Burning Mountain but those cases were mainly battery, theft and fraud. I have heard of alien peoples whose males are so much larger than females that rape is only too common, but here the idea is ridiculous—my husband was half my weight! and I have heard of only three such cases in my whole life."

Hasso said with a bitter smile, "I'm afraid that Gorodek was behaving the way he would be expected to do in Western Sealand. I know little about their ancient Scrolls and I am not an anthropologist, because these actions refer to customs, not laws. Some who lived there have told me that the bridegroom is often expected to take the bride immediately before marriage, in a sense to put his signet on her, to claim lineage if she has been fertilized. And she is supposed to resist to show that she is pure. But." He paused to put words more exactly. "He must make a ceremonial announcement of betrothal as soon as she accepts him, and there's no evidence that the 'bride' has ever agreed. And those guardsmen constraining her while he forced her—but they will all claim diplomatic immunity!"

Tharma sniffed and gulped air. "And she's from Center Point, one of those little Isthmus territories. He could be held on it, I know that much. However, I don't want to punish him, I want him to shut up and get away from here."

"Even if he were willing, you will need him for a witness in the murder of his aide, that pitiable Sketh."

"I have no pity for him. It is that child . . . it is just as well she burst out like that, because it showed how much she was being forced, and that chaperone's trying to control her by laying hands on her was a mistake . . . and she will have to be tested for pregnancy, and even if she is not pregnant her people may believe she is infertile and that will do her no good either—ek! this is a most difficult situation."

Hasso said slowly, "She may be a child in her country, and even in his, but if it's provable that she was wronged, WorldCourt law will give her adult status for the sake of redress. That will free her from both Gorodek and her mother. But both of them will be furious over Ekket, and—"

"That's what I am here for, Hasso, to make sure there is no 'and'." Tharma dipped her full-jawed head for emphasis. "But Hasso, there is another, and I think deeper, matter. Are you recovered from that strange experience up on the Mesa? Other people feel something else strange happened there."

Hasso was uneasy about discussing what he felt had been an out-of-mind experience; and was just about to feel relieved that she had not seized upon him as a witness. But because he was a truthteller he said haltingly, "I went along on the tour because I felt it was expected of me . . . I was quite bored and left the ship to look through those railings out across the canyons, thinking that it would be vastly more interesting to explore them . . . and had—it was not sudden but gradual—a sense that some, that someone or something was looking . . . at me, not at but *through* me at, I guess, at the world, and saying, *no really it is people who—*" He stopped, feeling as if his head was full of clouds, and shook it. "What it meant was, I suppose—and what is *it*!—that people are more, eki! important and interesting, and that is true enough, though I did not quite feel it at that moment, and then Ekket came rushing out in terrible distress with that woman clutching at her—and all others seem to have gone into hysterics!" He was trembling. "For a while I could not move and thought I was going mad."

"Others felt so of themselves," Tharma said dryly. "If not mad, then certainly disoriented. Eh, many religious and scientific authorities have thought long and hard about that ship and its possible connection with the origin of our species. Since we have never been found to relate to any other animal here, all our religions have expected to find that burning gods had carried us here in huge eggs, or else that we simply had not dug deep enough for fossils. If that ship brought us here it seems that both were half true. . . .

"Lately there has been a push to bring some Ungrukh people to look at the ship because they actually did begin as animals plucked off another world, by a powerful energy being called a Qumedon who somehow twisted them into a form of humanity—you understand where I am leading?"

"In short," Hasso said bluntly, "have I been contacted by a Qumedon?"

"Have all of the persons on that ship? Could that have caused Ekket's outburst, and their panic? I need to know that we didn't neglect any action that would have avoided it."

"Whatever I sensed may have stirred that panic . . . I don't know. I can't be sure that my feelings were caused by anything but normal fugues of the brain, but from what I have heard of Qumedni—they are like the Ix in that nobody wants to know much about them—they are cruel and capricious as well as being powerful shape-shifters, and I am as certain as an ignorant man can be that nothing I felt could have come from a Qumedon."

"Thank you, Hasso."

Rising from his squat he said, "Tharma, did anyone else hear this, *voice?*"

Almost reluctantly Tharma said, "No."

"I thought not."

Hasso was left feeling very uncomfortable: if his not-quite-vision had been evidence of a Qumedon, or the same as made no difference, it might, through him, have caused a disturbance that made Ekket pull herself free of Gorodek, causing a scandal in both countries, and leading to Saints knew what retribution on Gorodek's part.

Gorodek had pointed a finger and accused him—of what? *Doing a deal of thinking about the Quadzulls manufactured on Five Point Island, probably!* He had already been falsely accused by Sketh of trying to seduce Ekket and been cleared. If Gorodek had really believed this he would have considered Ekket impure and rebuffed her. Truly, he had gotten himself into trouble without help from anyone, least of all Hasso. And Ekket's hearts had been knocking together in fury for a long while. Perhaps this was why Gorodek burned to put his mark on her before she could break away.

Hasso wished he had not gone on that disastrous tour when he ought to have been with Reddow discussing the supposed Lyhhrt threat to Khagodis, surely still the most important matter in the world—

If only Gorodek had married that woman in Center Point, who would have been a real match for him in nastiness, and left her daughter alone!

. . . And Center Point was an Isthmuses state, wasn't it? Not far from that gold-bearing shore where everything began, and those iridium fields . . . ten times a fool, that Gorodek.

But Hasso, you are no better. You have only made an even greater enemy of Gorodek, and that old man's fury will become even more savage.

And I am more adrift, and farther away than ever.

Fthel IV, the Garden State of Bonzador

The State of Bonzador was a vast expanse of tropical brush down in the Southern Continent due west of the Serpentine River. Its southeast corner was called Garden Vale, though it produced no fruits or flowers and its differences from the rest of the country were in trees more gnarled and twisted, and weeds and insects more poisonous. Its first colonists had dreamed of resorts and casinos, but their plans had withered until the colonies became stunted into isolated villages drowning in thorny branches.

Ned Gattes knew this district too well. He had come one time looking for shelter and found a hell.

"This place is no nearer to Khagodis, Ned," Spartakos said at first look, "we have been here before and were hardly able to get out whole."

Ned grunted; he also felt the Lyhhrt's grinding impatience. They had arrived in a rusty aircar smelling of whatever it had transported earlier, that had gone rancid. The barracks were camouflaged tents with inflatable mattresses, the paper fatigues ("You'll get cloth when we board,") were the same kind Ned had been given during his year in the reserve at school, the packaged food was edible, the insecticides worked half the time, and the experience so far was much like the training and fighting routines he'd gone through in game-plexes on five worlds.

The area was thick bush brought down by defoliating agents to a scrubby and slightly rolling terrain that might have seemed dry but for its thickly moist air, and the verges of still-encroaching thornbush that had to be cleared daily. Rains came down almost every day before sunset, just as they did on equatorial Khagodis, and when the sun shone it did so through mist. No ancient civilization had ever gained a foothold in this country.

There were no more than a few hundred troops in this camp; occasionally Ned heard noises in the distance, muffled explosions or echoing voices that suggested others. Of the recruits around him were a few that Ned had a smacking acquaintance with, but he was still a pug who'd rather fight for money, had no bones to pick out of the ring.

These recruits were a very mixed lot, a few Varvani wrestlers who also could not find matches, some small but very wiry Bengtvadi with complex clan insignia tattooed on their hairless heads, a Dabiri male the size of a Clydesdale with one hind quarter replaced by robotics, and a Meshar woman from Barrazan V, a species Ned had never before seen, with coal-black fur and an arrow-tipped tail. By some mischance she had been marooned here and saw no other hope of getting offworld. He had heard rumors that the Meshar were teleports, but if this one was, her talent could not help her, or she had given up trying.

He counted more than forty O'e, and, surprised at first, Ned thought that to come here and risk being despised by the cruel and stupid they must have been desperate or their recruiters were. Then it occurred to him that the O'e had been well manufactured in one respect: they had a greater tolerance of variations in oxygen levels than the other hominids who needed the oxycap sockets behind one ear; these were hard to maintain and keep clean, and uncomfortable even when they worked well.

O'e did not mingle much, but they got fed and clothed like everyone else, and were willing to fight anywhere. The Lyhhrt did not shy away from them, but he did not let them come too close either, and made sure no one noticed. The woman, Azzah, so eager to be with these other O'e, was perhaps happier than she had ever been. "Maybe I am home at last," she said, and no one was cruel enough to deny her.

Spartakos had managed—or the Lyhhrt had managed for him—to comport himself in such a way that he did not stand out like a beacon; the O'e stayed close to him and he did whatever was asked of him.

After the troops had been fed and clothed as well as they could be for their shapes and sizes, they were harangued about prophylaxis and sanitation by a very old army man looking much like Gretorix, who had bossed the fighters in Zamos's arenas long years ago.

"That is your Gretorix," the Lyhhrt said.

"Jeez you'd think he'd be puttin 'is feet up an wrappin himself around a jug by now," one woman said, and Ned looked at her flashing cyber arm, modest compared to the Dabiri's limb, and thought he remembered knowing her a long time ago.

In the first evenings, nodding over campfires, the recruits told their dreams, or their lack of them in an endless mutter like leaves in wind. . . .

. . . can't find nothing that pays and im fucking tired of shoveling shit/lost job bitch of a wife grabbed kids and ran to maw/my children are lost without me and here is no whirling storm to soothe me/told that thumbsucker of a man to pull it out and get some cash/what work i come for aint no more/no place else to find a fight/dunno what that cat is doing here/listen if i was you i wouldnt ask neither/you chukkers look at this steel fist flashing i can fight as good as any man does shove my fist through a brick wall an come out clean/you think a cyber leg's a good thing you should feel how this one hurts/never had money my whole life an i'll kill if i have to i don' mind at all . . .

"Aah, one time in our lives we all had something," the cyborg woman said. "Not great, but good. Hey you iron man, what are you here for?"

"I go with my-friend-Ned-Gattes anywhere," Spartakos said.

. . . darkness and stealth are my territory . . .

Rrengha, dreaming in the limbic brainform of her ancient ancestors.

AND WHERE IS THE DAMNED SHIP THAT WILL TAKE ME TO KHAGODIS?

Ned wrapped his arms around his head and wondered why in all the pits of hell he had come on this useless journey with this only too alien being who despised him so deeply. Then he slid into the Lyhhrt's dream of hideous Ix, soulless Zamos, endless slavery, and eventually somehow he slept.

The next morning three men and a woman stepped out of a buzzer and began to curse the insects.

The Gardeners

They were thick-bodied and wrapped in dark clothes, and with massive aerial-sprouting comms buckled to their shoulders. The Lyhhrt knew them:

:Look now! So much for Brezant not telling us to keep our backs straight! Those four were the ones with Brezant in Montador City, before my Other was killed. Then they tried to destroy us where we were hiding. Now they have murdered their employer and hope to get more wealth. Eventually someone else who wants more wealth will kill them too. All fleshly beings act so.:

Ned wiped down his night's sweat with his kerchief. "All I want is to get my flesh out of here in one lump," he muttered. "You can keep the wealth." The sky was the same as yesterday's, with sunlight slowly clearing the mist.

"This the new batch?" The three men went walkabout, staring at the recruits, most of whom had been lining up for breakfast. Ned kept his head down. The Lyhhrt helped their eyes slide over him and Spartakos but they paused in front of Rrengha, who was fitting on the prosthetic 'fingers' that made her able to open her food packet.

"Lookit this one, I never saw one of them before. Hey you, you go talk-talk?"

Rrengha looked up at them—

:Go someplace else,: the Lyhhrt said quickly, and they went, without noticing.

Ned cracked his knuckles. *Dunno how long we're gonna last here.*

But the Lyhhrt was thinking of something else: that Other who he was sure had killed his mate and his contact, the one who could only be an even more corrupted Lyhhrt than those who had planned to attack Khagodis. He saw the image of that wrought-iron shape in the minds of these men.

"These three Earthers also know of your past," the Lyhhrt said. "You struck one of them on some other world."

"I don't start fights."

"You must have finished one." *:That one called Oxman, with the lenses on his eyes, has caught sight of you. He has forgotten about it now, but—what does 'He'll die as good as the rest of them,' mean to you? That is what he is thinking.:*

Ned swallowed. "I don't like to think."

"What does it mean, Earther?"

"I don't know. Maybe you'd better tell me what you think."

:They are going to send everyone here to be killed on Khagodis.:

Ned whispered, "What? That sounds—" He stopped himself from saying 'crazy'. "How could they? What's the point? Who'd kill us, Khagodi? Everybody thinks Khagodi are as straight as—as—eh . . ."

:Lyhhrt.:

"Right. I guess not." Of course not. *What everybody thinks, isn't.* Ned had known Khagodi arena fighters, men who hadn't settled into any kind of society: they docked their tails to make them fork, and fitted the tips with spikes. Usually they fought each other, because no one else could match their size, and their heavy-helmeted bouts were clumsy and listless.

But except for those fights they had almost never been physically violent . . . and Lyhhrt had become so. Zamos had smeared whole worlds with new forms of corruption.

:Suppose it means that the brave Khagodi are going to defend themselves against attack by slaughtering invaders hired by Lyhhr. . . . :

"If you really believe this, tell me how long, Lyhhrt?"

"I believe. No more than two tendays."

Shit, if that's right I've just led us into a trap.

In the morning there were the usual jaw-jaws and drills and during the afternoon Ned found himself hooking loose brush into the robot loaders that compacted and hauled the garbage, and used the helmet as his guard against thorns; he took care to retract the sensor antenna and leave himself alone in the universe. Trying to pull himself together.

Rrengha came to work alongside him, or go through the motions; though she was a powerful and intelligent weapon, even with prostheses she had no more than half-hands. Aside from the Lyhhrt, she was the only other ESP he knew of here, and she took care to shield hard and wear the copper mesh.

Ned found her silent company good during the long afternoon. He said, to take his mind off everything else, "I guess you must be missing good food and a better place to sleep, Rrengha."

Rrengha canted her head to one side, a massive negative. "Not everybody likes me the way you do, Ned, and working in that place there is too much flesh around me, all those women and men eating and drinking, eating and drinking . . ." She paused to swallow a mouthful of saliva, "too many big bites of meat." She grinned. "Not lean like you, Ned."

Ned laughed. "You're takin' away my appetite." Her appetite was one of the few things he wasn't scared of.

In the evening after dinner he asked the Lyhhrt: "If we had to get out, how would we do it?"

But the Lyhhrt had pulled away and closed his mind.

To get the chill off his spine Ned said, "I think I'll go walkabout and check the fences."

"Take care," the Lyhhrt said.

Ned rubbed himself slick with insecticides and began his walk in a slow spiral around the fires and murmuring groups, talking casually to anyone he knew, gradually working his way through the tents area, taking the offer of a dopestick and squatting to smoke it, moving further out among the scrubby trees that had been left standing, past several couples among the bushes grunting their way into whatever temporary paradise was available, until he heard the deep vibration and came up against the bulk of the cycler.

The windowless gray block went deep into the ground, once-and-a-half Ned's height above it, and eight armspans to a side. All waste went into its bay doors, but the stinging smell of it came from its solvents and vaporizers. All the money that was not spent on uniforms, barracks and ground-clearing machines was fed into it; its roof was covered with branches and was almost invisible from above. The loaders that collected brush carried it here, and Ned realized that some had come from other camps, the ones whose noises he had heard. Ned wondered if this Company was a business that ran other kinds of illegal militias and did not see why not . . . but sending them to death? How much money had been spent and would be spent for this, and so many lives . . . where was the payoff coming from?

He pulled himself away from these thoughts and wound his spiral past the watchtower, that did not rise far above the trees, and along a narrow path through them. The sun had dropped and the mists were rising; the stars were fuzzy and twinkled wildly in the still-hot air.

Insects were sticking to his face and that air was hard breathing; every once in a while some unsuspected flower would burst from a thorny bed with a waft of fragrance that was almost too sweet. Ned paused to listen for footsteps through the endless insect buzzings that were drowning out the cycler's rumble, and was turning his head to look back when something hit him hard between the shoulders and he was face down in dirt.

He stayed there, with a foot holding him down. The voice snarled, "What d'you think you're doing here?" Woman's voice.

His teeth were gritting with the dirt and he snorted it from his bruised nose. The foot lifted and flipped him like a stone. "Whatsis, Chrissake, I come for a walk!"

Another of the heavy ones, she had arms as thick as the Beer Goddess's, a zapstick in one hand instead of a lightning bolt, and a heavy stunner slung over her shoulder. Her hair was blond, chopped short.

Ned, cringing in a pose he had learned the hard way as a cheap pimp, recognized her with an extra twist of the gut: the one called Hummer, who had landed earlier with the three men, and even earlier had come in a fireproof fighting suit to kill him and the Lyhhrt back near the cave in Miramar, he had seen her hard face and yellow chopped hair through the suit's headpiece. She would have slaughtered him gladly, but now she did not recognize his face through the dirt and the blood running from his nose.

"G't up!"

Everything hurt but nothing was broken. He scrambled up, rubbing the dirt deeper into his face. "I wasn't doin' nothin' miss, what's wrong with walkin'?"

"Lessee your tag." She was raising the zapstick.

"It's in my kit, I got a rash on my neck an—Please don't—I'm Tommy Longjeans, Tent Alpha-Seventeen!" Tommy had been the biggest bully in Ned's school, and Ned would have been glad to trade places.

She grabbed his arm with her free hand and shoved her face close. "You looked like you were trying to go AWOL, Mister Longjeans, we don't like that, next time we'll push your face into the fence for a real good shave, and just to remind—" The stick was sparking the stubble of his jaw—

"Halloo, Hummer! You got trouble?" The voice was not far away in the bush, too close for Ned.

She turned her head to yell back, "Nothing, just a—"

Ned gave a hard edge-hand chop to her wrist that loosed her grip, wrenched his arm free and ran. He heard yells and cracking branches, but he was a lot lighter on his feet than Hummer and he ran as if demons were after him until he reached the cycler, then kept up a fast walk through the trees, past the lovers and when he was surrounded by tents, slowed to a limp, panting.

Suddenly he had a hideous mental image of her and all of the other brutes standing at the ship's bays driving out all their load like cattle, to be slaughtered before they hit Khagodi ground. But he did not know whether it came from his own paranoia or the Lyhhrt's.

The Lyhhrt was inside the tent doing his awkward best to refresh his liquids without being seen. He did not care to be near fires where he might boil in his own juice. After he had finished he lay down beside Spartakos, both of them in straight lines.

Ned thumped down beside him, groaning. "Found the fence, got scratched . . . Lyrhht, how many people and camps would you say there are here?"

The Lyhhrt stirred himself reluctantly and said, "In your enumeration, fourteen hundred and seventy-one persons in five groups."

"Any more coming?"

"There are no more signs of recruiting."

Fifteen hundred. A distance away from the Duke of York's ten thousand. Ned had been almost certain that Brezant was spritzing. "You're certain they mean to kill us." Fact, not question.

"Almost certain."

Ned swallowed on panic. "Lyhhrt, we gotta find a way out of here." He waited out the silence.

"I can leave," the Lyhhrt said. "I might be able to bring out all of those that I led in, but I would be lying to myself and everyone else if I promised." There was a dark withdrawing depth in his mind.

"I don't want to make any move without being sure they mean to do that," Ned said. "Make sure really soon and move fast. But, Lyhhrt . . . can we run out of here and leave everybody else to be murdered?"

He crawled off to the showers. The good news was, if what the Lyhhrt believed was true, as long as they needn't go to Khagodis, he needn't get that damned oxycap socket reamed out again, if only he got out of here.

FIVE *

Khagodis, New Interworld Court: *Choices*

Tharma was squatting at her desk eating a trencher of bread and a slab of cold myth-ox as usual for the late morning meal, but no matter what else she thought about, her eyes could not move away from that air-freight package on the desk just beyond the food. She found herself holding the spice-cellar over her tea-bowl without being able to remember whether she had shaken it, took a sip of tea and found it was already over-flavored, drank it anyway, in two gulps, and followed by gulping her food, and having it sit in her belly in a congealed lump. All ceremonies ended today and everyone would be leaving in two days at the most, but there was endless unfinished business.

The murder of that fellow Sketh, whatever his worth, needed a solution; the insistence of minor officials who had meant well, on imprisoning both Sketh and Hasso without formal charge, did not encourage confidence in public institutions of the public who lived and worked here. The problem of calming Gorodek and protecting Ekket. And that truly peculiar occurrence on the Mesa . . .

She set her teeth, swept the crumbs aside, drew the package toward herself, and pulled the sealer's tab. Stared at the symbo*lingua* text: *Report concerning the evidence of force.* The title stopped there, because no one had dared fill it in further.

If this had been one of her old cases in Burning Mountain reported in cuneiform on clay tablets, she could simply have maintained privacy by stamping them out of existence. Not so now, when every thought could be engraved as solidly on electronic record as it might be on stone.

She nerved herself to pull the file from its wrappings, break the seals and pluck out the sheaf of thin and crinkly papers. They whispered in her hands.

The good news was *victim not penetrated* embedded in a lot of elegant language: so then Ekket was safer than she might have been—but what followed no elegance could alleviate: *seed of perpetrator immature, suggest testing for Kartenat's Syndrome.* The genetic defect that caused male sterility in Khagodi.

"By Saint Gresskow's Seven Bastards, why do I need to know this!" She wrapped the package up again, sealed it with her personal signet and handed it to the most trusted aide to lock up. This was one she would push upstairs to her Prime. Let him gnaw on the problem of keeping Gorodek from exploding in even more furious embarrassment.

Then a message burst in her ear with such force that it nearly blew the comm button out of her gill-slit: "Have I heard you correctly, Prime Director?"

Ravat, a good sensible fellow from Tharma's own West Oceania, said, "I am afraid you have. Governor Gorodek has demanded—ek! replace that with 'requested'!—the privilege of making an announcement"—pause for a gulp of air—"of great importance to the whole assembly in the Hall of Communication and Telegraphy, at the beginning of the fourth quarter, just between Refreshment Hour and Farewell Dinner." Another gulp. "I'm sure you know what this means."

She did: a carefully crafted information leak to the media and an unobtrusive increase in security at the Hall. Heavier duty for herself and an increased expense in keeping on extra forces when there was nothing left to the gathering but a dinner. "What else do you believe it might mean, Director?"

"So much has been happening that I don't dare think."

Tharma said slowly, "One of my brothers has a charming wife-house standing empty in Burning Mountain. I had thought of retiring there, but I hate the summer heat."

"I don't mind it. Perhaps I'll buy it from him."

Of course the news spread hissing among all the whisperers munching and sipping at the end of third quarter. It simply added to the gossip about everything that had happened the day before. Hasso did not attend Refreshment Hour, too afraid of being a public spectacle like the one he had already taken part in. When the time came to convene in the Hall of Communication he remained in his room and watched on the TriV.

Tharma watched from her office on several displays that commanded views of all guardposts.

Everything in the New Interworld Court was grand, its marble walls and floors, its stained-glass skylights, its Khagodi-sized staircases with broad deep steps; even the narrow glass-walled escalator for diminutive outworlders managed a touch of grandeur.

The Hall of Communication had all of this and more; even in the media gallery, and barely enough room for its avid listeners. Gorodek mounted the great steps to the huge dais and elaborately carved lectern. He did not bother with the lectern but came around in front of it so that it framed him. And after the techs had set up the speakers he said without preamble:

"I have learned from sources I trust that factions from the world Lyhhr are planning to launch an attack, a senseless attack on territories in the Isthmuses district abutting my state, Western Sealand. They claim that this is necessary to redress our inaction during our crisis with the Ix. I do not care what they claim: I will do everything in my power to defend my state and its borders, and I deliver this warning as a service to the world."

This said, he stepped down from the dais, and with his guards around him, left the Hall.

Tharma did not wait to see the melee or hear the buzz. She switched off the TriV, but before she had time to act, her comm sounded its chime and an aide said, "Osset, an official of Governor Gorodek, demands to speak with you."

She did not like that "demands" but on the principle of getting it over with said, "Let him in."

Osset, a man of rather reserved appearance, was rather more civil than Gorodek.

"Firstly, the Governor wishes to know what is being done to find the murderer of his aide Sketh, which was obviously committed by a Lyhhrt, and why, when there is a Lyhhrt present here, he has not been sequestered."

"The Lyrrht in question was twenty-seven thousand siguu from the crime scene at the time it took place, asking me for help," Tharma said. "We are not certain there is no other Lyhhrt here. We are well occupied with examining the case."

Osset took a step back, and time to draw air. "I know that you are occupied, Supervisor. Principally I am here to tell you that the Governor wishes to leave and demands the presence of his bride-elect Ekket, to accompany him to Western Sealand."

Tharma smiled at the boldness of this demand. "At this

moment that—eh, request, is impossible to fulfill. I believe that we can prove that Ekket was wronged, by the statutes of her own country as well as local ones, and since she has claimed that a felony was executed on her and asked for justice, the Court will give her status as an adult, no longer under the authority of any parent or guardian but the Law."

"You smile now but you will not smile later," Osset said.

"I don't know whose words those are. But watch yourself," Tharma said, "and tell your master the same."

Osset left and Tharma did not take time to consider his threat, but turned her mind back to her visit with Hasso in the Hospital, so few days ago, particularly during those moments after he had pulled off his helmet and flung it aside. . . .

"Bring me Hasso, if you can find him," she told the aide.

While she waited Tharma looked around her office, which was not grand but a small cubicle lined temporarily in fiberboard and furnished with no more than a desk and shelves. Perhaps one day its walls and floor would be gracious and marbled. *By then I will be retired or dead.*

For now it and the other offices were the backside of grandeur.

Hasso was weary of everything in this place, even of his yearning for Ekket, and leaned heavily on his staff.

"Hasso, excuse me for having to say this, but when I was with you in the Hospital a few days ago—" *Only a few days!* "—you pulled off your helmet, and I caught traces of some thoughts that I at first believed were part of the feverish dreams I am sure you were having. Now, with Gorodek's astonishing declaration, I have come to believe you know something of its background. I am making a request. You must choose whether to answer."

Hasso crouched, laying his staff aside.

"I have long wanted to unburden myself, but could not

find a way to bring it to anyone's attention. It began three tendays ago in Burning Mountain . . ."

He relaxed, and began to brighten before her eyes: he told her his story, beginning with the dinner on his rooftop, through the journey on which he had met Ekket, and ending, given Reddow's permission, with mind-tampering and his certainty of the presence of one more Lyhhrt.

"I meant to bring up this matter with the Interworld Council, but then Reddow was so distressed, and the situation has become so chaotic I was afraid to ask them to convene for my affairs."

"You had reason," Tharma said sadly. "What message did the Lyhhrt bring you?"

"He said, exactly: 'I have been advised by the world Lyrrh to inform you that you will be called as a witness in an action being brought against your government for negligence in refusing to support and defend Lyhhrt action against the attack of the world Iyax in local year 7514.' And then he told me, they have begun this action and will arrive on Khagodis within three thirtydays to bring it to Interworld Court, and if Lyhhr is not satisfied there will be an actual attack."

"Did he tell you how he knew all this?"

"He seemed to be afraid to say more."

"I understand. That will explain something at least. But we have had no official warning and I don't know of any ships in orbit except those of media from the moons and from Fthel worlds. Why did this Lyhhrt choose to contact you, Hasso?"

"Partly because I have official connections, and the rest because he is the only Lyhhrt citizen onland and I am the only one he knows of with one heart and a wasted leg, so he believed I might be equally lonely." Hasso smiled. "That is not quite the case."

She looked at him for a long moment, and said, "Thank you, Hasso. I will take these matters to my Prime."

She did not want to bring up the case of Ekket then, though it was a burning question, but left Hasso, and his Lyhhrt as well, to take a little comfort in having her strength added to theirs.

She stayed alone in her office for an hour before going to dinner, with communications shut down, building her resolve to prevent Gorodek from becoming a master at setting worlds against each other, and remembering also those Lyhhrt, who had given their lives to the destruction of Ix power as simply as if they had snuffed a candle.

Fthel IV, Bonzador: *A Little Learning . . .*

"Next time let me search for fences," Rrengha said.

"You were asleep."

Dreaming terrible dreams of starvation and disease on Ungruarkh, the ancient curses of strangers in a savage world. Ned, aching in every muscle and half the bones, dragged himself out of his own nightmares, sloshed toothcleaner and wiped his face unevenly with depilatory, eyes half closed, mind stiff as his body, and staggered out of his tent.

"Hullo!"

Ned looked up and saw Lek. "Haven't seen you around."

Lek, wearing the same fatigues as everybody else, came up to Azzah, who was rolling up her bedding, with a "Hello, sweetheart!" and a chuck under the chin and then "Hey!" and a good wrap around the neck in the coil of Spartakos's arm.

Ned cried, "Let go, Spartakos!"

Spartakos let go, Lek rubbed his neck and coughed. "I like her! I didn't mean any harm."

"Something wrong with your approach, Lek. Spartakos couldn't tell that."

"Ouch. Believe me, I really do like this one. That other one you got with you is something else."

"Yeh. He is. You get a lot of money for recruiting, Lek? Maybe I'll try that line myself."

"Whatever I get, I can't do much with it until I get back."

Lek wandered off and Azzah snapped, "You let me take care of myself, Spartakos!"

Spartakos said kindly, "You can't have 'take me with you' and 'leave me alone' at the same time."

Rrengha said, *:I don't like that one, he is a thief, and gets a brand for it on the world Ahrgonsit.:*

Ned felt kinder toward the man now. "If he went about it the way he makes friends with women, I'm not surprised. But if he's going along with us he's just an ordinary pisser in the same boat, and if he'd meant to harm her you'd know for sure." Ned picked up his ration and headed for a squat in the mess tent and a cup of weak tea.

Rrengha followed. "And where is that other one who is something else?"

"He's just—eh—"

Ned realized that the Lyhhrt was gone. He found a place to sit and ate in a daze. "He said nothing to you?"

"He does not invite me into his mind."

"You think he deserted?"

"I don't know what." Rrengha had not much enjoyed being upstaged by the Lyhhrt.

Trying to pull his ragged thoughts together, Ned found himself chewing his paper fork and threw it in the trash along with the empty container. Rrengha added grudgingly, "I cannot believe that one is a deserter."

From the watchtower, Gretorix called, "All you sinners, Work Area Number One!"

This was the largest of the fields Ned and the others had been working to keep clear, and carriers crowded with recruits from other camps were rapidly filling it.

"Awright now," Gretorix yelled, "you know you've been hired by the Lyhhrt to take a bite out of Khagodis, in sharp and out soon. You need training for that, an here's where we start—you, Esser and Yokoah, bring that over here!"

Two burly NCOs unloaded and wheeled what looked like a big metal cage into the center of the field. "There now! We need a volunteer—you, Ned Gattes, I remember you from old days, you get to try this first! In you go!"

"Wha—?" Esser and Yokoah grabbed Ned by the arms and stuffed him into the cage. "I never—"

"Don't mind the electrodes and that bit of a needle won't hurt—"

Before Ned could say his prayers, he felt a great jolt and at the same time Rrengha's reassurance, *:No fear, they are not killing you yet,:* and then as if the whole contents of his skull had been sucked out, dumped into a giant mixer with the power on high, and poured back in.

In one standard minute he opened his eyes with the ability to load, aim, fire, field-strip, clean, and assemble a GuentherMMV. A very old mercenaries' standby.

Gretorix thrust the Guenther with its cleaning pack into Ned's hands and Ned went through all of the maneuvers zipzap.

"Neat," he said. It was all he had breath for. He handed back the Guenther. "I hope I don't have to do that every day."

"You'll find out," Gretorix slapped him on the back. "Now who goes next?"

Ned did not want to watch the next victim's fear. He threaded his way through the crowd and headed for the mess tent, where he found Rrengha drinking from a bowl, the i.d. tag around her neck rattling against it. No one else was there except a Varvani named Orbo who was sweeping the rough floorboards.

"That tea you got?"

:Maybe.:

Ned filled himself a cup from the tank and muttered, "Christ, you're as cranky as he was."

:He sends a message.:

It fell into Ned's mind that moment, the way the ability to handle a rifle had done:

My fission-sibling saved your life on Shen IV and gave his life for you when you tried to save his in return. I found him in your memory and saw through your eyes what happened to him. I hope you will forgive me if I seemed angry. I am angry at myself for taking you from your life to do my/our work for me/us. I must do it for myself to give you back your lives.

Ned sighed. *I dunno what he thinks he can do.* He had never felt nearer to Nowhere than he was now.

The Lyhhrt might have caught a ride by boarding any air or ground vehicle in the camp, but he was weary from being with the minds there and had no trouble passing the armed guardians at the edges, they blinked and he had passed. And just as easily he went through the barbed wire fence that Ned had not reached by cutting it with his laser and rewelding it when he was on the other side. The thornbushes caught at his clothing and false skin, so he slipped them off and used the laser to vaporize them. The glass eyes popped when they exploded, and someone far back called, "What was that? You hear that?" By then he was gone into darkness.

His brushed silver carapace was unencumbered, but he did not feel more free. He was a being confined to a cramped cell with small windows, burdened with a task beyond his stability that he could not give up, and weighted further with the sense that he had taken a dreadful wrong turn that led him to conscript Ned Gattes, and draw him into the camp in Bonzador.

The nearest village was ten kilometers distant; he lengthened his legs and began walking toward it, using his radio to search for unoccupied land or aircars. He was not quite as good at this as Spartakos, but eventually he was able to summon a buzzer and direct it to take him to Montador.

Montador was more sophisticated than Port City, much less of a company town, and the capital of the Cinnabar Keys. For the Lyhhrt everything had begun here. *Here is the center.*

There were Lyhhrt here who worked at the embassies, or for businesses, and he would be one more. He would be allowed to obtain drugs that were illegal for fleshers in order to mix his food, and buy the expensive power cells that were vital to his workshell's operation; he did not dare go back to that cavern in Miramar.

Here was where he would find—no, be found by, the Other who wanted him dead.

He landed in a car park as the sun cleared the horizon, sent the buzzer home and walked the streets of the city. There were open-air markets, leafy trees, glassy towers that even the Lyhhrt might have enjoyed observing when he first came. He paid no attention to them now, but walked through the markets and down the main avenue scanning the crowded minds to sharpen his sight and hearing.

He saw through alien eyes that there were brilliant holographic advertisements swarming among the people, urging, pleading, admonishing, but they appeared to his vision as flickering mists, and he was concentrating intensely on what was in the minds, what the eyes had seen, the ears heard, that would point him where he was going.

Projected on the walls of tall buildings there were other kinds of messages, printed newsstrips telling of games won and lost, wars in distant places. The Lyhhrt did not read, but the minds of readers who stopped to look told him what was being said, a great deal that was of no importance to him, and suddenly, a report that the Ambassadors from Lyhhr had been called home for gross misuse of their authority, and the Embassy closed. There were no other details.

He caught this message just before it scrolled out of sight, and stood stunned, feeling faint while streams of people heading to work swarmed around him muttering. Finally he withdrew the feelers of his mind into himself. *What does this mean?* Of course that pair well deserved to be sent home, and good riddance.

But he was not sure now that the murderer in wrought-iron was a cohort of those ambassadors, Brass and Bronze, and he was struggling to put the two parties in relation to each other.

The matter had begun with those ambassadors and Brezant planning a neat coup against Khagodis. Now Brezant was dead, the two ambassadors displaced; that murderer, who had come out of nowhere, was now running the Company. He wondered if that one had been in control all along, had used Brezant as a puppet. Brezant had been a man with no control and little talent in an organization of any size, the controlling Lyhhrt had seen that, had seen that his underlings were contemptuous of him and let them—perhaps even encouraged them—to kill him. That death made no difference.

The difference is that my Other is dead, and Willson.

If I do not destroy that dark sibling, all of those in that camp will die, Ned Gattes, Spartakos and Rrengha, and all of the poor fools that the world could not find a use for, they will die horribly and I will die for shame. . . .

But for all of his casting about, the Lyhhrt found nothing in the minds of the news-gathering passersby to suggest that any threat had been made against Khagodis. *Then what is going on?*

The woman Greisbach had run for her life, he did not even have any one of the Embassy staff to reach out for and the ground was rapidly shearing away beneath him.

Tracks

Jesus God how did I ever get into this / being too pissed off with the old man / falling into a whorehouse and letting myself be / not having enough guts to sit out him and his lectures till I could earn a real / picked up because anything was better than that knockshop and ended just as much of a whore. . . .

Tyloe pulled himself away from his thoughts and hers, they glanced at each other, one blink, and turned their heads to look out the windows. They had left their aircar at the monorail junction and boarded for Montador. The windows showed an autumn landscape, what passed for autumn in Cinnabar Keys, a slight yellowing of thin leaves in the rich growth, a dark thickening in the succulents that rose like city towers.

"There's no reason we have to go there just because he said so," Tyloe said.

"I'm so afraid of him," Lorrice whispered. "My esp is almost zero on Lyhhrt, they can shield so you don't see them coming."

"I bet you'll know that one. Just how far can he esp anyway?"

"It's not how far he can esp, it's how well he can find." Then with an obvious effort to pull herself together, "Listen, you don't have to stay with me. If you give me half of that cashbook I can find a place to dig in."

"You think he planted anything on us?" Tyloe pulled the cashbook from his pocket and flicked its gold foil leaves. "Think that's giving him a buzz right now?"

"It's possible, every one of those could have a tracer on it." She said reluctantly, "Maybe you'd better throw it away."

Tyloe thought for a minute: "No. Let's stick together for

a while, your esp must be good for something, and we're less conspicuous as a couple, we'll just spend it around town for a day, get a hotel room, go through the motions laying a trail and then leave it in the street for somebody else to find and get the hell out."

Lorrice couldn't think of any better plan.

From the mono they took the aircab and looked down on the city and its tall towers, many of which had been built in the foundations of ancient stone ruins and rose like stemmed flowers from their beds of leaves. "I don't want to go back to that damned Lyhhr place we went to that night," she said.

"There's plenty others." Tyloe plucked the first gold leaf for cabfare, the slot spat a cashcard for change.

They walked along the avenue among the crowds for a while, shaking off the air kisses of the hologram sirens and spending the cashcard on iced drinks. Tyloe found the brightness of the sun and sky, the reflections of glass and steel, almost painful after the long days in the forest. "That one there looks good." He was pointing to an establishment that was a branch of an Earther chain known for expensive elegance.

"It looks awfully snobbish." Lorrice was wearing the gray silk suit that had made her look powerful, and she was pushing at herself to keep from shrinking.

Tyloe's clothes were barely good enough. "We're not on anybody else's wanted list yet."

"How much time d'you think we've got?"

Tyloe put on an air of recklessness to match her efforts. "Let's pretend we have a day."

"Only a day?"

"A day, to start with. I don't think he's wasting time playing with us right now."

Neither of them dared ask, *What does he want with us?*

* * *

In the crowd of minds the Lyhhrt scanned, searching for GalFed agents and workers he had known, traces of feeling-tones he could not describe, did not quite know what he was looking for, wondering if he had gone really mad now . . . and sensed a something, he thought first only the whispery pulses of his heart, no, a signal, yes, by its frequency and resonance a Lyhhrt tracking device, he had used them himself working for GalFed, and he said to the empty air: *I have you now.* A pleasure to form those soundless words with his metal lips.

Wait. *I am deceiving myself.* Any Lyhhrt in the city could be using one of those. No matter, there was nothing else for him, nowhere to go and no more time. He followed.

Tyloe and Lorrice took a hotel suite and slept for two hours, woke up, ate lunch and went shopping for three hours, spending a lot of money on clothes that did not look expensive, consulted an InfoDesk to find the most pretentious restaurant and spent precious time on drinks and dinner for nearly three hours.

"We're killing time," Lorrice said suddenly. "I don't like that expression."

"You don't have to use it."

"My mother always used it. When my father left us it would have been all right because she had her own money, but she'd never been educated for much, and she was always saying, let's do this or that, go here or there, to kill time, and when she died, it turned out she'd spent so much money doing it there wasn't any left."

"My father spent his like it was his life's blood . . . we're taking up space here—let's get out before the staff kills us with dirty looks."

One more gold leaf.

Back at the hotel they began to change into the mufti they had bought for anonymity.

And in mid-change a spark of sexual feeling flamed between them and—

Lorrice cried, "No no, God, what am I thinking, it's just one day! Damn you!"

"I'm not coming at you! I can't help what I feel!" *It's the danger, a maybe-never-again feeling.* He zipped his pants and top and flung open the doors to the balcony; the city lights flared below, the stars above. A last false taste of wealth. Just as the leaves of money were not really gold. "We've got too many of these left. I don't want to use them for the underground." The tram would take them to the hotel at the edge of the city, a place for one-night stands, where they would pretend to be moneyless lovers.

She said in an exhausted voice, "Let's order up some drinks, then, and toss the rest of them over the balcony one by one."

"Why not? Let's."

The Lyhhrt followed the signal into the store where clothing was being sold. It stopped there. Whatever was carrying it had been locked in metal. His fear deepened. He left quickly before people could begin to stare at a Lyhhrt in a clothing store. Out in the street he picked it up again, thin and thready, surely not the original one, which had stopped so abruptly. He followed it as if he were lost in the deepest of caverns searching out one footprint, across the street into a small arcade that sold iced drinks, where it stopped again; he scanned the minds of the servers there and they gave him a glimpse of a man and that ESP woman he knew from seeing them through the eyes of those Earthers, in that eating-place that claimed to show his world Lyhhr.

He was far from sure of the time when these passages had taken place, but he knew that he had landed his buzzer in the western outskirts of the city and from there to the center he had found nothing; so he kept walking, eastward, slowly, down side streets and back to the avenue, crossing to explore streets off the other side, back again, as the sun arched over him and fell behind him, searching the minds of the passersby and straining to catch a signal once more. There was no reason that another tracer should exist, but since there had been more than one, why not? He followed on, led by thready hope.

Tyloe drank the last drop of whiskey and crunched the ice. Took up the cashbook from the table, it was three-quarters empty by now, went to the balcony railing and breathed in the soft heavy air. Lorrice joined him, he tore the leaves out one at a time and let the evening wind pull them from his hand.

They leaned over the balcony and watched them floating down in ripples of light.

"That's that."

The Lyhhrt found it: a signal that was multiplied like a sung chord came from the restaurant across the way. He crossed the street. The windows were curtained now but he knew what was inside.

The server was saying, "That three hours was worth it, they never stopped ordering and gave me a tip big enough to start a small business . . . just wish I could keep it all . . ."

The Lyhhrt could see him, could feel him waving the sheaf of gold leaves, shutting them into the strongbox, stopping the signal.

:Which way did they go? Tell me that!: the Lyhhrt cried in desperate silence.

"They went back up the street the way they came," the server said. "Now why the hell did I say that!"

The Lyhhrt was moving up the street with lengthened strides, where would they go? Expensive clothes, expensive dinner, expensive *what* now? He did not know why they were spending money in this way, he wondered whether he really knew anything about aliens at all and wished he had never been forced to learn.

Then the signal sang and sang and the gold leaves came blowing across the pavement at his feet.

"Let's go," Tyloe said. "What's the matter?"

Lorrice was standing still. She had dropped her bag and was clasping her hands. "I feel so . . ."

"Lorrice, what is it!"

"I . . ." She raised one hand and bit the knuckle of her forefinger. She had the same look on her face that she had when the Lyhhrt arrived to meet Brezant.

Tyloe sweated ice.

The Lyhhrt opened the door and came in holding up the five gold leaves in his hand as if they were four aces and a wild deuce.

"No," he said quietly. "I am not the one you are so afraid of."

Lorrice and Tyloe looked only too ready to be afraid of him. Lorrice wet her lips and said tremblingly, "Who are you, then?"

The Lyhhrt placed himself into a chair and quietly, quickly opened his mind to them as he had done with Ned, but rather more slowly, because he had learned so much more, and told them everything, beginning with the meal in that restaurant that looked something like Lyhhr, and watched the expressions flickering over their faces under the assault of information. The weight of it made them sit down.

"I see all that," Tyloe said slowly. And as Ned had done, added, "All this sounds like highly official business. And we're not quite on the right side of the law, are we?"

The Lyhhrt said, as he had done to Ned, "If necessary, I will see that you forget."

"But you want something."

The Lyhhrt folded the leaves in two and held them out.

"You lead me to that one."

Khagodis, New Interworld Court:
One Man's Meat

Tharma's dreams were thorny and terrible; Ekket wept in them, Gorodek's flunky Osset leered and threatened, Hasso was wrapped in a cloud of something altogether sinister. A restless twisting sleep that sent her arms knocking on the edge of the basin, pinched her breathing siphon, squirted water into her ear.

A low but powerful *zzukk!* made her jump up with a tremendous splash that shot half the water over the floor.

:I have him, Supervisor, but get out of there quickly!:

Tharma jumped from her basin doubly fast. "What is it, Dritta? What do you have?"

The young woman, who had been waiting with the stunner for three hours, flashed her belt light and was bending over the dark figure sprawled by the basin. "I am trying to see whether it's a weapon he has or a poison flask—I see it is some kind of container—you had better shower down, Supervisor."

"Just make sure that flask is stoppered . . . here is a washing rag to wrap it in." She added, "And thank you for volunteering yourself, Dritta."

"I serve willingly, Supervisor."

Tharma stared down at the intruder. He was a stringy old man with faded scales, wearing a heavy helmet that surely must have burdened him. "A servant," Tharma said. "Too worn down to match any of our diplomats." Also there were no documented felons, as yet, in the New Interworld institution, and whoever killed Sketh would be the first—if found. This beaten-down specimen had not killed Sketh.

"I have called for a platform to pick him up," Dritta said.

"When he comes to we'll get that helmet off and see what . . ." Especially what kind of poison.

"You might call this poison," the chemist said. "It's methotrimeprazine, a hypnotic that causes staggering and hiccups in Bengtvadi and Varvani. It must be a cheap intoxicant if they're willing to take those effects." He knew of it only by hearsay and had no idea what it would have done to Tharma. "It was a rather stupid kind of attack, you know. No one would believe you of all people took this kind of drug on purpose."

"I hope not," Tharma said.

"Calm of you to go to sleep with that on your mind."

"I trust Dritta. See what DNA you can get off that bottle."

"Everyone will be gone by the time we find out, but we'll do it."

The attacker had willingly removed his helmet. His mind was a blank. Not a great surprise for Tharma, considering what Hasso had been telling her about his suspicions of a Lyhhrt in hiding.

Yet, there were many home-grown telepaths who could have done this mind-work. *You smile now but you will not smile later.* It just was possible that Osset was not carrying out his threat. *Though the Saints know that if it had succeeded, I may well have been lunging about with hiccups and giggling fits . . . far from not smiling.* And Gorodek may even had nothing to do with this.

Maybe so. But Tharma did not try to sleep again.

She broke the fast with her usual bowl of yagha-root tea and some soured curd, and went down to the holding cells where she found her attacker taking his. There was no basin for him to sleep in and he was propped in a corner with his tail curled around him. He was looking very ragged, and did not want to meet her eyes.

She opened his door with the pressure of a fingerprint and squatted before him as it rolled shut behind her. "Old man," she took off her helmet and set it on the floor, "do you know who I am?"

He did not look up. "I know now." He took his last lick of the yagha bowl as if he would never eat again.

"You have a name?"

"I am Aggar."

"Where do you work?"

"I unload freight from the railroad cars."

"I am the Supervisor of Security in this Court Center, where I try to keep people safe. You didn't know that, did you? I have never harmed you, so you have no reason for coming to my room to put drugs in my water. Is that true?"

"Yes." Eyes down to his yagha bowl wishing for more.

"Now, Aggar, you tell me who sent you to my room."

"Nobody."

"What! Then why—"

"I dreamed," Aggar said almost eagerly, gulping air as he gulped yagha. "My dream told me, if I did this trick, everyone would say how clever I was."

"Eki! I understand." Tharma sat back. "Then where did you get the drug bottle?"

"It was in my hand when I woke."

"Yes," Tharma said, picked up her helmet and got up to close the cell door behind her. Freight-handlers were a rowdy lot, but not subtle enough for a trick like that. No legal way to esp out the trickster, and every other way too risky for that dim mind.

"Give this fellow some more of that yagha and a slice of glauber, Constable—eh, go ahead. I've never seen a scrawnier freight-handler!"

Outside the Security offices was a cluster of chapels for six or seven of the world's religions. Tharma had just faith enough to swear by the Saints, and she chose their chapel to rest in and think.

She found an empty space and accepted a communication wafer. She set it into her gill-slit where it emitted words of wisdom from the Saints. Khagodi languages in spoken form are a late development and do not take well to recording. The Saints who addressed her in bland croakings did not go near enlightening the great puzzle, of which this attack was not the biggest piece, or have the vigor of her own favorite, Saint Gresskow of the Seven Bastards, who had earned sainthood by refusing to have her fetuses aborted after a violent rape; Ekket's case made the legend particularly pertinent. Gresskow had refused the abortion allowed by law because of the eternal problem of infertility on Khagodis: there never have been more than seventy-five million people on the world.

Gresskow's bastards had begotten fifty children and become the only male saints of Tharma's religion.

But: the total number of the bastards had been nine. Two had been violent rebels who were punished by being dropped into Screaming Demons Chasm, where their anguished cries resounded forever.

Tharma was well aware that in Screaming Demons Chasm, which the locals pretended was haunted to lure outworld tourists, the demons were only echoes. But except for those two there were no other demons in Khagodi culture. No tricksters, no Underworld gods. Only giant eggs in plenty, bearing multitudes.

She wondered if the Lyhhrt had become these demons, out of their anguish had truly made a rebellion that was not merely an empty threat, on the worlds where they had become known, in the midst of hot lives far from their own cold sightless world. Whether the attack on her had been part of it. Or if there really were Qumedni here, ready to find mischief among the stodgy Khagodi, or make it.

Qumedni had been very fond of tweaking the Ungrukh at one time, but the Cats had discovered that joining three or four tens of their telepaths could send a Qumedon somewhere else fast, and none had been heard from since. Hasso was sure that the presence he had felt was not one.

But I believe that there is at least one other Lyhhrt here, and I am only an ordinary woman. Not someone with a real talent or great importance in this world . . . a district supervisor who has risen as far as she can go. I might become Prime if Ravat retires or transfers, but I doubt I will wait that long. . . .

"Eh, Supervisor, you've found a good quiet place for yourself." Ravat had come in soundlessly and settled in beside her. He civilly refused the wafer and said, "I heard what happened last night. That was sharp work."

"Thank you, Director, but it would have been sharper to have found the source."

"Yes, but you are unharmed, and that is most important. I'm sorry I cannot give you any time off, with so much happening."

"I will be glad to have some when this affair is over," Tharma said. "In the meantime I would like a favor."

"Ask."

"I worry about the young woman Ekket, and I would

like to assign an officer to guard her and perhaps even escort her when she leaves here."

Ravat looked at her wisely, "That young one who stood guard for you, a new one, isn't it?"

"Head of her class, yes. And I can spare her now that some of the guests have gone."

"If you find her so trustworthy, certainly," Ravat said, and left her to her Saints.

But Tharma gave the demons one more thought.

Suppose that foreign drug was deadly to Khagodi? She had heard of no cases of such poisoning—and no one was likely to test it. And unwillingly she had come to know that Gorodek was probably sterile.

Would that be worth poisoning me?

The report suggesting that Gorodek might have Kartenat's Syndrome did not mention him by name, but was identified by number. *I am the only connection to it.*

And only a Lyhhrt telepath could find that out . . . why? Something to put away for the future? And if that was so that Lyhhrt could be hiding anywhere here, even in someone's body. . . .

Eki, Tharma, you have more questions than there are answers and some may never be found. But I was right to choose Dritta . . . yes, and her work is cut out for her. . . .

Friendships

Hasso felt that in these past few days he had been broken and badly patched together. He said to the Lyhhrt, "Neither of us has gained much by coming here."

The Lyhhrt said, "A few hours ago there was a triV news report that the Lyhhrt ambassadors on Fthel Four had been called home. I don't know what that means."

"It's useless to bring the matter to the Council now that Gorodek has made that announcement. People all over the world will be hissing over it . . . but no one takes a Lyhhrt threat seriously."

"Gorodek does," The Lyhhrt had wrapped himself in his wrinkled cloth again. "There are so many factions now on Lyhhr that even I could not tell friend from enemy. But I know that Lyhhrt is mine if he is working for Gorodek."

"What will it matter? He must leave soon to lead his forces, and so will we." *Tomorrow . . . and Ekket?*

"I will never be safe as long as that other is alive."

"Surely he will leave with Gorodek."

"Sooner or later we will meet."

Hasso stared. "Please don't think in that way. You may be destroyed!"

"So will that Other," the Lyhhrt said calmly. "Two more dead Lyhhrt that your world will not miss."

Hasso had no rational word to answer this. He wanted to say, *I found a friend in you that I valued,* but he knew that he could never be the kind of other the Lyhhrt needed, and turned away to open the glass doors and step out onto the esplanade.

Around the mesa fifteen or twenty of the giant flying reptiles called greater thouk were lifting off in practice for their winter flight to West Oceania. The lesser thouk was common in Burning Mountain, but these vast-winged air-beasts here had been thought of as Lesser Known Thouk until the New Interworld Court was built, and they were found in increasing numbers.

Lifting off in light morning haze and barely flapping their huge translucent wings the thouk were one by one swooping into the canyons where Hasso had been wishing he could wander as he looked down from the mesa, before the strange *voice* spoke.

There was nothing to stop him from doing this exploring

in the mind of a thouk, that one drifting so smoothly almost touching the canyon walls . . . as in a dream he took off his helmet and focussed his mind to launch—

The thouk stopped dead in midair and flapped furiously.

Hasso—magnifying glass *again*—found himself trapped beating his wings staring unseeing along with *someone* examining bones, wing membranes, blood vessels, muscles, digestive system, mechanics of flight—what is fear?—and freed now suddenly flying, twitching head and tail to made sure they were working . . . Hasso himself watching the

not people

yes, if people could fly they'd—

:Hasso?: The Lyhhrt had seen or felt nothing of this.

Hasso backed into the room and slammed the door panel into its socket. He was trembling, angry at himself for his fear which had doubled itself along with the thouk's. *:You tell me what is that, Lyhhrt!:*

The Lyhhrt answered aloud but quietly, "That *voice* you seemed to hear up on the mesa, was that it?"

"No no! It was using my eyes and mind to examine that thouk! Stopped it in mid-air! And—I think—decided that it was not a *person*, and I foolishly began to say, 'Yes, if people could fly they'd travel much more easily.' Who was I speaking to? Everything has gone wrong since I came here. I hope I am not going crazy as well!"

"You are not crazy, Archivist, but I think you have attracted a very odd friend."

Choices

At noon Tharma called on Dritta once more. "Have you been able to rest, Dritta?"

"As much as I needed, thank you, Supervisor." Dritta had an air about her of limitless calm, and Tharma envied it deeply.

"I am going to ask something you may refuse." She paused, thinking how to put it. "I am trying to make sure everyone either goes home or remains here peacefully. The young lady Ekket needs protection and I have got permission from Prime Ravat to free you for the purpose. You may need to escort her to her home country."

Dritta considered for one beat. "I believe I could do that properly."

"Good. Bring her here, then."

Ekket's shame and humiliation still showed in her swollen eyes and trembling mouth, but Tharma trusted the spark she had shown in her defiance of Gorodek. She noticed the lock on Ekket's helmet and was relieved that she did not have to put on her own.

"I know you have had a difficult time, dems'l, but I must go forward with this case while those concerned are still here. The young woman I sent to bring you will be your guardian until you are safe. I have to ask, do you want to charge Gorodek for what he has done?"

"No," Ekket said immediately. "It wouldn't make me feel better and it would only make Gorodek angrier."

"Would you rather go home?"

"Never. I'd rather be in Screaming Demons Chasm than with my mother."

"We narrow the choices. Hasso's stepmother Skerow would be very happy to have you stay with her—"

Ekket, shyly but with firmness, said, "There is a young man who cares—we care for each other very much. His parents offered me their shelter before I was dragged away by my mother and that awful Sketh. They have sent word that they still . . ."

"So, and where do these people live?"

"In Port Dewpoint, a short way down river from Burning Mountain."

"My old territory and Hasso's. I will see what arrangements . . ." *Alas for Hasso! But he knew he had no claims. . . .*

That was the easy part. Dealing with Gorodek would be somewhat harder. Tharma was trying to decide which of his attendants would listen to reason. Osset was not the one, if only because her own anger would get in the way. But then she would not be the one to deal with him. Someone smooth from Vannar's office . . .

"Eh, Supervisor!" Ravat burst in on her. "We have another situation—" He stopped to swallow air.

"What now?"

Ravat calmed himself. "The Isthmus States Federation governors were to leave today, but they've received instructions from their Joint Executive Council to warn Gorodek that if he brings armed forces near their shores—" another swallow, "I can't believe this—there might be a war!"

"I doubt that will happen," Tharma said quietly.

"If we can't settle this and keep them apart I'm afraid the damned fools are going to battle it out right here!"

"They have no weapons. The extra security we hired left on the midnight barge, but we can deputize some of our clerking staff. The Isthmus people are not upset without some reason: Gorodek owns property there that's believed to have been an Ix headquarters at some time . . . a West Sealander holding outland territory, always a bone in the craw of the Federation."

"I see you have been speaking with Hasso."

"He knows what's going on." She switched on display screens. "Hall of Communication, is it?"

"Yes."

"They have their helmets on, no microphones. Banging on the floor with walking-sticks, they seem to have lost their voices and will burn out soon. Has Vannar given orders?"

"He has no idea what to do!"

"You want to separate the combatants and send them home as soon as we can pack them up. I'll make up a squad. Dritta and my aide Kevvar are the strongest women here, I can find another one or two."

"Good."

"I can think of a few things you might have Vannar tell Gorodek, if he has the nerve—or I will call in Osset and tell him myself."

"Thank you, Tharma, you are invaluable. Faugh, you have such a musty little closet for an office, we must stir up those builders to give you some real space."

Tharma sent for Osset. She was drinking a bowl of tea, not too spiced this time. With effort she kept her face expressionless and she was sure he was doing the same.

"I am sure you are glad to see me in good health, Courtier. Do help yourself to a bowl of tea."

"No thank you, I don't drink it. You wanted to tell me—"

"First I want to say that we will continue to investigate the murder of Sketh. Then I will tell you this, Osset, and you must tell your Governor: in her country Ekket is a child who can be married off by her parents. In your country it may be legal to force sexual attentions on a bride, but a young person of Ekket's age is too young to marry in your country. I know what your laws say. For legal purposes right now, Ekket is not a child and may go where she wishes, and while she refuses to press charges against your Governor, neither will she agree to go with him under any circumstance.

If he cannot accept that decision I will have my superiors repeat it to him."

Osset left without a word.

So, Ravat, I did your work for you.

Vannar, I did your work for you.

Sleep, sleep . . . Tharma, you need sleep.

Beyond

Is this manifestation of an alien Mind actual or some mental dysfunction?

The Lyhhrt answered the unspoken thought: "It is actual."

"Could that possibly be the alien who created the ship?"

"I don't know what its nature is, Archivist. You are the one that seems to have caught its attention."

The door-chime sounded.

"A young woman we do not know," the Lyhhrt said. For some reason the words added to the dread Hasso was already feeling.

"Come in," he called, and when the door slid open the young woman stood there smiling.

"I'm Officer Dritta," she said. "My Supervisor Tharma has requested that I guard the lady Ekket while she travels to her friends in Port Dewpoint—"

The Lyhhrt could not keep his young impulsive mind from whispering, (*:she has an Other:*) . . . and Hasso thought his heart would explode—

"—and that she hoped both of you would join us on the train tomorrow to make a safer company for everyone."

Hasso's heart *beat* and *beat*—

The Lyhhrt said quickly, "We would be very glad to join you, Officer."

"Good." At the door she turned for a moment to say to Hasso, "You are Hasso the Archivist, are you not?"

Hasso swallowed hard. "Yes."

"We studied much of your work in our Records courses. My Supervisor Tharma greatly respects you."

Hasso saw that her young face was full of joy. "Thank you, Officer . . . and thank your Supervisor for me."

After the door shut, Hasso said nothing for a few moments. Then, "You told me that you would never leave while that Lyhhrt was here."

"I don't believe he will be much longer. The Isthmuses group has been accusing Gorodek of threatening their shores and Tharma has ordered him to leave. They will be on the same train and the same ship up to the Equatorial River. I will keep good track of that one."

"Our whole mission has strangely dissolved itself."

"Not mine."

Once again Hasso had no answer, and looked out at the deep sky and its noon stars. *Being, take care how you use me, for your glass may crack and shatter.*

SIX *

Fthel IV, Bonzador: *Stirring*

Rrengha had taken to running at night: her ancestors had been nocturnal, and running stilled the nightmares. No one saw her run, her red fur vanished in darkness. Sometimes her mind reached Ned's along with a scent, a sound, a stray thought she had picked up in the tracts of brush she was traversing among the five camps.

Looking, esping, listening for trouble.

One night Ruah, the Meshar woman, crept into Ned's tent. She had been barracked with Rrengha on the presumption that because both had fur they would get on together. She curled up against Ned's back like a cat, or the local animal his people called a cat, for there were no world-grown ones. More like a cat than fierce Rrengha.

She whispered in Ned's ear, "When the Big One was here I couldn't bear to be with her, now she's not here I don't want to be alone." Her breath smelled like cloves, but her canines were as long as her claws and her ears high and pointed. In daylight her eyes were like black seeds swimming in red membrane. She wrapped her black arrow of a tail around Ned's hip and he felt only his daily fear and fell asleep while she murmured of her love for her fiercely storm-beaten world. In the morning she was gone, either to another camp or perhaps teleported to somewhere else entirely.

Yawning, he asked Rrengha, *:What have you found?:* But she was asleep by then and made sure no one roused her.

When she woke she said, "Watch Spartakos."

"Whatsit?"

"Look." She raised a forefoot, he followed the direction and saw Spartakos herding a score of O'e to breakfast in straight ranks and files with others running to join them, and Azzah skipping along the lines to keep them in order. She was laughing.

"First time I've seen her laughing," Ned said.

"That is not what I mean."

"Yeh."

"There are more O'e here than there were when we come. They move from other camps to be with Spartakos. They persuade others to fill their places." There were head-counts but no roll-calls in the camps.

"Eh, the screws here will think it's a challenge?"

"What do you think?" Rrengha asked, wanting to know.

Ned thought so, and went to stand in the breakfast line with Spartakos. "Not too military, friend, or you'll be mistaken for the real original."

"What do you mean, Ned? This is our friend Azzah leading all her people together."

Ned clenched his teeth, but there were no watchers nearby; the wind was licking up thick clouds from the east and there was a flurry to crowd into the mess tent. "I know that, Spartakos, but you don't want our employers to think we're building a private army."

"It may be that we will need one," Spartakos said.

Ned stared at him for an instant before the first fat raindrops spattered down hard and all the rigid lines broke up.

I wonder if you've heard from your Maker? He did not want to know the answer, and robots are not telepaths. He watched Lek trying to make conversation with Azzah, and Azzah trying to decide if he was genuine or not. Ned did not know that either. But he turned back to Spartakos before he joined the breakfast line. He did not want to know the answer but asked anyway: "Did your Maker tell you he was coming back here?"

"No, but he had promised before that he would never desert us," Spartakos said quietly, subdued now.

The reply sounded cooked and packaged to Ned; still, he believed it. Spartakos could choose to lie, but the lie would nullify his esthetic purity, and that of Lyhhr too.

Not much use for that in these surroundings. *Two ten-days,* the Lyhhrt had said . . . *Maybe seventeen days left* . . .

Spartakos said, as if he had read Ned's mind, "The *Zarandu of Thanamar* is in orbit around Fthel Five."

"You heard—?"

"The *Zarandu* computer told me one-half chron ago. It always connects with me when we are in range."

As far as Ned knew a chron could be a day, an hour or a minute. "You could call for help!" He had traveled to Khagodis on the *Zarandu,* its first destination on the way to deeper reaches of the Galaxy.

"It is a machine with limited duties, not a person. And my call out of here would be intercepted. That is what the watchtower is for."

Ned grunted. "I wonder how they can afford to ship on that." The *Zarandu* was the greatest ship Ned knew of.

"The ore carrier *Raghavendra* will be riding it—"

"Heh, put us in a container? Thought they'd do it on the cheap."

* * *

The rain stopped in mid-morning, leaving the sky overcast and the ground covered with the scummy clay mud that comes up fast when thick growth eats loam.

In early afternoon Ned was going for lunch, pulling off work gloves after a morning practicing guerilla tactics in the brush, followed by the usual session of cutting brush, when a gaunt man named Cawdor, whom Ned had met in the air-car on the way down, drove up in a tractor and pulled up by the mess tent splashing, stunner on shoulder and yelling, "You there!"

Ned turned. Cawdor was pointing with a shaking finger at a group of O'e. "I mean that one there, that little fucker that's trying to skin off! What the hell's he doing here, he's supposed to be in my camp! He stole my comm!" Jumping out running to grab the skinny O'e by the shirtfront, ripping the paper, "Where is it! You got it here somewhere!" Whacking him across the face forehand and backhand, Spartakos in mighty organ voice calling "STOP!" surging forward—

Ned yelled, "Stop, Spartakos!" He'd been through this kind of thing once before and ended up with a badly bruised kidney.

Cawdor yelled back at him, "You fucking better keep hold of Tin Man, Gattes!"

"He's a citizen, Cawdor, he does what he wants."

Spartakos stood still, and spoke calmly. "If he stole your comm, you will have it back."

The O'e clutched his shirt about him and cried in a thin wail, "I stole nothing! I have nothing!"

Cawdor rounded on Spartakos, snarling, "You got all them coming here to hang around with you! What you think this is, a playground? I want everybody belongs in my camp in my camp an' if I don't get that comm back you don't know the trouble you'll get!"

Behind Ned the other O'e were clamoring in their high thin voices and he began to be afraid that Azzah might lead them into battle. Gretorix pushed through them yelling for order. "Your comm isn't here, now get back where you belong, Cawdor!"

Cawdor opened his mouth and—Rrengha appeared from among the forest of legs and looked him up and down. "You give your comm to the Bengtvadi woman in your camp that you smoke the ge'inn with after dinner."

Cawdor closed his mouth. Blood rose into his rawboned face like wine poured into a pitcher. Without a word he jumped on his tractor and sheared off.

The beaten O'e, half Cawdor's size, was bleeding from his bruised mouth, thin pink blood. "I'll get you first-aid for that, soldier," Gretorix said, and took him by the shoulder.

Spartakos seemed about to follow, and Ned said, "Wait."

Spartakos turned half of his body by a hundred and eighty degrees. "Yes, Ned?"

Ned said very carefully, "Please, send your O'e friends back to their own camps tonight, Spartakos. They're becoming a target, and if they ever do move out of line they'll be hammered twice as hard."

"They need me."

"You don't want them hurt. If they march around with you leading them it looks to those chukkers like they're being threatened, and it's just too hard to protect each one. If they need you so much they'll do what you ask."

Azzah cried, "How are we going to live together in this place if we're treated like that? And you say we mustn't defend ourselves."

"Not yet. Not by marching in straight lines. I don't like the way things are going here, and I think we will have to defend ourselves, but in the meantime don't ever forget we're dependent on the enemy for food and water, they're armed and they can get out of here whenever they want and we can't, and even if we could we'd have a damned long way to walk."

The O'e muttered among themselves for a few moments until Spartakos waved his hands and they dispersed. Ned broke into a sweat and ran off to get lunch before anybody picked a fight with him.

The afternoon passed with weapons drills and more brush-cutting, and after dinner the camps were quiet enough with recruits playing zodostix or skambi for not much stakes, telling hard luck stories of seventeen worlds, and boasting of old conquests made only in the imagination.

But Ned's mind was running and running around the possibilities: they were a closed perimeter. Spartakos could break through fences, but only in one place at a time; Rrengha could control minds, but only a few at once. The big powerful Dabiri had a cyber hindquarter that did not work very well. The O'e were stronger than they looked, but no stronger than anyone else here.

"Spartakos," he whispered, "can you disrupt the electronics in any of those weapons they carry here?"

"Some. Most of the long-arms you train with are mechanical, except for their sighting mechanisms." After a moment he added, "I will use weapons to defend you and others but only to disable, not kill."

"I've never killed anyone yet, except once by accident. But you can't create an army and then tell the troops not to kill anybody."

Spartakos had nothing to answer.

Montador City: *Bait*

Tyloe said, "You want us to go out there in that wilderness and let him catch us. What will you do if we refuse?"

"Not what I will do, it's what he will do," the Lyhhrt said. "Perhaps something like using your body for his workshell." At this point Lorrice ran for the bathroom to throw up. "That will let him move freely without being noticed. Or he can split and make two of himself quite easily. They will be much younger versions but quite as evil. I could have done that myself when he murdered my Other, but that one would not be *other*, and though we might like to believe that we are all the same person, your friend here has realized that there are differences, there are identities, and we need them."

"And you could do to us what you say he—the non-Other can—"

"No! He has lost his sense of sin because he is so alone. I have not, yet. That's one point of difference."

"Maybe, but you're still asking us to let ourselves be killed."

"I did not cause you to be in this situation, and I am certain that you could not have escaped for long with the plans you made."

"I'm not so sure of that," Tyloe said sharply. "He'd have had no way to track us."

"Whatever he would have done, I have found you now," the Lyhhrt said. "It is better than being found by the police and the government, and I will do everything in my power to keep you safe. I have only a few days to find that one and only a few more to take care of some others."

Lorrice had come back into the room, looking pale and dabbing at her mouth. "What have we got to do?"

The Lyhhrt held out the gold leaves: "Stay here tonight, then take this money, go out into the city and do as you were doing, but keep the money with you. I will give you some of my own to spend. I'll stay out of sight but always within five spans of you, you will sense it with your telepathy. Likely he will find us all at the same time, but he will be much more interested in me."

"You hope," she said.

Tyloe took the folded leaves as if they were poison.

"Maybe this money was meant to lead your enemy to you."

"If it was, so be it," the Lyhhrt said.

With a deep rasping breath, Lorrice said, "Back where we started." They were in bed, Tyloe keeping his hands to himself, only too tired now. "I feel as if I'm in one of those stories where you're condemned to live the same day over again forever. Repentance doesn't do much good either." She touched his shoulder, a light virginal touch. "I'm sorry I bit your head off. I knew exactly what Andres Brezant was. Loving never improved him, and I was scared of him one half of every minute."

"Yeh, now we can be scared shitless the whole time."

The Lyhhrt had gone, but was hovering somewhere. Both Lyhhrt were.

Moving targets, they spent a second day in the same activities, shopped for wilder clothes, bought more colorful drinks, ate at even more pretentious restaurants and left even bigger tips with Lyhhrt money. Always they sensed the light touch of the Lyhhrt's mind, but they were frozen numb, and hardly spoke.

Tyloe thought only of what Lorrice was thinking as she scanned the milling crowds of vacationers, beggars marooned as Lorrice had been, diplomats in locked security helmets, other Lyhhrt who could esp anyone but would rather not fight through the press of minds, the clouds of thought like nebulae among bodies, holograms, blinking neons, walls shrieking bulletins.

For relief they fled into a theater where they took the cheapest back-row seat and thankfully did not hear or see much of the morbid drama of alien incest and revenge or its five-language subtitles.

It was when they were coming out that Lorrice felt the knuckle-biting hollow-chested dread that approaching

Lyhhrt gave her. When they were focussed on her.

Tyloe felt those chills again. "That's him?"

She whispered, "There's two of them, oh my God." Then she said, "I know them." The ambassadors in bronze and silver-scrolled brass who had left Brezant in that Lyhhrt-world restaurant to snarl and smash glass.

The Lyhhrt, now in his half-visible brushed silver, had been crouching on the curb that night in O'e's clothing. He came from behind to stand between Lorrice and Tyloe: "So do I."

In Deep in Bonzador

Rrengha kept prowling at night, like her ancestor the leopard on Earth. She made Ned uneasy. "You're gonna get a big poke with a zap if you keep that up." Since he'd whacked Hummer she was going around with a plexiplast wristband and an even meaner look on her face. Ned was always on the dodge.

"She is no match," Rrengha said. She was not boasting.

But Ned tossed on his mattress ever more restlessly. He felt enclosed, and his mind beat at its walls.

Enclosed. A country with no city, no government, only hundreds of villages and each with, at the most, one or two peace officers. Spartakos might reach them by radio but they had no forces. *Who would believe us? And if they're anything like the police in Miramar they'll join in running the place with the rest of these yobbos.*

A country where people came to lose their identities, become unidentified . . .

And Rrengha endangering herself. Spartakos commanding his O'e cohort like some half-mad general. The stupidity of his own choices. Zel and the kids whom he might never see again. The Lyhhrt's departure/desertion: *Will he bring us help?*

:If he does not it is because he is dead.:

There's a thought to hold on to.

:Time to break that cycle,: Rrengha said, and it broke. As he was falling asleep he found himself in her mind:

Ground under her feet . . . an ingrown claw to bite off, tail slung along flank, *:Nobody can grab that.:* Shoulder-blades pistons in oil—*:Only to Earthers! These are my bones in meat.:* Filthy air stinking of rotten leaves, too much water in it . . . all those strange minds trying to sleep or looking for trouble, *There's a murderer, those two are thieves, and all the snoring lot of them are lost spirits far from no home. Why do they come here? Why am I here?*

Something else: sudden air currents, winds. Gates opening. An air carrier with a silent engine, whose only sign is in the movement of air, landing in a small field cleared in the brush beyond the fences. . . . It trundles through the gateway, no pilot, it is a drone . . . Hummer and Oxman waiting there, the bay doors open, the ramp slides out like a tongue, containers on noiseless casters roll down and settle on the ground.

Weapons. The vision of thermoplastics and blued steel is in Hummer's mind. She thumbs her comm, the ramp pulls in, doors shut on it, the car rises in silence. The electric gates close with a crackle. She aims a hypnoform gun at the containers, and they blend with the shadows. *Double the watch.*

Oxman reads the manifests. *None of them Quadzulls.*

Plenty on Khagodis.

Yeh. Oxman licks his lips: *Now we're in business.*

Ned twisted on his mattress, fighting the dream. Rrengha touched his mind and his sleep deepened.

When he woke, stretching and yawning, it was another thick moist day. The dream . . . when he raised the tent flap she was there.

:That is no dream,: Rrengha said.

"I was afraid not. I don't think all of those guns were meant for us to use. . . ."

:I don't believe so either.:

There was a low rustle of ill feeling along with the daily struggles against the brush. Rrengha was sleeping off her night's efforts and none of the caretakers was likely to give her a poke. She had pulled in and shielded her thoughts and dreams as the Lyhhrt had done, and Ned became even more uneasy.

He knew now who the thieves were and the murderer, but somehow wished that Rrengha had not shown him. At times he had put on the Lyhhrt helmet, pulled its knobs and pushed its buttons, but it was built to let him communicate with Spartakos, who was right within arm's reach; arrogant Lyhhrt were not to be contacted at will. He was afraid to use his wrist comm: he had no other contacts than the Lyhhrt who would not communicate, and he did not dare to try reaching Zella. If the call was intercepted he would be putting her in danger.

Now he put on the helmet to keep his mind to himself and went on doing whatever was asked, busy work that could have been done cheaper and easier with machines or chemicals, beating his brains against the problems.

"Spartakos, could you call down an aircar for us to board?"

"We are killed before it lands."

"Yeh, I thought so—"

"—and we cannot load all those fourteen hundred and seventy no matter how much you like to save them."

The grand old Duke of York, he had ten thousand men . . . try getting all of them out of here. "We—hey, wha—"

The cyborg woman had whacked him full length with an

armful of scratchy branches. "Watch it, Grushka!" The armful was obviously too big to keep hold of, but there were other places to drop it.

She put a hand to her mouth, not the metal one. "Sorry, Ned, sorry!" Then, in a low voice, "It's so hot and dirty and bloody boring here I'm off my crock. I come to fight but it's more like a prison with hard labor."

Ned picked leaves off his face. "You want a fight you won't get it from me."

"Maybe I'll go look up your friend Metallo Man, we can fight cyber to cyber."

"He'd probably like a fight, but I don't think he'd want to play at it." He wondered if she'd been doing ge'inn, she had that smoky look in her eyes.

"Well, I'll just ask him—" Spartakos was somewhere nearby working his corner of the forest.

"No!" He found himself growling and forced cold urgency into his voice. "You don't want one of those yobbos coming down on you like yesterday for chrissake!"

"Yaah! Did I hear somebody wants a fight?"

Ned recognized one of the thieves in the stubbled face grinning over Grushka's shoulder. Grushka turned. "I want a friendly fight, and you aren't one of my friends."

"Well, you can pretend I'm one." He grabbed her shoulder. "Come on."

"No!" She gave his nose a couple of taps with a metal forefinger, and he backed off.

The thief turned to Ned. "Can't I find a fight with anybody here? You're supposed to be a pug."

Ned kicked a stack of branches. "I'm fighting this stuff here and you can help."

"You're scared!"

"You're damned right! If I fight for no money and get my head cracked, I can't fight for money, can I?"

The thief's friend, a skinny long-face with a scraggy chin

beard, came along to join the argument. "Fight going on?"

"You two can fight, but leave me out," Ned said, but he knew there was no way out.

"I like that helmet," the thief said.

"I'm sure you do. It's not for sale."

"Give you mine for it."

"This one won't work for you." *:If you want to join a militia you will need this,:* says Lyhhrt.

"Yer puttin' me on."

"Unless you're my twin and I doubt it."

The thief and his friend laughed in unison. "How do you know I ain't your twin? At least let me try it on."

"It might hurt you."

More laughter. They began slapping Ned back and forth between them in a semi-friendly manner. Ned kicked one in the shin and elbowed the other in the windpipe, and was immediately sorry. They fell back, recovered fast and came at him harder.

He slid away out of their grip and let them bang their heads together, then Grushka caught one in the shoulder with her cyber hand, but the other kicked her out of combat, and pushed Ned face down on the ground. He was slow about trying to get up because he'd already had this done to him within the last half-tenday.

Gretorix came running to break up the fight and the thief punched him hard in the chest, snarling, "Get outa this, you old bastard!" then rolled Ned over, straddled him and pulled out a knife.

Hummer came then. "Hey! Whatsis!"

Hummer was the one that scared him. Ned grabbed a mouthful of air and gasped, "Awright, awright, you can have it!" He fumbled to unclasp the helmet, and the attacker moved away to let him.

Hummer stared at them and Ned. "What is this?"

"Just a friendly argument, ma'am." The thief's friend was fading into the distance.

There was a look in Hummer's eyes when they rested on Ned.

"Go ahead, take it!" Ned thought his time was up.

The thief said, "How d'you close this thing?"

"That dirty face looks familiar," Hummer muttered, and her eyes opened wider.

"Push that lever," Ned said breathlessly; his heart was beating enough for two.

Hummer said, "You—"

The thief pushed the lever.

He screamed, then choked and fell to the ground.

Everything went still.

Rrengha padded up and looked at the fallen man. "Dead." *:I sleep too long.:*

"What's going on?" Hummer yelled and dropped to her knees beside the body. She seemed to have forgotten Ned, and Ned did not wonder why. Rrengha could not make people do what she wanted but, like the Lyhhrt, she was a master at making them forget what they wanted.

He realized that Grushka was crying, and as he slowly picked himself up saw that she was kneeling beside Gretorix, who had not been able to pick himself up, nor was he moving at all. She pointed at the thief: "That sonofabitch punched him good."

Hummer yelled, "But why is he dead?"

"He pushed the wrong button," Ned muttered.

Grushka said, sobbing, "He wanted to try on that helmet and said if he couldn't he'd kill my friend here, he had a knife, and when Gretorix tried to stop the fight he gave him a punch and Gretorix fell down and then he put on the helmet and something went wrong in it and killed him."

Hummer's eyes were rolling in her head. "Don't move,"

she said, and dinged her comm. Nobody came, and finally she ran off.

She did not hear Grushka whisper, "And I started it all."

Ned knelt to retrieve the helmet. "He said it wouldn't work for anybody else, but I didn't know it was a weapon." He gave it a nervous touch . . .

"Yes," Rrengha said, "Likely you are the one person in the universe that helmet doesn't hurt." Answering Ned's unasked question, "I doubt he knows that either. Lyhhrt always make better than they know."

"And sometimes worse." Ned folded it and clamped it on his arm under the sleeve. "I'm not wearing this for a while." He looked down at Gretorix, curled up in his death spasm. "What happened here, Rrengha?"

"Something in heart or veins, we don't need to know. Stop crying, woman! These things must happen in a place like this."

Spartakos, Azzah, and all the O'e in the field were gathering around the tableau, and Ned put a hand on Grushka's shoulder. She was wiping her eyes with the back of her hand. "He was too damned old for this."

Ned looked around at all the hopeful and the needy. He wanted to say, *Let's get out of here . . .* but not to be overheard.

"Spartakos, we might have some use for that army of yours."

"I knew that you would," Spartakos said.

"But guerillas, not chessmen."

A couple of recruits were deputized to carry Gretorix's body on a stretcher. The dead thief was dragged away by the feet.

"We have to move out some way before the roll call shrinks any more. Tell your Maker that."

"I do my best, but—he is like your God. He does not answer."

Khagodis: *Secrets*

Hasso's spirit was very sore. He had accomplished nothing, had deceived himself into half-believing, if only for a moment, that someone could truly care for him, had acquired a deadly enemy and the attention of a powerful being who was only too interested in him.

He and the Lyhhrt were up late in his marble-lined room, finding rest difficult with a long tense voyage facing them next day.

"Why in the name of all the Saints is *it* interested in *me*?"

The Lyhhrt said patiently, "Because *it* wants to know—"

"But why not find somebody else!"

"Because everyone else exploded, Hasso! Isn't it possible that *it* touched Gorodek, and Ekket, and who knows how many others, and they couldn't bear the touch?"

"I would have thought that one like you would have been most interesting of all to such a being," Hasso said stubbornly.

The Lyhhrt said with a bit of sadness, "My people are not great explorers of the exterior world, Archivist. Their senses are dim and they cannot see unless they make themselves eyes. Because of my youth I am untrained and inexperienced. Only when I put myself in your mind do I know what you saw and felt, no more."

"I would help that *being* find what it wants if I knew how, but in the meantime I am just afraid of offending it."

"Evidently you have not done that so far."

"It seems to be a bodiless energy being, and if it came from that ship I wonder why it needed one."

"I am afraid we will not know until it tells you, Hasso."

Tells me, indeed!

"From your experience, it appears to want to know something about a world where people need flesh."

And what do I know of the world, always imprisoned in my flesh? Hasso leaned on his staff and looked out into the night.

After a few moments, the Lyhhrt said, *:Since we have spoken so much of this other Lyhhrt I must tell you something that you may not want to know.:*

The dark tone of the thought made Hasso uneasy. *:Only if you must, friend.:*

:When I first came here I was sure I had made a terrible mistake. Loneliness and fear are weak and simple expressions of what I felt . . . and when I was finishing my work for Galactic Federation I thought I might really go mad in the particular way that isolated Lyhhrt do . . . and then one day I heard a voice that was not one of madness, in the same way that you have been called by that . . . being. But this was an Other. I was filled with joy. Yet . . .

:I am not altogether foolish and I did not accept its invitation at once. But after many days in which the Other urged me to give some acknowledgment, finally I answered. I refused to meet this one or have more than an informal change of thoughts, but I believed there was no one in the world happier than I . . . alone no longer!

:Then, when I finally agreed to meet him he withdrew for some while and after a day or so he very carefully explained his circumstances. He was living inside a fleshly being, and this being had an acquaintance who would be glad to accommodate me.:

Hasso gulped, and had nothing to say, or think.

:I tried not to be horrified, I was afraid to make him angry, and when I begged him to tell me why he chose to do this, he said that fleshers have more power and influence than we do in clumsy metal workshells that only frighten and repel others.

:When he kept pressing me to join in this perversion I began to feel threatened and put distance between us very quickly, and I have been spending a whole year trying to calm myself. I have no proof but cannot help believing that the one here is the same.:

"Is that the person who warned you of an attack by Lyhhr?"

"No, that came from outworld. This one seems to be part of the attack plan, another part of the population altogether! And, Hasso, I came down here with you because I thought it was time to conquer my fear and make myself useful. And some day I might be able to cure myself of hiding in these stupid clothes, which are not quite as bad as living in a flesher's body."

Hasso said fervently, "I hope that *being* who is so interested in 'people' does not decide to inhabit one!" And added, "But you, friend, will you go home eventually?"

"I cannot tell you. But somehow I will find an Other."

A clamor rose in the hallways and the lights went off, and then on again.

The TriV burst into light and sound with a flash image of two groups striking at each other with sticks. Hasso could not identify any of the combatants, but one of them fell with a bloody head. After that the screen blackened, a robotic voice said: BE CALM AND DO NOT PANIC, and clicked into silence.

"What's happening?" Hasso pushed the TriV's ON button but it remained dead, then pulled himself up and hurried to the esplanade doors to make sure they opened. "Come quickly, Lyhhrt, whatever is happening, I want to be out of this!"

Silence. The cloth-wrapped figure stood against the wall and did not move. "Lyhhrt, what's the matter, Lyhhrt!" Hasso was struck with horrible fear. Someone began to beat on the door with a staff or weapon. With great effort Hasso stilled himself and opened his mind.

:It is Dritta! Please let me in quickly!:

He recognized her face through the spy-way and let her in. She was followed by Ekket, but Hasso did not have time to let his heart flutter. Both were carrying packed travel-cases. "What is going on?"

"Someone has tried to attack the Speaker for the Governors of Isthmus States, and there is such a great disturbance in all the Assembly Halls that my chief, Tharma, has sent me to bring you and Ekket away right now, along with—what is the matter?"

Hasso had crouched and taken off his helmet in order to part the clothing, and put his ear against the Lyhhrt's body. "One moment I was speaking to him, and the next—"

He could hear faint humming, but did not know whether it came from the machines or the pulse of a tiny heart. "There are small sounds, but—"

"He fainted?"

"He stopped. One moment we were speaking together and then nothing. . . ."

"You must come, Hasso." Dritta was as firm in her way as her mentor Tharma. "My chief has ordered it and there is no more time."

"No! I cannot go without him! He put himself at risk for me. Even if he is dead I must bring him."

For a moment Dritta stood looking Hasso up and down, and Hasso noticed for the first time that she was slung with a heavy collection of stunners, zaps and serious firearms.

She went over to the wall, opened a door that Hasso had not known was there, and pulled out a small wheeled baggage-cart. "If we must, we will take him."

She laid the soft-skin cases on the wagon for a bed and began to lower the Lyhhrt's standing figure. Ekket, who had been waiting in the corner with tear-filled eyes, came forward. "Let me help," and the two women set the Lyhhrt on the wagon with a great deal of both strength and gentleness. Hasso could not help wondering if the Lyhhrt might ever have appreciated being treated in this way.

"Come." Dritta picked up the remote and slid open the glass door; the wagon with its burden followed the remote's signal on silent wheels. Hasso locked his helmet and came after Ekket, leaving his marble chamber without regret. The stars and moons glared down and Hasso did not turn his head for a glance. His spirit was with that clumsy heap of cloth and metal.

The esplanade tapered off down a ramp which was a collector lane from other rooms, but their occupants were either quarreling in the halls or had hurried away to avoid the conflict. Dritta said quietly, "This ramp leads to the underground station platform. We will not be travelling on a passenger train, I apologize for the inconvenience, but secrecy is safer. We will board a freight train that brings in food and building materials and takes away processed waste. We'll leave on the barge that carries it to Dead Moon Crater to be burnt, and the cruiser *Ocean Star* will pick us up from there."

The air turned cold in the dimly lit tunnel at the end of the ramp, and the sounds were muffled, pattering clogs and sandals, the tick of Hasso's staff, and the thin skim of wheels on stone. The Lyhhrt was all too silent. If he had dared, Hasso would have stopped and lifted the Lyhhrt's body in his hands to breathe life into it somehow, but the thought was madness, and he hurried with the others.

Hasso had never needed to take an underground train and there were few of them in the world: membership in Galactic Federation had made Khagodi a traveling species willy-nilly. The cold vault looked old and dusty because of its newness. The dust came from hewn stones and the oily spills from the engines that brought them. "The train is coming," Dritta said.

The railway car was a framework for carrying freight; and a pair of laborers hung tarpaulins over it to shelter the travelers and laid woven straw mattresses to carpet the splintered floor. When they were done, Dritta gave them money and they put their tongues out in thanks and crept away. Hasso spread his cloak on the floor of the car and Dritta placed the Lyhhrt's awkward metal-and-cloth body on it; then she reprogrammed the remote and sent the baggage carrier back to its home in the wall. "Nobody will trace us with that," she said.

Hasso removed his helmet, got down on his good knee and gave his whole mind to the Lyhhrt. He did not notice when the train began moving.

Lyhhrt, Lyhhrt, you are a metal box of mind I cannot open. . . .

Dritta crouched beside him. "He stopped speaking—and—perhaps living for no reason at all?"

"I must believe he is alive . . . It is as if he has been struck dumb, paralyzed, there is a pulse, a whisper of something there. . . . I'm afraid it is only the noise of his ventilators."

"Can his shell support him?"

"Yes, if he is alive in it."

"I've seen this effect from ESP attacks—but none of our people have the power to attack a Lyhhrt that way."

For a moment Hasso had a horrible fear that the *being*, who was all energy and no mass, might have become curious about the Lyhhrt and—

But no, my friend told me a terrible secret, and it was perhaps one secret too many in this crisis. Only another Lyhhrt could do this . . . "Your chief may have told you of my suspicion—"

"That there is another Lyhhrt in this area? Yes. She said it was her obligation to warn me of all possible dangers." She touched her stunner and dipped her head. "I'm afraid I have no defense and no treatment for this condition."

Hasso closed his eyes to keep the tears in and reached out for the touch and texture of Lyhhrt mind, friend or enemy, listened intensely but could hear nothing beyond his own heartbeat except the puffing of the steam engine and a faint whirr of circulation in the shell's vents. His back and leg ached fiercely, and he fought the pain desperately though he knew that it was foolish to believe that his touch or nearness would do good.

And felt something. *Again.*

Again began to feel the peculiar terrifying sense of *Other* that was nothing like the Lyhhrt sense of the word—

No no whatever you are leave me with my friend you have nothing to know here!

Once more his mind was magnified, clarified, every thought flung against his inner eye in a lurid intense glare, he was dizzy, disoriented, wanted to sink into sleep, lose consciousness, whatever would stop the attack, the red lightnings of terror in—his mind? the Lyhhrt's?—found, somewhere, the merest strength, as much as would press finger and thumb together, as much as might crack an eggshell, set himself against fear to look into the maelstrom the attacker had made of the Lyhhrt's mind, an abyss of hate where the icy cold waters of his world thrashed and spun. . . .

Shivering with fear and at the same time savage with determination, Hasso let himself fall into the eye of the storm and made himself hover until his passion forced calm on it, searched for the small pulses of the heart and the minuscule impulses of the brain. After endless time they shimmered to life and the Lyhhrt's essence returned. His limbs vibrated slightly. *:Archivist . . . :*

"You are quite safe now," Hasso said, *I think, I hope.*

"Archivist . . ." The word came through the voder with an odd warble.

"No, no, don't stir yourself. Rest."

He hauled up on his staff to stretch and crouched again,

everything used up, opened his eyes and found Dritta beside him. She looked at Hasso, then at the Lyhhrt, who had become still again, and he saw that she had taken off her helmet. She said, "I think he must be sleeping now."

Hasso moved away from the Lyhhrt, from whatever forces had opened his mind for him, or given him strength, and pulled on and locked his own helmet quickly, wanting only to keep his thoughts to himself. There was a question waiting at the edge of his mind that he could not ask yet.

Then he noticed that Ekket had been huddled in a corner, weeping. He was wordless, but Dritta crept over to her as quickly as the lurching and rattling of the car would let her. "What is upsetting you, dems'l?"

"Eki, I can't help myself, it was Gorodek tonight, telling the whole world through the TriV that because I was not found pregnant after his horrible attack I must be sterile!"

Hasso cried out, "He truly said that?"

"Yes," Dritta said. "I tried to shut it off before he came out with it, but . . ."

Hasso said quickly, "You must not think anything of the sort, dems'l! If anyone is sterile it must be Gorodek—he is old enough to be my father's father and he has no children!"

"That's an idea that is better left unspoken," Dritta said uneasily, "Better forgotten. Eh, friends, we have two hours to embarkation. Let us find a place to lean on and get some sleep."

Tharma and Ravat and Vannar

Tharma had been looking for opportunities to sleep without finding more than an hour at a time, and when she received the urgent summons from Ravat near midnight, she and her scratch of a security force were at wit's end trying to keep elderly and dignified diplomats from waging war with staffs, walking sticks, and crutches. Both her hearts were heavy; Ravat had been aging beyond his years, and she felt the same of herself.

"This is extraordinary," he said. "They cannot be quieted and I'm sure they will drop from exhaustion, if not apoplexy." He was watching from several screens; one or two of them were showing replays of Tharma's efforts. "If we succeed in sending them home they might actually raise forces, and we haven't seen that for three hundred years. My grandfather remembered the last battle in his childhood. Here is where the world is supposed to be at one with itself!" Ravat's office was a cut above Tharma's: three of its walls were marble and only the fourth fiberboard, with a heap of marble slabs leaning against it waiting to be set in.

"I have done everything I could," Tharma said firmly.

"I know," Ravat said. "I realize that you have been doing much of my work for me as well. What I ask of you now is that you come with me, rouse up your aide Kevvar, I will bring my secretary Iskar and we will battle our way through Vannar's guards and secretaries and disturb his sleep for a change."

Tharma did not need to answer.

Vannar was roused, but carefully, and after a report and a view of the conflict, wrapped himself in his fluffy drying blanket and marched down the long halls and between the ranks of combatants through a lane cleared for him by Tharma. He insisted on doing this alone and punctuated himself with hard raps of his thaqwood staff of office.

"No, I will face them alone, and nobody will call me a fool or a shirker!"

"But do leave that blanket behind, Director!"

Rather than climb the dais he stopped at the entrance of the Hall of Assembly, took a great mouthful of air, and hit the floor rat-a-tat.

"Good people! Are you going to break the peace now after you have been tending it so carefully all these years!"

Tharma felt a surge of respect for Vannar for the first time. The noise ebbed. Someone handed him a microphone.

"You, Governor of West Sealand, and you, Speaker for the Confederation of Isthmus States! You came to celebrate the wholeness of the world! Now what are you telling me— that you are going to declare war?"

The Speaker drew himself up. "We have reason enough to worry!" he called out after several breaths and a draught of air. "If the Governor brings forces to our shores to fight off an invasion we have no reason to believe exists, he will find an entirely different kind of battle facing him!"

Gorodek answered hotly, "If the Speaker is daring to call me liar—"

Vannar broke in quickly, "If your concerns are so great that you need to air them before the world, and if you are willing to stay here one more day, I will call a full session right here at the beginning of second quarter tomorrow and—"

But Gorodek could not keep himself still any longer and cried out: "I have more than one concern, I tell you! I came here with a friend and a bride, and my friend is murdered and my bride is lost!"

Vannar said slowly and quietly, "All parties, it is past midnight. Tomorrow we will discuss—"

"And that woman—" Gorodek was pointing at Tharma, "—has taken—"

"Security Chief Tharma has taken extraordinary risks to keep peace."

Tharma came up to Gorodek quickly and said in a low voice, "Governor, we are acting according to law, there is no other way." She would have liked to say, *We could not make her love you*, but not here, and was aware that any pity for the old man was dangerous.

"I swear to you that we will do everything with all our resources to avoid any more conflict!" Vannar declared.

By now his intervention had at least broken the rhythms of the fractious parties and they were drifting off, glad of an excuse to be peaceful; even Gorodek's aides were not hurrying to surround him, and he backed away.

With one more tap of his staff Vannar left them.

In the morning Gorodek and his party were gone.

No Love Lost

The sky was brilliantly starred, with a faint line to the east, dawn barely into the day's first quarter. The barge was a coal-fired vessel fitted with shutters instead of awnings, because the sea-wind was fierce at night, and it whistled through the laths.

Inside the cabin the lights were as dim as they had been in the tunnel; the other half-score places were taken by laborers off duty or replacement crew and all settled down to sleep as well as they could, squatting, except for the one Varvani who unrolled a mat, flung himself down on it and was soon snoring.

Dritta opened her case and handed out bowls which she filled from a hot-jug of sprigwort tea, and shared out a packet of dried sea-stars.

The tea was Hasso's favorite drink and reminded him that he had an ordinary life somewhere on the world. Eventually he asked the question that had been waiting at the back of his mind: "Lyhhrt, when you received the message that sent you to me, you said, 'I have been advised by the world Lyhhr.' Did it come directly from Lyhhr?"

The Lyhhrt moved and spoke slowly. "All I know is that I was summoned by the Galactic Federation local office in

Burning Mountain and given this message by an official there. She read it to me, put a seal on the paper and gave it to me, then told me that it had come from Headquarters in the Twelveworlds and there was no further information she could give me because Khagodis no longer accepted communications from Lyhhr. I couldn't read it properly through her eyes because I am deficient in symbo*lingua* but there did not seem to be much matter in it. They were eager to be rid of me and so I came to you. I was desperate. As you can see there is still no one who wants to talk of Lyhhr."

"I have seen," Hasso said. "But—do you believe that came from Lyhhr?"

"No! It would need a whole trading consortium to mount a war effort, and now that Lyhhr has curtailed trade and Zamos has been dismembered, Interworld Trade has no impetus to fuel Lyhhrt 'revenge,' whatever that is. But I had to take it seriously just the same, and so I came to you."

Could his frustrated Other have had some part in that? Is it possible that other Lyhhrt was harboring himself in Sketh? Sketh had poisoned himself with karynon and other drugs. . . . Hasso left the questions in limbo: he already knew much more about private lives than he wanted; folded his hands and closed his eyes.

As he was drowsing he heard quick footsteps and an urgent voice: "Officer! Officer!" He opened his eyes. The shipmaster in his oilskin cape was swinging his lantern, searching.

"Here I am, Shipmaster!" Dritta said clearly.

"Officer, we are being followed by a motor yacht that just now sent a message demanding we stop and hand over your party."

"Are they threatening you in any way?"

"No, madam, but it claims to be a vessel owned by the Governor of Western Sealand."

"Does he have any authority in these waters?"

"No, he doesn't."

"Can you outrun him?"

"I . . . likely could."

"Why do you hesitate, Shipmaster?"

"It takes more fuel and harder labor, Madam Officer."

Hasso raised his heavy head. "I will pay for the extra fuel and labor."

"Outrun him," Dritta said.

"Right."

The lantern swung away, and Dritta said, "My department is quite able to pay for extra supplies."

"Allow me, dems'l. I already have enough clay tablets and spools and vellum scrolls."

Dritta was silent for a moment. "The young lady is sleeping. It's a good thing when sleep outruns fear."

Hasso was quick to agree, and fell asleep.

Three Heads

"Gorodek has left! So much for getting up at midnight to make peace." Vannar cast sardonic looks at Ravat and Tharma. "I'm beginning to believe it might have been better to let them thrash it out and keep Gorodek's faction occupied." The three were leaning on elbows at Vannar's great marble escritoire and trying to hold up their heads.

Tharma said, "I believe his faction has run out of steam. Hasso had the idea that Gorodek was intent on raiding the Isthmus mining fields. If that was true, the Lyhhrt threat he conjured up would have been an excuse for going ahead. But of course the Isthmus States quite rightly read his declaration as a threat to themselves, and I suspect that he didn't count on their taking quite so much offense. He has landed himself in the grokkli's nest and he's running home, trying still to collect his bride—"

"Can't the damned fool give up!"

"I was told earlier that Gorodek's cruiser had been pursuing their party, but in the past hour I've had a message that the barge is within sight of Dead Moon Crater, and Gorodek has no clearance to land there, so unless he prefers to hang about thumping his tail he might as well go home. Also . . . young Ekket comes from Center Point, that little Isthmus state—"

"Eki, yes!" Ravat said. "And all of the Isthmuses will be here making cases and demanding reparations . . . but let us at least try to send them all home safely first, so we can sleep."

Fthel IV, Montador City: *Meetings*

:You.: The Lyhhrt, having no recourse to humor, have to make do with irony. "You who met with the wealthy and powerful!" He was facing Bronze and Brass, whose meeting with Brezant had led them into the shame of dismissal.

"You were called home!"

"We did not go." Brass-and-silver said. Each of the two was holding a gold leaf.

"That would have been best for you. Where did you find that lump of evil that killed my Other and my friend?"

The five, three Lyhhrt and two Earthers, were standing stiffly in the middle of the walk, where passers, laughing and talking, streamed around them without seeming to notice their brush with fear and fury. Tyloe and Lorrice would have sidled off then, but their Lyhhrt held them firmly in his mind's grip.

Bronze said, "Galactic Federation would have nothing to do with us because our world canceled its trading pacts. We were bitter, both at them and our world, we wanted a taste of revenge—"

"And that one came saying he was an emissary from Fthel Five," Brass said, "and told us we would have power and revenge if we joined with Brezant. Brezant and his people wanted only the gold but—"

"We had nothing to do with killing! When we heard of the killings we hurried away from Brezant and his company! When we found this money lying here and giving out signals we were afraid he was tracking us, trying to control us."

The three Lyhhrt were silent for a moment in furious thought. Tyloe, who at least had control of his eyes, was looking for any avenue of escape, and saw with a peculiar feeling, that Zella Stoyko, one of those two who had tried teaching him to fight like a pug, was coming down the street toward them, three children in tow. . . .

Lorrice caught on. *:Call out to them, Tyloe, that's the distraction we need!:*

. . . Zella, tired and frustrated, was on her way to the train that would take her back to Miramar on the cheap midnight run. As usual on these visits her mother had not died, good, but she and her sisters had kept yammering at Zella about her way of life and her no-good husband. *Hypersledges will not drag me there again.* The kids were jumping up and down and jabbering in imitation of their grandmother and aunts. "Awright, kids! Maybe I should have left you there, how'd you like that?"

Tyloe could hear the faint sighing in her voice, and for a moment felt he was in a parallel world. . . .

:Not with those kids there. No way.:

:Damn you.: But the curse was half-hearted.

Tyloe muttered to his silver Lyhhrt, "Someone is going to come along that you don't want to meet. . . ."

But the Lyhhrt had picked up the thought; he did not want Zella asking him what had happened to Ned, and was already saying, "Here is a hotel. Let us go inside." He turned to the hotel entrance. "Come."

When they had settled themselves among potted trees and velvet chairs, Lorrice said to the silver-shelled Lyhhrt, in a trembling voice that was like slowly cracking porcelain, "For God's sake, you don't need us any more! We never knew about any of this, we never hurt anybody! Can't you let us go?"

The words formed in his mind and speech: *You were content enough to live with murderers.* But for a moment the Lyhhrt did not answer, and could not. The glimpse of Zella and her children, Ned's children, had unnerved him, for he had dragged Ned away from them. Their presence mocked him for claiming superiority over his enemy, boasting about his sense of sin.

"If I let you go now you will still be in danger, and I made myself responsible for your safety. When the one who gave you this money is found you will go.

"Now you two . . ." Confronting Bronze and Brass in their shame, he was almost envious of them, because they had each other.

But they were defiant. "What do you want from us? We don't need your money." They thrust the gold leaves at him.

"But I need your help, and if you help me now I will praise you on our world."

:We may consider that.:

He said, *:You must know that there is an other One who has taken Brezant's place.:*

They did not answer, and he followed up: *:You do know, and you are in contact with him then . . . what is he doing? Why is he behaving this way?:*

:On Khagodis there is a powerful ruler who wants to raid the wealthy mines on his neighbors' territory, he is going to claim the threat of a Lyhhrt attack as an excuse to "defend" his land. That other One agreed to arrange this "attack," to

be carried out by some hundreds of alien hirelings gathered on this world, who have no future, and will be killed on their world by his heroic defence. But we were exposed by what you told the embassy and his plans may change.:

:If you are free to tell me this, then tell me where he is.:

:He never tells us that. He comes when he chooses.:

:Why does he come to you?:

:To stop being alone.:

:But he did not try to attack you?:

:There are two of us. You cannot attack us either.:

:I am well aware of it. But I want to know where he is.:

:We cannot tell you.:

Lorrice said suddenly, "He told us he liked Montador." Her esp antenna had picked up the drift.

Tyloe said, "He owns that house in the south where you were staying. Why would he want to come here?"

"And he had a big cache of weapons there," Lorrice said.

Tyloe added, "All of them new, most in cases."

Both were now uncomfortably aware that the two Lyhhrt in bronze and brass had shifted attention to them, and wondered why they had spoken up at all.

But their Lyhhrt's mind was elsewhere and he answered his own question. "Perhaps here is where he is going to be paid for them . . . or pay. In either case he will be meeting someone—"

"Us, if no one else," Tyloe said.

"And soon, before the last tender lifts."

The two Lyhhrt in bronze and brass rose and sat themselves to either side of Silver. "You need not worry about that."

Lorrice cried, "No!"

"What?"

"Do you really believe that being praised on our own world is more valuable to us than joining him and owning worlds?"

"He told you that, did he?" The Lyhhrt was powerless between them.

"You needn't speak any more," Bronze said in a conversational tone. "He sent us to find you and finish what he had not done. Just down that stairway over there it is dark and quiet, and you will find rest/in/prayer at one with your forebears."

Brass-with-silver said to Lorrice and Tyloe, "You two will stay where you are, and we'll be back."

Three Lyhhrt rose as one and walked on the deep green carpet toward a wall covered in green plush with its dark opening that might have been the entrance to a hedge maze.

Balancing on the edge of the step, one foot extended to step down, Brass and Bronze Lyhhrt so intent on their silver one that they seemed to weigh him down.

Tyloe realized that the pressure of their control had lifted from him to let in one sharp instant of freedom—

Lorrice shivered.

And, *For God's sake, Tyloe, what—*

Tyloe leaped up and ran one-two-three-four-five-six bent-kneed steps jumped in the air and straightened legs to slam feet smashing into the back of left-hand Bronze. Bronze went down in a hideous boiling crash—

Tyloe landed third step down with a jolt that nearly bit his tongue off. Brass just stood there rattling.

Lyhhrt-in-silver recovered quickly, and when Tyloe jumped the three steps and raised his arms to send Brass down as well, pulled him away. "Come! That one is no match."

Downstairs people screamed and lights were coming on. Tyloe grabbed Lorrice by the arm, and when she pulled back caught her around the shoulders: "Get going! All the bouncers'll be after us and the police coming!" He could feel blood from his bitten tongue drizzling from the corner of his mouth. He found a tissue and wiped it quickly to avoid stares.

Outside when they were among all the ordinary people, and lights and fluttering holograms, Lorrice found breath and said, "It's those bouncers and all the others the police will be after."

"Why?"

"They're running an unlicensed drug bar down that stairway, ge'inn, karynon, other things. They had it shielded but I guess everybody heard the noise."

Tyloe was beginning to find speaking slow with his bitten tongue. "Karynon? Um, that wouldn't have been the place Brezant found you, would it?"

"If it had been as high-priced as that I might not have gone with him."

Tyloe suddenly realized that he had probably killed a Lyhhrt and began to shudder.

"Repent later!" the Lyhhrt said sharply. "Come along now!"

Tyloe snarled, "Come where!"

"To the District Port Complex, where you landed when you first came here. Where the one I spared just now told me to look for that other one. Because you broke his shielding when you—"

"Don't! What are *we* doing then!"

"You are acting as my hands and feet, that run and jump without having to plan every slightest move! I have found a use for fleshly beings! Somehow I will reward you for that—now, would you rather serve me or that other?"

Neither Tyloe nor Lorrice answered.

"Here is an aircab, we will take that to the monorail station and you may sleep for one or two of your hours."

Lorrice fell asleep immediately in the monorail. Tyloe was afraid to close his eyes, but exhaustion forced him into a hot and sickly sleep in which he could feel the Lyhhrt muffling his terrible dreams.

Bonzador: *Pickers and Choosers*

The day after Gretorix and the thief were killed the aircar flew in with a fresh load of beer; nobody refused it but it did nothing to lighten the sullen atmosphere. The sky fit the mood, the clouds were thick and so was the air. There was no funeral for Gretorix, an old soldier who had studied war too long; just a day of tactics, maneuvers, arms drills and cutting brush. Ned was thinking, *He'll be lucky if they bury him. Yeh, lucky.*

By mid-afternoon the rain came pelting and everybody took shelter to keep the paper uniforms from dissolving. Grushka was still red-eyed at dinner time, and Ned said, "No use beating yourself for it, it's a mean lot they got here, better to duck out of the way."

"Wish I hadn't come, it was just there was nothing fucking else."

Spartakos said: "I have heard from my Maker."

"Sends his good wishes, does he?"

"It's no use directing anger at him, Ned. He always wishes us well. But he wants me to ask the *Zarandu* computer when the last lading boards."

"Why are you telling me that, Spartakos?"

"Partly to show that I don't keep secrets from you—"

"I never believed you did—"

"—and partly to let you know what time we need to be ready to leave this place."

"And that's—"

"Seven days local time."

"Doesn't give us much time to dig a tunnel."

"If you had told me in advance that—"

"I never expected you to build a tunnel, Spartakos, and if we'd tried I doubt we'd still be alive." Ned had been gnawing at the problem since the Lyhhrt decamped. "Whatever we do it's gotta be soon and quick."

Why'd they want to spend so much shipping people to be killed? . . . There must be an awful lot of money involved in it.

Next morning Rrengha nudged Ned awake. "In camp number three," she growled. "Someone you know." She gave him the mind-picture: in the center of the clearing the body of a man beaten to death, skin blackened with bruises, blood seeping into the mud he was half buried in.

"I can't tell who," Ned said.

"You give him one or two of those bruises." Rrengha said.

"The thief's friend?"

"He has an idea to steal arms and get out of here."

"Ran into somebody first . . ."

"I think they don't care for those ideas."

"Teach us a lesson. Yeh. It's time we left."

"Do you have an idea, Ned Gattes?"

"First, we can't take even half of everybody. There's some who're gonna die no matter what we do. . . ."

"And others don't believe there is any danger at all."

"They're not the ones I'm worried about. Who don't we want to take, aside from everybody that's running this place?"

"You mean, who gives us away? The only other telepaths here, of all that come to fight, are one or two low-grade Bengtvadi. They are part of a group of collaborators in the camp to the southwest that supplies bullies like Cawdor, that kill fools like the one lying there, and they have privilege to keep weapons with them—but there is no plan to save them. What I see is that all fates here are alike inside these fences."

"We know that, but none of these poor juddars do."

"Perhaps. But I make sure everyone knows the choices." After a moment she added, "Those weapons that come by night are for the Khagodi to kill us with and think they are gaining great honor and revenge."

Ned swallowed. "Then we better hurry. Spartakos, we have five days to get out of here, and it doesn't look like your maker's gonna rescue us." *Only somebody who wasn't in his right mind would come back to this place, wouldn't he, Spartakos? And I think he was already far out of it when he left.*

"I don't intend to wait for him, Ned. I have free choice—and I am in this place, and so are you."

Some time during the day the body was dragged away, and otherwise the world went on as usual, except that the work took more time and energy because of the rain. Ned's NCO's mind thrashed in a whirlpool of strategy, tactics, logistics, and terror. Gathering forces, breaking out, finding vehicles, food, weapons—someone who would listen to a story told by an army of ragtag warriors.

That night Rrengha roused out of her sleep and began a survey of dreams.

No one in this camp dreamed of home except Ned, not even Rrengha, who had given her world everything she owed it. Only the Meshar woman Ruah had longed for home, and perhaps she had found her way there, for Rrengha could not sense her. She had no need or desire to esp the armed sentinels who watched with helmets on or slept in shielded quarters, and the O'e would follow Spartakos anywhere without needing persuasion. One group of half a score dreamers in the southwestern camp, who were ready to kill beside their masters and were privileged to sleep with weapons beside them, took up phantom arms to join the killers in their dreams, and Rrengha did not let her mind touch them this night.

Ned slept in his helmet; he had enough of his own dreams. And no one had ever asked Spartakos about his.

As for the rest, that daily lot, she gathered their thoughts and dreams, frightened, angry, sexual, indescribable, into a slowly forming network.

Once she had them netted she slipped in the idea: *prisoner* and let it run its course among them, sparking fences, brutal guards, beaten O'e . . .

Then she added *cold sleep*, a long needle and a semi-death from Fthel to Darhei, the nearby star that Khagodis circled.

Once her dreamers were chilled in long sleep Rrengha warmed them into fresh hot life and dropped them into bloody blazing gunfire. As she had done with hostile tribes over long cold nights on Ungruwarkh.

But she was not on Ungruwarkh. She left the sleepers alone then, a few to twist on their beds or wake startled, and some to find greater depths where monsters did not swim.

When Ned woke she said, "I tell them what they need to know as far as I can without scaring them into panic."

"Thanks, Rrengha."

"Another matter. The woman Hummer keeps being about to remember who you are, and I cannot divert her forever."

"I know." He said to Spartakos, "We may need to leave here on short notice, and I think you ought to tell your troops."

"I have already done that, Ned."

"You have! Are all of them ready to go?"

"There are a few who don't believe in the danger, but they are more afraid of Azzah."

"Have you found an aircar for us?"

"I have been surveying Montador and Port City by satellite, but whatever I find we cannot evacuate the whole camp."

Ned rubbed the wrinkles the helmet had left on the back of his neck, raised his hands to take it off, hesitated, and wrenched it off for good. It was a killer that had never protected him from anything, and for all its ventilators was too damned hot. Couldn't throw it away either; he clipped it on his arm. And didn't bother with depilatory; it would have run off his wet face. *Weapons, food, the rest of the hundreds? And this being a criminal operation, maybe prison?* "And where would you have it land here?"

"At the end of the road, beyond the fence. And nearest our camp."

"And it will take us to—"

"Whatever port I call the aircar from. They will know that I am Spartakos, because everyone knows Spartakos. That is simple enough."

"Yeh." Ned went off to find breakfast, as usual, as if he'd spent a thousand days in this place.

SEVEN ✷ *EXITS*

Montador: *One for the Money*

At the same hour in which Rrengha was taking stock of dreams, the few sleepers in the halls of the District Port Complex, ticket-holders waiting for late connections, were tucked up in cramped SleepLets, little more than slots in the wall.

In the center of the vast chamber was a great column of streaming lights from the hundreds of built-in screens that announced arrivals, departures, cancellations of aircar flights around the world and connecting shuttles to and from Port City for liftoff. The column's security cameras and spy-eyes watched sharply from all angles. The Lyhhrt stood with Lorrice and Tyloe, wondering who might be watching through all those eyes.

Even in the hours just past midnight the station was never less than busy, and travelers ran to keep pace with the robot porters skimming the plasmix floors. An old Earther woman come to a strange world to meet grandchildren, a pair of tattooed Bengtvadi in long robes that automatically rippled and pleated themselves in complex patterns, a harassed Dabiri nickering at a trio of little ones with plaited tails.

Scores of others lined up at terminals that were checking passports and identifications, dispensing tickets and inter-world credit, tokens for renting chairs, slings and leaning-frames. A team of robot cleaners waited for the crowd to thin. A line of sniffer machines stood in whatever wall space was left. There were very few human workers in this temple of automata.

"He is here, somewhere," the Lyhhrt said.

That's not saying much. Lorrice was wondering if she would ever reach beyond fear. Even Tyloe sensed that. They felt grotesquely out of place, though she and Tyloe looked presentable enough for what they were: visitors, not passengers. Even the Lyhhrt was not so far out of place.

He paid Lorrice no attention. *:Wherever, he is waiting for a messenger from Khagodis to bring him an Interworld Bank Certificate for a great sum of money, to pay for the strike force, the weapons, the house you were staying in, and . . . :*

There! In that twisting corridor off the great chamber, a very thin Khagodi in a shadow-colored cloak, pushed ahead by a burst of exiting passengers, trying to flatten himself against the wall, terrified of coming out into the light—

. . . wakened out of cold sleep to find a waiting message from Khagodis that there was to be no action, no need for a strike force or its weapons, the bank certificate had been nullified, charges under newly passed Interworld Laws were pending . . .

Knowing that a murderous intelligence was stalking him.

:Not mine,: the Lyhhrt in misty silver said. *Can I save this one?* In a conversation that took less than ten seconds he asked Lorrice:

:You believe you can tell the difference between those Lyhhrt who say I/we and those who say only I.:

:I'm not sure—:

:You have met that one. Can you sense him? He will be enraged—not at you, because he still has some use for you—but because his plans have collapsed—:

The Khagodi was filled with panic—

:—and that Khagodi—you can see him through my eyes—is a victim of what happens when plans collapse—you should know how that feels!—and is many times more frightened than even you are . . . I want to save him. He will not like the justice the Law will give him but it is better than being dead. I need your help. He has a gun—that Quadzull I've nearly been killed with more than once—and I want to make sure he does not use it—:

Aloud, Lorrice said in a dull cold voice, "That's crazy. We'll both end up getting shot." Through the Lyhhrt's crystalline eyes she and Tyloe could see down the corridor where the Khagodi was crouched against the wall as if he was praying to his gods; that the Khagodi was helmeted, had drawn the Quadzull from his shoulder pack and was holding it in both hands, hidden by his body, with its muzzle pointed to the floor, desperate to defend himself and too frightened to raise it for fear of having it used against him.

:I'll make sure he does not shoot you, I'm more afraid that if he sees a Lyhhrt coming toward him he might die of fright.:

And the Lyhhrt himself was afraid. Tyloe knew, she let him know, that she could feel, almost taste, that touch of cold fog.

"Yes, I am afraid," the Lyhhrt said, "and I will not force you." *:But if you could follow me down the ramp out to the floor and keep watch while I go into that hallway where all those people are pouring out, because I need to reach him before everyone else sees that gun . . . :* He let himself onto the ramp without waiting for her answer.

A whisper of *perhaps that Khagodi's not worth* flickered

through her mind and was muffled. She turned toward Tyloe, and he returned the look. In a flash he thought he might have been training all his life for that one jump back there, but whether it would ever mean anything besides a bitten tongue—

Lorrice took one step onto the moving ramp and let it carry her down.

"I'll go along," Tyloe said.

:No,: the Lyhhrt said. *:You stay where you are.:*

She let Tyloe into her head, fear and sweat and sore feet from all the running. No past worth remembering.

:Not even Brezant when you come down to it. If I die doing this you try to remember me for a while. Nobody fucking else will.: Then she closed down her mind and walked slowly across the floor, letting the current of passers move her one way or another like driftwood.

The Lyhhrt reached the opening of the corridor, and in his mind the Other spoke for the first time.

:There you are! I did not expect you to last so long.:

He did not answer. He did not know where to search and so kept walking slowly.

:You believe I have been defeated because a stupid man on another world could not contain his greed. I can correct my mistakes with a storehouse of arms and fleshers to use them for me. And I have told them to rid me of that pathetic—but what do I know about pathos?—useless collection of fools who expected to find wealth on Khagodis. The universe runs on greed and everything is given to the one who uses it properly. You have no answer. Do you think you are invisible?:

The Lyhhrt in fact did believe he was invisible, at least to hurrying travelers, because he was shielding himself and Lorrice to keep from being noticed while they went forward so slowly. Now he had been told that the Other was within sight, though he could not see him.

Lorrice murmured, "I don't sense anyone out of the way here, you'd better not depend on me."

"He can see us through many eyes and I/we should be able to see him."

She scanned around herself, but her fear was only the kind she always lived with. She waited at the entrance to the corridor while the last stragglers came out to collect luggage. Beyond the Lyhhrt, halfway down the corridor, the Khagodi stayed slumped against the wall.

Lorrice took two steps into the corridor.

The travelers streamed away; half of the screens on the column flickered out and left a silent interval before the next swarm, a time halfway between midnight and dawn. The bounded universe of the vast hall and its corridors was populated by Lorrice, the Khagodi, the Lyhhrt, and Tyloe waiting back there. Nowhere else to look.

Lorrice took another step, and another. Tyloe could feel her twinges at the back of his neck.

But the inward voice told the Lyhhrt, *:That Khagodi you are trying to protect is nothing to me. You have nothing to say. In that case—:*

The Lyhhrt said, *:If you forego your plans I will leave you in peace.:*

:You are trying to make humor as the fleshers do. But you are also noth—:

And one last step that left her an arm's length from the Khagodi—

The silence exploded into Tyloe screaming, "Watch out! Behind you!"

The Lyhhrt swiveled his head backward.

The giant arm of a robot sweeper slammed down grazing his heel. The Khagodi's body twitched from head to foot and he slumped to the floor. *:Not quite dead.:*

In one movement Lorrice grabbed the Quadzull and shot the sweeper, its body parted at the seams with a sick muffled sound spurting bits of burning silicon, thermoplastic and steel as it reeled and crashed down while the echoes of gunfire were still flaring.

Another skimmed in after it, slewing and screeching in the hot fragments of the first. Whimpering, Lorrice fired again.

Then passengers flooded into the hall to catch early morning flights, the alarms started shrieking and the crowd turned back tangling and falling in panic. Harsh voices roared at them to keep still and stay where they were.

No one came near the corridor. One more sweeper, two buzzing porters, a sniffer, everything automatic was swarming—

The Lyhhrt had flattened his body against the wall, and was sidling away. *:He's in one of those! Don't waste shots!:* Lorrice, sweating beside him, could feel the heat bouncing off his workshell. The live machines were tangling in the wreckage of the fallen ones, but the smaller porters and sniffers were pulling away and skinning around them toward her, while more flailing sweepers crowded the entrance.

Because she was being shielded by the Lyhhrt with all of his power, the enemy could not reach her mind, but only the gun could protect her from being smashed. She was thinking rapidly that a Lyhhrt would not install itself in a clumsy sweeper or a puttering sniffer. That left one of three porters, and she was sure there were not three shots left. For all that the Lyhhrt thought that she would know the difference between Lyhhrt, she was sure she would not.

She tucked the gun down her jersey between her breasts, chose one of the three porters, she never knew why, ran up to it, grabbed the railings, jumped into the basket, and waited to see what happened. It began to spin and kept on spinning, the others shuddered in place.

Dizzy, she pulled the gun from the tangle of her underwear and shot the porter as she threw herself off over its railing.

A flash of psychic lightning turned the universe white for one instant.

The porter's plates split open *whuk!* and all of the machines stopped.

Tyloe sensed Lorrice lying there, bruised and still dizzy. He could not move except as the crowd moved, pushed by human guards, toward the exits.

The Lyhhrt peeled himself off the wall. He at least was free. He lifted Lorrice by one arm and steadied her for a moment. Snarling, she wrenched herself away, raised the gun toward the ceiling and pulled the trigger defiantly. It clicked with a *pstrung!* sound. Guards began climbing through the tangle of dead machines, and they had weapons of their own.

"No more bullets," the Lyhhrt said. *:Now run! Meet me at the monorail platform!:*

Lorrice dropped the Quadzull and ran. She did not want to know what the guards thought of the blasted porter that was dripping a pale pink liquid very nearly the color of an O'e's blood.

There was a calm and starry dawn when Tyloe and Lorrice reached the platform. The Lyhhrt was waiting for them. No one else had noticed him. Tyloe and Lorrice had asked themselves, *What are we here for?* and answered, *We need money.* Their possessions were waiting for them back at the overpriced hotel but they had none to travel on. As well, Lorrice was limping from the bruises she had collected when she fell, and the long dragging search for an exit. The Lyhhrt had made sure that no one stopped or questioned her.

Tyloe muttered, "That Khagodi . . ." He too had needed money.

"Not dead, but under arrest." The Lyhhrt did not stop

for conversation. "I need to go quickly now. Here is all the money I have, you can divide it. Whatever has the signal chip is still good money, and no one will answer its call. If I survive what I am going to do now, and if you have no criminal records, in half a year you will be able to go to any Interworld Bank, give a genome sample and be provided with whatever you need. You are free." He disappeared in that way the Lyhhrt have, and left their lives for good.

Lorrice sighed raggedly and said, "He does know how to use fleshers. You'll notice he didn't say, whatever you want."

Tyloe found his mind a blank except for one question. It kept him staring at Lorrice, she felt the look's intensity. "That Quadzull . . ."

She shrugged. "Before your time. We'd go out into the forest and he made me learn to shoot. You know Brezant liked to live dangerously. Then he wanted to fuck me lying on all the dead leaves and branches. He didn't know how dangerous . . ."

Khagodis, Dead Moon Crater: *Desperation*

Hasso's sleep under the engine's drumming was jolted and shuddering. If he had asked himself, *How many days since I left home?* He could not have answered. Or its alternate: *How many since I was so happy on my rooftop brewing tea and waiting for Skerow, when this frightened Lyhhrt called out to me and sent me on this mission, to be imprisoned in a cell for no good reason, find that my one heart was so weak, gather enemies for no reason, and then be chosen as a specimen of humanity by a Being that may not even exist! In all being so helpless, so helpless!* His dreams presented the memories in disjointed and surrealistic fragments.

He was startled awake by a sharp slapping noise that echoed over the water, and after an instant realized that it was a gunshot.

"That was fired into the air," Dritta said. "They are not aiming at us yet."

Hasso rubbed his eyes and tried to separate this new phenomenon from his dreams, and shift himself out of the stiffness in his limbs. "Would they really try to hit us?"

"I don't know, but Shipmaster has reported them to the Coastal Police."

The shutters on one side of the cabin had already been folded back, and the UnderMaster was going along the other, the planks slapped and cracked against each other with a noise almost as loud as the gunshot. The sun had burned off mist and rose through second quarter into the flat blue sky. Hasso could just make out the pursuing yacht, but had no line of sight to tell how near land the barge was.

The Lyhhrt said, "They don't yet mean to kill. They do mean to succeed."

"We'll see about that," Dritta said.

Hasso was about to say, *That they are willing to shoot*—and stopped.

He noticed for the first time a bracelet on Dritta's wrist, had a flash of thought that jewelry was incongruous on a police officer; then realized that the band, pewter studded with onyx, indicated sterility. In some countries, not his own, it was the obligatory brand of sterility, in men or women. A warning: *not worth marrying!* Skerow had not worn one.

Hasso shivered. In a way her burden, hidden under youth and health, was greater than his own. He turned his mind away and helped her gather baggage.

"Land in one half-hour!" Shipmaster said. "Officer! I am willing to put full effort into moving this vessel, but I will not put the lives of all my passengers in danger for your sake!"

"Do your best, please, Shipmaster!"

Now Hasso could see that there were stony arms of land rising to either side of the barge, and the quieter water let it slip toward the shore more quickly.

After a calm quarter-hour the noise of a shot cracked across the water once more, and in a few minutes the barge was gritting against a dock and the shipmaster rang his brass bell. "Out!" he barked through his microphone. "This here is Insight Island, just off Dead Moon Crater, and I am taking you no further for all your Offices and badges. I'm telling the Coastal Police where we're landing you, I will inform the *Ocean Star,* and I've taken as much risk as I can! Out, and let me get away from those damned murderers. Next time I would sooner give you up to them than let them shoot at me again!" He wound up the microphone to its loudest. "You with your guns out there! There's nothing for you on this barge!"

"I will report you!" Dritta said.

"Do that, Madam Officer, and you will see the twist of my tail and no more of me. Get off." He lifted his arm to his workers and they let fall a gangplank.

Hasso could smell from far off the stench of ancient fires that had never been allowed to go out. "Dems'l, the shipmaster is not completely out of order. This place probably smells better than that other and you are well armed to defend us."

"Gorodek has no clearance for Dead Moon Crater, but nobody can stop him from landing here," Dritta said.

There was little to see of Insight Island except a rocky barren slope topped with a square block of a building that may have once been white and inhabited by a watchman, but was now smoke-blackened and half-collapsed. The air was hot as well as fetid and the hard blue sky, smudged with smoke and ash, held nothing but the brazen sun.

Hasso pulled a handful of silver pistabat from his purse,

more than enough, tossed it to the shipmaster and said roughly, "We never chose to bring you into danger."

He stepped down on the gangplank and reached to help the Lyhhrt, who was still unsteady.

"I'd have had sharper words for him," Dritta said.

"What use?" A couple of workers were quickly pulling up the gangplank and the barge steamed away even faster than it had come.

Ekket pointed: "Look, they will land in a moment!" The yacht was only a few hundred siguu away from the shore and traveling fast. Dritta fired a shot into the air, but it would not slow.

"Get up the hill and hurry! Lyhhrt, can you climb?"

"I believe so."

"Then come." Dritta and Ekket, both strong enough and light-footed, took Hasso by one arm each before he could protest and half-carried him up the slope. But he was grateful; it was hard keeping his sandal-boots level on the sharp rocks.

The Lyhhrt climbed easily enough, but said to Hasso alone, *:Their Lyhhrt is inside the body of one on that boat.:*

Hasso could not tell if there was more fear than anger in the thought. *:You have more power in your shell than he in whatever body.:*

The hilltop gave way to more hills, folded and pleated by weather as well as earthquakes, with here and there a clump of semi-succulent thumbknuckle shrubs, most with spines, and one or two small stands of stunted trees. Hasso thought that the place was an outcropping that had been separated from the crater wall by earthquake, though the crater itself, unlike most on Khagodis, was caused not by volcano but from an ancient comet. A self-punishing place to look for insight.

"Plenty of hiding places," Dritta said.

"Best not to get backed up in them," Hasso muttered. Looking down, he could see that the yacht had reached the dock and one of its crew had jumped off to tie up. Two or three others were helping Gorodek disembark. "Is he actually coming to chase after us himself?"

"Good, he'll slow them," Dritta said. "Let's move."

Hasso was struck again with a sharp sense of unreality. His heart began to thud frighteningly, and he fought to force calm on himself, and keep moving with the others. Dritta took his hand; the onyx bracelet gave him a cold touch and he shivered again, for her sake.

There were voices calling, and one more shot.

So far they have not shot at us, but—

He was angry now.

"I can see a crease in the rock wall, down over there," Dritta said, "where we can watch for them."

"There is also a back way out, and that's good, but we can't afford to go too far . . ."

Would Gorodek order Ekket to be fired on? Go that far?

But someone fired into the air again, and even Hasso hurried toward the shelter of the rock crevice.

Dritta remained at its opening with her Uzi MarkVII harnessed on her shoulders and her eyes on its miniscreen, but all Hasso could see was a slate-colored wedge of sky with her at its lowest point, and could not keep from crying out, "Don't stay there, dems'l!"

A voice out of a loud-hailer called, "Come out and speak to us, we will not fire!"

Dritta switched off her helmet for one moment and said, "Just one of you come forward and we will both put down weapons."

Hasso said evenly, "What will you do if they do fire at us?"

"I will return fire."

But a great mindvoice swelled out and seemed to Hasso as if it struck sky, rocks and even the sun like a gong.

:Why did you desert me! Why do you hate me! Why will you not be my Other!:

The Lyhht began to tremble, both in his thoughts and in control of his workshell: its microscopic plates sang like the faintest of wind chimes.

Ekket and Dritta cried out in ragged chorus, "What's this? What's happening?"

Hasso did not know how to explain the outburst, but he forced himself to say, "One of those with Gorodek is harboring a Lyhhrt." *Or maybe Gorodek himself . . . but no, he would not let himself do that.*

"Eki, that's possible? I knew there might be another Lyhhrt, but not—"

That mind said, *:You know you want to be One with me, with me!:*

The Lyhhrt left Hasso's side, went to stand beside Dritta, and spoke. *:I longed to have an Other like you, but I cannot make myself live in the mind and body of another person.:* Just the same he stepped past Dritta and she was unable to stop him.

Hasso said, *:Friend! Think how hard you have fought against this! Every step you take away from us you are nearer to being taken, Lyhhrt.:*

The Lyhhrt paused. *:I want! I cannot help wanting, there is no one else—:*

"That one nearly killed you, Lyhhrt," Hasso said.

The Lyhhrt said, in the whisper of a thought, *:You saved me.:*

"You owe me nothing," Hasso said, "but whatever happens to you ought to be under your own control."

"I want to see what body this one is living in."

"You know he was living inside Sketh, it is obvious now when I think of it that he cut himself out of Sketh's body and called for his workshell to receive him! What else could have happened? Sketh died only because that other did not like his corrupted lodging . . . and where he is now is probably in Osset, because he is the one closest to Gorodek and most controllable."

The Lyhhrt paused.

:Lies! Lies!: The cry came from Gorodek himself, and his party began to swarm over the ridge and down, five armed guards, first, three of them women half again as tall as Dritta, and Gorodek supported between Osset and one other.

"Dritta, can you signal the *Ocean Star* on your comm?"

"I have been doing it since we landed." She was shaking now, if only for a moment, louder than the Lyhhrt with her chattering teeth. She was very young. "I will hold them off as long as possible." She pulled at herself and clamped her jaws.

:Don't deny you truly want to be my Other!: the mindvoice from Gorodek's troop called across the breadth of sliding rock. *:Living within flesh is one more kind of love!:*

Horrible, Hasso was thinking, *he means it, it's no lie.*

The Lyhhrt took one step back. And said, *:Not for me. Whatever I wanted once I do no longer.:* And to Hasso, *:Yes, it is Osset . . . see, he is sleepwalking . . . :* Osset was staring at emptiness.

Gorodek was now within hearing and called, "Ekket, you must come with me! I paid your mother for you! I have a right to you!"

Ekket said suddenly, "By all the Saints, I can't bear this, let me go to him and save yourselves."

Dritta said, "What makes you believe that will save us?"

Hasso added, "He's most dangerous now he has lost everything—he's a felon with charges against him and you will still be in danger."

"I must do some—"

Gorodek, a tiny figure among tall ones, waved his arms, half-dancing on sliding rocks as he balanced, drawing air desperately to scream, "If I can't have you no one will! Kill her, Osset, Lyrhht—"

Dritta said sharply, "Get back, Ekket, back—and you, Lyhhrt!" She undid the clasp of the heavy Uzi MarkVII and let it fall, pulled up her stunner and fired, the shot went wild and hit one of the men, who fell immediately into heavy sleep, another took his place and raised a weapon that was not a stunner, and—

—the greatest voice in the world said

are all people like this

The unbodied speaker! *Not now, whatever you are! I am not a magnifying glass!* Hasso's scales rose as his vision expanded into the universe and every object, being, bone, brain, blood vessel, rock-vein, cloud, thorn-bud, and—worst of all—thought, presented itself . . . to whom? . . . in one integrated panorama of existence. *Good Saints, not now!* He fought to keep balance and consciousness, mind darting like lightning through the other minds around him in dazzling mosaics of electric impulses—

—nothing changed, the guard's finger tightened on the trigger—

But Osset cried out, "No!" *:No! NO! Stop! By all of our Gods, STOP!:*

Everything stood still. Gorodek turned slowly and stared. "What, Osset?"

Osset pulled off his helmet and threw it away, burst into a torrent of garbled words, half esp, half choking voice:

"I can bear no more of this! For your sake I committed terrible crimes, I gave you the use of my body and even my soul to carry this enemy because I believed that your course would make us strong and wealthy, but you care nothing for anyone but yourself and you are nothing, nothing but an evil, self-deceiving and impotent old fool and I will defy you!" There was a knife in his hands, suddenly, and he drove it into his belly and fell to his knees, and then on his side, choking and retching.

"Osset!" Gorodek fell to his knees. "No, Osset." His eyes burst with tears and drops of blood.

Hasso could not move and could not prevent himself from watching alongside the disembodied Observer who had chosen him.

To see Gorodek observing his own shrunken life.

But the Lyhhrt was not paralyzed. He strode forward past Dritta and set himself beside Osset to raise his head and keep him from suffocating himself. "Help me! Osset is not dead, he killed only that—that one," he paused, shocked at what he had just said, and the words reverberated in the minds of the others. He was stammering a bit: "His organs are not badly harmed. Only leave the wound open a quarter-hour to drain." And added with faint bitterness, "Dead Lyhhrt turn to water easily enough. Now help me raise him." Paying no attention to the guard and his finger on the trigger. But then no other Lyhhrt was in control now.

The guards, who had been standing like stone columns, came alive and stared at their Governor kneeling, in tears, beside their bleeding and shivering Commander. They looked about as if wondering where they were, and why, found themselves inexplicably terrified, began to howl and turned toward their yacht.

Gorodek, still streaming bloody tears, twisted his body trying to catch at them. "Take me with you! I command you to take me with you, you fools!"

The guards paused and stared at him. "No! Old man, we are free now, and you are nothing!" They hurled themselves into the yacht and sped away.

Dritta dropped the rifles and stood gaping after them. "Now what are we—"

"We wait," Hasso said. "Better off without all their armaments." The sea washed the shores, Osset gasped in pain,

Gorodek wept. Dritta padded the wound with a cloth she had wrapped the food in, clean enough for the moment, and bandaged it with Osset's own sash. Ekket turned her back on everyone and watched the sea line. The sun passed its peak in the sky. No more than one endless quarter-hour.

"Our cruiser is here," the Lyhhrt said. "And that other over there is the police boat."

Ocean Star's whistle blasted, and her dark shape was breaking the flat line of the horizon, and soon joined by the police.

Are all people like this?

Being, spirit, whatever you are, I believe you have found out for yourself. . . .

Out of Sight

On Dritta's advisement Gorodek was carried away by the Coastal Police to be returned to the Interworld Court, and Osset taken aboard the *Ocean Star* under guard to be given medical help; Dritta had given a concise account of all that had happened and Hasso did not try to embellish it.

Hasso stood at the railing and looked out to sea, free of enemies and rubbing his head in relief at not needing a helmet, happy enough that he could not catch sight of Dead Moon Crater or its outcast island.

He had heard from Tharma through the ship's communication channels that Gorodek had actually arranged to gather a fighting force on one of the Fthel worlds in order to raid the Isthmuses in a hugely expensive and risky scheme, but she did not know any more of the details. She did add that Skerow, in spite of her unwillingness to travel, was coming down to meet him in Burning Mountain.

* * *

The Lyhhrt had gone to stay alone in a cabin and do his best at healing his battered self.

Ekket recovered her spirits; glowing with pleasure at her freedom, she came to thank Hasso.

"For what, dems'l? I am not any kind of hero. Only," he smiled to disarm her seriousness, "the same plain fellow who grew up by the Sea of Pitch."

Ekket smiled back at him, and he knew that though she would not love him she saw a dignity in him that he would never have looked for in himself.

She said, "You and Tharma helped more than anyone else in the world to stand between Gorodek and me. And she could not have done it without you." And added:

:when evil has turned
gold
into filth

even the Sea of
Pitch
smells sweeter:

"If I work at it perhaps I will write *seh* almost as good as your goodmother Skerow's."

Then she left, to walk and look about her through the ship's world without, as Hasso could not resist thinking, let or hindrance. He went on looking at the sea, though he was tired of it.

But Dritta appeared so soon after Ekket's leaving that Hasso wondered if she had not been standing in line. She was composed as usual, and Hasso thought of the years of effort that composure must have cost.

"Now I have someone to thank," he said.

"I'm not pleased with myself," Dritta said briskly. "I should have found some way to avoid endangering everyone."

"I don't know how, with so many circumstances beyond your control. I'm sure Tharma doesn't blame you."

"No, she doesn't, but my own standards are . . ." She fell silent.

"After all, we are unharmed, so don't make your standards into shackles."

She smiled then, briefly. And said very carefully, "I saw you taking notice of my bracelet . . ."

"Yes, I should not have let you see, but I couldn't help thinking of Skerow."

"My case was much the same. I married too young, had a difficult lying-in, and ended sterile and without a husband . . . I have a child, a girl six years old. My mother cares for her."

"You must have spent some time in Burning Mountain, where Tharma was stationed, since she knew of you."

"I served under her there for a year, after my divorce. It was easier then than now to visit my daughter, my mother's house is downriver near Port Dewpoint, where Ekket is going. But the pay at the new court is better for all of us."

Hasso said with great daring, so much so that it made his scales rise, "My goodmother would so much enjoy meeting you. And your daughter too, as would I."

She looked at and through him as clearly as the Being would do. "Tharma has given me generous time off," she smiled again, "with pay, and from Dewpoint to Burning Mountain is a sight-seeing day-trip . . . but now, I still have a great thirst for sleep. . . ."

Hasso stood alone at the rail again, not needing sleep yet, so filled with hope that he shook with fear.

But he had not finished the venture he set out on.

He closed his eyes and leaned on his staff. He thought

of the monstrous gargaranda in the Great Equatorial River's depth that rose to draw air through its flute-shaped nostrils, and sank to blow an underwater mist of froth that masked it from its prey as it drove forward with wide-hinged jaws. Almost he thought he might see it astern in its trail of bubbles, though he knew that these waters were not its territory . . . and again of the greater thouk and the blue small-winged scavengers that flew under its great sails to catch the scraps that fell from its horned mouth. As he leaned with an arm on the rail and the staff in his hand he could feel sleep gathering behind his eyes, though that was not what he was after. . . .

Presently the voice formed itself:

yes i found what people are and not alike

What do you want with us?

i want to know

About people—

about myself i knew no other like me people

Did you come in that ship on the mesa, and bring us here?

what is a ship i know yes it is not

Are you saying that vessel is not a ship?

it has no energy to move itself

True . . . no one has been able to explain that yet.

i made that when i was looking for others like me and i picked them off their worlds and put them in something so i could bring them with me

And how did you make—

i looked inside the structure of the stones and they told me how to form but it was too hard for me to carry and too far from any sun

And you put—those who were not people but—

ones like those under the water and in the sky

—Into a specimen case!

i found your originators on another world i was

very young then and knew no better or i would not have taken them without thinking

But you lost the . . .

i only meant to take them away to some place where i could make them move for me and see if they were like me when i stopped to rest here first some of those creatures ran away or fell out of it and then the world opened up and it fell in the world closed over it i did not know how to get it back and i was very tired and shrinking and needed the sun but i did not make your people perhaps i may have been ignorant enough to try that if i thought of it but you became people by the way they become i know nothing else

My people are not going to like that explanation . . . and I'm damned if I am going to tell them!

when they truly want to know they will discover but i know nothing i do not know if there are others of my kind i do not know where i came from or where they are and i will go to the limit of the universe and look until i know perhaps they are asleep in the cores of the stars that feed them as they feed me dreaming of us i am tired and want sleep now and perhaps i will dream of them I have not found them on this world and I am leaving now

Wait—why did you choose to speak to me?

no one else would let me you seemed to know so much and i thought you might really know

Being, I wish I did.

Hasso opened his eyes. There was no voice and no Being. The sea and sky were as empty of that presence as they were of the gargaranda and the blue scavenger. Perhaps he had been dreaming.

"You were not dreaming," the Lyhhrt said from beside him. "I hope you are not offended when I confess that I shared your experience."

"I'm grateful," Hasso said. "Otherwise I might have lived the rest of my life believing I was a bit crazy. Perhaps I have been honored in some way, and wonderfully fascinated too . . . but I must confess I will not miss that Being." He was thinking of the horrifying possibilities of religious unrest and violence as the Diggers, Watchers, Hatchlings contended over a Truth that only might exist somewhere out beyond the stars. Of course he would tell Tharma everything. Perhaps she would know what to say to the world, if anything.

"I want to tell you something else." The Lyhhrt hesitated, and Hasso waited.

"That crevice we were trying to hide in led to a hollow, not quite large enough to call a cavern. . . . I don't know how he came there, but I sensed that an Ix was living in that place. He had built a small fire, its smoke was drowned out for you by the smell of trash burning. He was roasting thumbknuckle buds and eating them when they popped . . ."

This homely picture could not but resonate in Hasso's mind. Horribly. He could hardly manage to choke back air enough to say, "That might have been the one who murdered my father."

"No. He was a child. Born accidentally in an impossible time. With nowhere to go, no way to breed, nothing to do but die . . . perhaps you believe I should have destroyed him."

They looked at each other steadily, and Hasso said: "You know I could never destroy anyone."

"I know it, and as for myself, I want to go home to Lyhhr in peace."

"I thought you would. I hope you find peace and much more on your world, even though I will miss you deeply."

"I may come back. I am your friend wherever I am."

Bonzador: *The Briar Patch*

Ned was reaching for his breakfast pack when Spartakos came up quickly. "Change of plans."

Ned stopped dead and whispered, "What?"

"My Maker has destroyed the Other but not before he told his captains to kill us."

Ned could feel the grafted skin on his polymer jaw turning white and then red. His mind kept saying, *yes, it is real, it's real, yes—*

His mouth said, "Jeez, is this the way to make a living." And then, "When, Spartakos?"

"As soon as possible."

"And they don't know here that 'other' is out of the way."

"It won't matter if they have the weapons to use or sell."

"They'd use them first. These chukkers wouldn't want witnesses. You've got to bring a carrier down here, Spartakos."

"My Maker is returning."

"Is he? I won't count on that. There's that aircar we came in, but it doesn't hold more than fifty."

"And it's a drone they keep out of the camp. Eat your meal, my-friend-Ned-Gattes. And another, if you can find one."

"Not very hungry . . . Spartakos, you and Rrengha could get out of here."

"I am your weapon," Spartakos said. "And my people are here."

Rrengha said, *:And I have nothing better to do.:*

These two could take me out of here—if I didn't mind being sick of myself for ever. His face was plastered with every version of insect in the district, and he wiped at it distractedly, leaving a smear on his arm.

The sky was almost clear, for once; sun and wind had left the ground baked hard.

He was squatting by his tent eating when Lek came running, battling his own cloud of insects. "Listen, I had that dream, then Azzah told me—was that our big red friend at work?"

"That's the kind of dream Rrengha has."

"God damn it, I brought a hundred people into this hellpit! You've got to tell me if it's true!"

Ned looked hard at Lek, and said, "It's worse than true. It's going to happen here, not there. And any time."

Lek froze for a moment. He had been in as many dark corners as Ned. "You're not skinning me . . . if we got out, there's nowhere to go."

"Spartakos might be able to call in some kind of ship that could get us out of here."

"They'd kill us first. Just when do you think is 'any time'?"

"The easiest'd be when we're sleeping."

"Nobody's gonna sleep tonight." He added, half-whispering, "We've got to get out somehow. There's no time to make real plans."

"The alternative may be dying without knowing or trying to fight."

"Who do I tell about this?"

"Anybody you trust, just keep Rrengha alongside."

A loud voice yelled, "Awright, you, it's worktime, you forgot it?"

Ned looked up to see if the work-boss was that rouser, Cawdor, but it was only somebody come out of the same factory. This one liked to go round waving his zapstick and touching leaves to hear the sizzle. The look in his eyes said, *You'll die as good as the rest of them.*

Ned became conscious of the dull rumble of the cycler. It seemed louder today, as if it expected to dispose of more waste. Like dead bodies. . . . He went off to go through the motions of work, in the same patch where he had done the same thing yesterday, trying to watch all sixty-four points of the compass. There were no masses of movement among any of those around him, though the looks were furtive and the greetings mumbled.

Azzah worked her way over to whack at branches beside him. Something about her made him wary, and he knew what: the boiling anger of a slave people had reached a particular intensity in her.

"When I went to talk to my people in the southwest camp I saw a gate, and Rrengha says it opens on a path and maybe leads to an old landing field. What do you think?"

He stood and looked out toward the southwest where he could see no more than milky sky and the dark lines of useless growth, occasionally broken by stands of thin trees. Between the southwest and northwest camps was the gated compound where the self-styled captains and most of the NCOs lived and stored their weapons.

"Eh, the ones that live in the southwest are a lot worse than that bunch you used to serve, you'd have to plough through them before you got out." Not likely to lead anywhere, either. *But hope, Azzah, hope.*

She was a lot sharper than that. "You don't believe in that. I don't know you, do I." She rubbed sweat off her forehead, smearing her arm as Ned had done. "Some of those worse ones are looking for you, but Spartakos calls you my-friend-Ned, and you came with that other one of us Folk that is gone now. What was he, and what are you?"

Breathing hard, Ned forced himself away from fear and said, "That one of you that you thought was Folk is really a Lyhhrt who was trying to get to Khagodis to stop an attack there, now he's trying to stop a massacre here. Of us, you and me and everybody else here, even the worst. I'm just a pug who did some work for GalFed and Spartakos was my partner. I was trying to help, and I got us stuck here, didn't I? You may have a better chance if you keep away from me, so you don't get caught in the crossfire."

She seemed about to say something, but didn't. He turned back to push sticks into the loader and drag out as many as he had dumped, trying to put together a plan at least as good as Azzah's. *We might just get some breathing space if we had distractions. And some weapons—*

Then he caught a whack on the side of his head, one hand was grabbed and dragged up behind his back and a heavy arm came around his neck.

"Tommy Longjeans, is it?" a voice bellowed. "Let's have some good times together, Tommy!" That was Hummer, recovering from memory loss.

Shit. Looking in the wrong direction.

Hummer growling: "I'm gonna show you off, Tommy, some people want to have a better look at you, let's have some fun!"

He choked, gasped for air, tried to claw at the meaty arm with his free hand—

—and *whulk*, a sound like a hammer striking a melon. Hummer fell like a grain sack.

Ned fell with her, and when he looked up in terror, he found Grushka examining her cyber arm. "Never did that before." She pulled him up with her other hand. "I think my shoulder's out of its socket." Then, "Azzah sent me to keep an eye out for you."

He stared down at Hummer's bloody head, rubbed his sore neck and couldn't find his voice.

She said, "Ayeh, I know you thank me, now let's get'r out of the way, we can't carry'er far an she's too heavy to boost into the loader, so let's shove her under this stuff."

Ned found a voice among his painfully swollen throat muscles. "Where's Rrengha?"

"Sleeping. She has to sleep some time."

Times she picks. "Who's looking at us?" He didn't dare turn his head.

"Nobody that's gonna tell. Can you give me a hand here?"

"She dead?"

"I'm not gonna ask. Come on—"

"She's got weapons." He squatted to examine Hummer's armory.

"What's that little thing?"

He unhooked it carefully and lifted it by the loop. "It's a Zepp." Zepp dart: agony, madness and death in ten seconds. *Not my kind of weapon.* He dropped it down his shirt front, afraid to handle it, afraid to leave it about. "Nobody uses them but people like her."

Would she have used it on me?

:Yes,: Rrengha said, waking from her own dreams in the shadow of the mess tent.

Ned picked Hummer's comm off her wrist, stood up and ground it under his heel. "Got a direction finder. Now she's not anywhere." *Especially if she's dead.* "Take the stunner and the zap, I'll keep the baton. Tie up her hands with that belt, just in case." He helped Grushka lift and carry the body, alive or dead, and push it into uncleared brush that was unlikely to be cut down now. "Just don't wave them around."

As he moved down the line of workers he found Spartakos. Spartakos said, "I was monitoring her comm unit. I see that violence has begun."

Ned showed the Zepp. "Nobody else has been carrying these." *They will now, if she's opened up those containers, they'll feel free.*

Spartakos touched it with an iridium-plated finger. "Taken from that store of weapons . . . she stole it."

"Yeh." Ned ran a hand through the sweaty mess of his hair. *Violence has begun.* He held out the Zepp. "I'm afraid to carry this around."

Spartakos took it from him. Lightning flashed between his hands and a drift of powder sifted down. *Violence.*

"I will make arrangements for the rest of those," Spartakos said.

Cinnabar Keys: *Identity*

While Ned Gattes was eating breakfast, a half-forgotten woman in a safe house on the edge of a small satellite town near Altamir, the other main city of Cinnabar Keys, was wakened by the holstered man who was guarding her.

"Madam Greisbach, a call from GalFed HQ, very urgent."

She pulled herself up slowly and rubbed her eyes, still shadowed by fear. "They're not supposed to know I'm here."

"Can't help that, ma'am, someone has to know I'm here, and it's a secure line."

He was a thin sharp man with a sneering voice. Eufemia Greisbach was a gentle-faced but hard-headed woman who did not like Secret Service agents even when they were cheerful and polite, or safe houses, for that matter. She took the comm from his hand and waited until he left.

A mechanical voice said, GIVE PASSWORD.

She pressed the long series of keys on the pad. The voice that came through the earpiece said: "Greisbach, is that you?"

((*Greisbach is that you*)) The words in the Lyhhrt voder-voice echoed and reechoed, she felt blood reddening and then draining from her face.

That evening days and days ago, she had not heard those

words addressed to her at the GalFed Headquarters in Montador. Her friend and colleague Willson had spoken them, his last words, and the answer had come from his Lyhhrt murderer: *No, but I will do instead.*

That exchange had festered in the mind of the surviving Lyrhht and forced itself into her mind while he waited for her along with his dead Other and Willson's body to give his burden of information.

She said, "Yes, this is she. You have survived then. Where are you?"

"Headquarters is rerouting this call but I am not there. You needn't know, any more than I need know where you are."

"Is it really you? How do I know you aren't the killer?"

"Galactic Federation is content with my genome sample." She was silent, and he added, "Would anyone else know how much you desired Willson, and respect you for not taking him from his family?"

She felt her face flaming again. "Not the respect, no." Nor the agony she and the Lyhhrt had shared over their losses. No more powerful password could ever have been uttered. "Why have you called?"

"Galactic Federation accepts me as I am. Your identification will give me access to help from World Police."

"I see." She did not want to know what for.

"The murderer is dead, and you will be free soon," he said, and the line clicked.

The mechanical voice said: REPEAT PASSWORD IF YOU ACCEPT THIS IDENTIFICATION, and after she had done that the line went dead.

The agent came to collect the comm. She said dully, "He said I'd be free soon. I guess that's good enough."

He stood looking at her for a moment. "There's a good breakfast for you, waiting."

Bonzador: *Seek and Hide*

:They are missing the woman and the hunt is beginning,: Rrengha said.

Ned saw only moving figures grunting with effort, some working as if they had not heard any of the news and others as if they might be spared for obeying, still others beginning to collect in threes and fours; the O'e had gathered into separate orchestrated groups that kept sight of each other as they moved. Spartakos was shepherding them; Azzah was their leader.

He caught sight of Ned, approached him through the clustering workers who did not know quite where to go, and called out, "Keep filling that loader!"

One of the women, who had stopped working to ease her back, yelled, "What's the fucking good of that? If all the stuff we've been hearing is true they'll cut us down while we're doing their work!"

Spartakos said, "I need the loader. It's a weapon."

Ned stared at him, wondering if he had gone mad, like his maker. He had dulled his surface by rearranging its infinitesimal plates so that light did not jump back from them, and looked almost like a stranger.

The woman who had been yelling at Spartakos said, "You got a plan?"

"I have a course of action," Spartakos said. "Stay away from me—and Ned, my friend, you too. Go find Azzah."

Ned, dazed, limping from his fall under Hummer's weight, went to find Azzah. The sun beat down hard now, the insects swarmed to drink the sweat of the laborers, and the O'e group were looking as dazed as he.

"I don't know what," Azzah said. "He told me to move

southward and take as many as I could with me. That's farther away from the main gate . . ." She called out to her cohort, "Come with, come with!"

Ned stared back the way he had come but could not see Spartakos. He was very far away . . . *What's going on with him?*

:Why ask me?: Rrengha said. *:I cannot esp him.:*

He had not asked, but was relieved to connect with her worldview, because he could feel his group unraveling. "Go ahead, Azzah, do it!"

Azzah cried, "Spartakos has a plan! Let's do what he wants, come on!" Each of the O'e looked ragged, skin puckering with heat, but they followed in ranks and files. "Bring others!"

Cawdor, the real one, drove up screeching and kicking dust in a wheeled pickup and began yelling, "I told you goddam dumb oinks to stay in your own camps!" He was red-faced and his words slurred.

Azzah suppressed her rage and said, "We do your work better on our own."

"You giving me orders you piece of shit! I'll show you—" He jumped out of the carry-all with stunner sprung to fire, Ned threw himself between the two with his baton swinging at Cawdor's wrist but could do no more than graze his elbow.

Cawdor sneered, "*You!* Got something else for you!" and unholstered something that Ned could not identify except that it was a gun, raised and cocked—

—Cawdor did not see the crew of O'e at his back, and the O'e had knives—

—and his face wrenched with shock, then went blank and he fell, knees, hands, head. The crew picked his body clean of weapons, and Azzah pulled at Ned's arm, urging him, "Come with us! Come!"

But Ned could not. He pulled away. "You go and I'll be with you in a—"

Turning back he could just see in strobe blinks among the moving friezes of trampling bodies that Spartakos was unhooking the auxiliary fuel tank from the loader. *Oh my God.*

Before he could move again he felt a savage pain in his left shoulder, one of the few places he hadn't been battered. No one was near him, his shoulder was untouched, but he found himself looking through Rrengha's eyes as she licked at a bloody wound in her shoulder. The eyes shut for a moment and his heart jumped, they blinked on again with the bass rumble of a snarl, *alive right now,* he closed his mind to it and ran after Spartakos pushing bodies to right and left, shouting, "No, for God's sake! Don't!"

Everything happening at once, noise of riotous movement growing by the second, no way to tell friend or enemy in the mix, those who had found weapons firing them off in foolish rebellious bursts that wasted ammunition; others without weapons knocked down tents and set them on fire.

The thug Oxman ran right by Ned without seeing him, Istvan and Demarest followed a moment later, struggling through tangles of fighters thrashing and screaming, and after them a straggle of their NCOs with frightened faces—at full force they were outnumbered nearly ten to one—heading for the corner between the gate and the watchtower that seemed to have nothing in it, and had all the striking power they needed now.

Ned was diverging from them at a narrow angle toward Spartakos, who was standing on the hood of the loader, calmly pouring ethanol from the tank over the heaps of brush.

"No, Spartakos!" Ned found himself screaming.

Spartakos swiveled his head by a hundred and eighty degrees to look down at him and said kindly, "You have always been my friend, Ned Gattes. Now keep back and everything will be well." He turned away and bent his head forward to open its laser panel.

Ned sensed Rrengha running forward lopsided on three legs with her pain flickering around her, the laser light flashing out like an arrow, the heap of brush in instant flame, the loader with its blaze began to move, roared straight-lined at the weapons cache.

Because hypnoforming meant nothing to Spartakos. He himself had slid down from the loader and was running now, as swiftly as if he were on wheels, to place himself between the conflagration behind him and the streaming crowds before him, calling out, "Keep back, all of you, keep back!" with his voice at its fullest and most melodious.

A score of shooters yelling defiance aimed and shot.

Spartakos became a dazzling flash and a rain of bright dust.

The loader rammed into the corner and the mob turned and ran as thousands of bullets, grenades and gas canisters exploded, the watchtower teetered and crashed down, and greenish black smoke billowed.

Ned found himself lying on the ground and deaf in both ears.

The gate was open and its electric current broken, but nobody hurried out through the flames and stinking smoke.

Rrengha? Ned pulled himself up and staggered over and around bodies that were dead, wounded or unconscious, feeling sickeningly alone among them. He caught sight of the Dabiri, whose tail had caught a spark he was trying to beat out, and then Grushka, who seemed to be whole and sane. The sun kept shining over all of this, casting the smoke cloud in a yellow-green light. *Rrengha?*

Ned's hearing was coming back in echoes and popping.

After some panicky moments he found Rrengha crouching; her eyes were closed but she was panting. There was blood in her claws. "A few scratches, no bites," she said, and managed to grin.

A low roaring sound was rising over the crackle of fire and the popping of explosives. After a moment the sun was occluded by a great dark shape, a behemoth of a carrier with police markings, as gray-green as the cloud of smoke. It slowed and hovered.

WORLD POLICE, a robot voice said. DROP ALL WEAPONS AND REMAIN STILL. The voice did not stop the flurries among the scared and wounded, nor the sudden flights of those who realized there were no more fences and were willing to risk the bush.

"You can't take all of us!" someone yelled, firing. A bullet's flash cracked and ricocheted off the undercarriage of the ship.

Another voice spoke then, in resonant tones echoing between ground and ship: "Your employer is dead. I saw him die. Your weapons are destroyed. There is no work for you on Khagodis and the money that was to be paid for it has been seized. You have nothing. Put down arms or be put to sleep." A bay door opened and three ladders extended to the ground. The Lyhhrt in silver spattered with something like blood, descended one of them and said, "You there, Ned Gattes, come here, and whoever can do it, bring over that wounded Ungrukh."

Ned walked up to him and as they met he pulled the folded helmet from his arm and held it out. The Lyhhrt took it and it also flashed and became dust between his hands.

Port City: *Rounding Up*

Rrengha became the patient of a doctor and a veterinarian; the doctor for respect and the veterinarian for treatment. The police kept everyone else in a holding area, except for the twenty-three dead and the hundreds wounded, who were treated at whatever hospitals found room for them. Some hundreds, who preferred to avoid any authorities, had taken Azzah's advice and pressed southward, broken through the fences and found their way to villages with a population much like themselves.

The Lyhhrt, after consulting with others of his kind who held office on Fthel IV, promised that his world would pay for all treatments and transportation. Then he helped the police sort out the rotten apples that were left.

The media descended, whacking around the sky when they were not allowed into the compounds, but during the few days until the story deflated, Ned had a cubicle to himself and spent it sitting on his bed, knees and arms folded and head down on them, thinking of Spartakos. *A flash and a fall of dust* . . . He didn't know whether Spartakos had been hit by the shots or self-destructed to keep control over himself to the end. *Everything will be well.* Famous last words.

When he called Zella her voice trembled more than his. "They didn't show you on the trivvy—"

"I was hiding from them and—eh, I'm all right, Zel. . . ."

He forced himself to get up and go into the compound where most of the others that he knew were gathered, Grushka laughing now and arm-wrestling with anyone who took the challenge; over in the corner of the yard Azzah, joshing with her corps, and Lek beside her.

Ned paused to console the Dabiri over the damage to his tail, and finally learned to pronounce his name, Hrihranyi, then went to speak to Azzah. He found himself unable to utter the name, Spartakos.

She looked at him wisely. "Spartakos said he wanted to lead us freely into the world . . . but, in the end we are the only ones who can lead ourselves. He let me make myself a leader. . . ."

Ned said to Lek, "Are you going to follow the leader?"

Lek grinned. "What'm I gonna do, recruit for murder gangs? I done that already. Wherever we can find work . . . and if we need children we'll find some of them, somewhere, too."

Ned smiled. "Don't look at me, I haven't got any to spare."

Finally realizing that he was truly free to look homeward.

When he visited Rrengha in the infirmary, she said, "Doctors tell me they believe I walk on four legs again. If not, three must do. Let some other lucky one from my land go to Khagodis and give them our story, I have enough. My bartender tells me my place is open still, and there is red meat too, so I don't want to eat the customers. That is better than being useless on my own world.

"I am glad to know you, Ned Gattsss, and I wish you safe home."

When his i.d. had been established and the police had found no reason to hold him, Ned was let go and the Lyhhrt booked him into the biggest hotel in Port City, a clean place of modest size where the food was good instead of merely edible. The Lyhhrt went off and Ned took three baths, one after the other, until the water ran clean.

In the late afternoon the Lyhhrt came back with beer and clothing for Ned, as well as travelling money.

Ned, not yet feeling grateful, could not keep himself from saying: "If you ever make another robot citizen I hope to God you don't name him Spartakos."

The Lyhhrt said, "That Earther one died fighting as well, according to your history."

"Ours told me more than once that he was a guide and lighthouse, to keep you safe, and free the O'e. Did you make him to ease your guilt, Lyhhrt?"

The Lyhhrt answered nothing for a moment, because he owed Ned much. Then, patiently, "You must answer that for yourself," and while Ned drank the beer told him everything. About Brezant, his shadowy staff, Lorrice and Tyloe, the murders, the plots and their failures, whatever he knew of the plans on Khagodis, the story that branched off in so many directions, and folded in on itself and became something entirely different; not an exhaustive story, but enough to set Ned into the landscape for the first and only time in his career.

Ned heard him out in silence. He had become a different Lyhhrt from the one Ned had met in Dusky Dell's.

After that the Lyhhrt said, "I/we made promises to you."

"Damned little I did," Ned said.

"You risked your life to do what I asked. And without you and Spartakos those hundreds would be dead. I told you what I did for Tyloe and Lorrice. I will do the same for you, and whatever else you ask."

Ned shook his head. "I don't need wealth to the umpteenth generation. If you want to reward me right now you can help me find a job and one for Zel if she wants it, so we can keep sending the kids to school. I don't need to be plated with rhodium."

"Not quite done, but will be done."

"And you can take care of the O'e the way you promised Spartakos . . ."

"I/we will."

Before the Lyhhrt could slip away, Ned asked, "What do you think your world is going to do about itself, Lyhhrt?"

"I alone cannot speak for us/them. I can only say: we don't know if that poisonous growth Zamos has been extirpated root and branch throughout the Galaxy and its poisons washed away, but we no longer need fear it.

"We are creators of science, healing and artistry. Worlds are begging us for our talents, and the more we trade with them the more power and protection we have and less likely we are to be enslaved ever again, forced to create slaves, or have our bodies used for egg yolks by peoples like the Ix. Whether we like it or not we will never again be ignorant enough to be content."

"That should spin their brains for them," Ned said.

"And," the Lyhhrt added hesitantly, "I will tell them that as long as we live among worlds and must work with them we cannot keep from becoming many minds in many gatherings of them, and cannot go on believing that differences among us are heresies. At the same time we must no longer travel only in pairs . . . it leads to agony. There must be more of us to absorb . . . losses."

Ned was sitting in the city's Port Complex over a drink, impatiently waiting for his lift home, when his transcomm signal beeped. Ned clicked on nervously. Zel? But the message was from his agent Manador. He had not asked her for work in years.

NED GATTES, I HAVE A JOB FOR YOU, THEY NEED A TOUGH PUG ON KEMALAN V TO TAKE CARE OF.

Ned had signed off.

He sat there drinking and listening to a slim young woman with long fair hair and a dress of iridescent uki scales who was singing:

and sometimes I feel like the mermaid
walking on footsteps of pain
crossing bridges over rivers I was born to swim
down to the sea
and I want to be
free to swim the rivers to the sea again

and fleetingly he thought of the Lyhhrt before his mind turned once again toward home.

Then someone sat down beside him and said, "Hello, thought you lived up in Miramar." Tyloe, by himself.

"Thought you lived around there too. What's doing?"

Tyloe smiled. He and Lorrice had returned to the hotel, packed all their purchases and rigorously divided the Lyhhrt's money.

And she had said, "One last drink?"

"Why not?"

The bar, just before noon, had been empty except for two women drinking coffee and a gray-haired man wearing a diamond ring and a silk shirt with pearl buttons. He was drinking a BlueVine cocktail with zimb slices and she had her eyes on him right away, smiled and esped him down to the last cred; eventually he noticed her.

Tyloe nodded and murmured, "It's been nice knowing you," and went off to pay the check.

Since then he'd hung around Port City waiting for a ship but not sure where he wanted it to take him. "Dunno what I want to do, go home and listen to Daddo earbanging or somewhere else on my own."

Ned dared to say, "Didn't you once have a lady friend?"

"Not really. She found somebody older and wealthier than me."

Ned grinned. "Here's an address." He clicked a couple of buttons on his comm. "Look."

Tyloe squinted at the tiny display:

Manador of Pinaxer, Registered Gladiatorial Agent.

"Eh, one of those blue women . . ."

"Yeh. She won't make you a pug, but she'll damn right find something for you to do. Just don't let her get you into bed." Tyloe's reddening face made Ned raise his eyebrows. "You go there, tell her Ned Gattes sent you, tell her, thanks for the memories, but I'm outa this life. I've had some gaudy times, but this THE END."

All's Well That Ends

The Lyhhrt went home and decontaminated until the grit and filth of other worlds washed out of him in waters of welcome salt and bitterness. He gave his people one of those mind-crimping reports that Lyhhrt specialize in, and told them what he had told Ned. Then immersed himself in long years of dreaming.

Eventually the world Lyhhr fulfilled all promises. They established trades workshops for the O'e on five worlds, and for Ned they bought Waxers Works, renovated it until it esthetically matched the ancient grotto it had been built inside, and gave it to him. Ned and Zella hired Knuck and Ham, and found customers among the embassies who enjoyed working out in a safe place that looked dangerous.

The world Lyhhr sent a delegation of five, a good working unit, to Khagodis, apologizing for their murderous extremists and asking for a resumption of trade . . . but that was deeper into the future.

And gradually the universe got used to existing without Zamos.

* * *

Sometimes in his mind's eye just before he falls asleep with his arm around Zella, Ned sees Spartakos as he must have looked when the Lyhhrt first created him, splendid in his gleaming chromium and gold, his iridium fingertips and pearl nails, burning with light like the sun.

He has never seen Spartakos so newly made, and wonders if the Lyhhrt has given him this vision.

Hasso is full of joy, Skerow waits beside him and he feels her joy redoubling his own, as the child comes forward with her young thoughts tinkling like a ring of bells, just learning to speak in the difficult way Khagodi do.

And he stoops to take her hand: *:We are so very pleased to meet you, dems'l!:* While Dritta smiles from above.

The Lyhhrt will never again reach out to find an Other, but when dreams of fire and blood threaten to pull his spirit down into the demonic Anti-Force he sends for his work-shell, encases himself to rise above the swamp and succulent growth of his world, and through his adamant eyes he watches the sundogs, the halos and at night the stars.